Happy Ever After at Romansa Castle

THE FIX UP

RAVEN MCALLAN

The Fix Up
ISBN # 978-1-80250-961-8
©Copyright Raven McAllan 2022
Cover Art by Kelly Martin ©Copyright June 2022
Interior text design by Claire Siemaszkiewicz
Totally Bound Publishing

Totally Bound Publishing books by Raven McAllan

Single Books
Hong Kong Heat
Taken Identity
Fairground Attraction
The Duke's Temptation
The Viscount Meets his Match

Diomhair
Secrets Shared
Secrets Uncovered
Secrets Remembered
Secrets Dispatched
Secrets Learned
Secrets Dispelled

Daring Ladies
The Earl and The Courtesan

Castle on the Loch
Love by the Stroke of Midnight
The Heather and the Plaid

Happy Ever After at Romansa Castle
The Fix Up

Anthologies
Bully for You: Chasing Charlie

Collections
A Little Bit Cupid: For One Night Only

With Cassie O'Brien

The Scots and the Sassenachs
The Earl of Callander's Secret Bride
The Baron's Saving Grace

THE FIX UP

Dedication

To Lisa Hall, who encouraged me all the way.

Chapter One

To add to the gloom of a storm where the end of the garden was hidden by mist, raindrops bounced off the terrace like golf balls. The pond overflow spout was akin to Niagara Falls in full spate and the postman brought bad news.

Two lots of bad news.

The first was a scribbled note, in a handwriting Arietta didn't recognise. That got her wondering even before she opened the envelope. Who sent notes like that these days? When she checked the signature she understood. It was from a so-called friend who did not and now never would have Arietta's phone number, saying she'd met Arietta's ex a few days before in Mauritius. Wasn't it fab, she gushed — if gushing in bright green ballpoint was possible — that he was loved-up and his partner expecting a baby in the very near future? As it hadn't been that long since he and Arietta had split, *and* he'd always been adamant he hated flying and asserted even from Glasgow to London brought him out in hives, Arietta decided she was entitled to be upset. Especially as it now appeared that the bloke who'd professed she was the love of his life and had been pressuring her to move in with him — or was it him with her? — had been bonking someone else at the same time.

Thank God for condoms. Okay, it was time to forget him, but that was easier said than done. Not that she ever wanted to see or speak to him again, but the bugger had hurt her big-time.

Bye-bye, Stu.

If that wasn't enough, she'd also received an invitation. A very unwelcome one.

What next? The roof to cave in? The electricity to be cut off? An alien invasion?

Dramatic or what? Enough already.

Arietta opened the other envelope, took out the contents, stared at the piece of very elegant, heavy and expensive card in her hands and grimaced.

"Mr and Mrs Arthur Berkley-Tong request the pleasure of Harriet Clare and partner to the wedding of their beloved daughter, Kristin Therese Maude, to The Honourable Tarquin Algernon Carstairs Kinsley Smith on November 13th at Pannerburn Castle…"

If she hadn't realised whom the invitation was from, the way her name was incorrect would have told her. She'd never bothered to correct them that Arietta wasn't and never had been a version of Harriet.

Honourable? Ha, not when I knew him. Tar…Tack for initials? Oh my, hahaha, that fits… Very tacky. Maude? She never mentioned that. Go to their wedding? Not in a million years. November? In Scotland? No chance, I might be stranded there in a snowstorm. Any Scottish snowstorm I'm stranded in is going to be here. The thirteenth, no way. That would be an unlucky thirteen and was a scary thought. Enough to make her shiver. Stuck with a load of people she didn't know for however long, in a hotel, however sumptuous, wasn't a scenario Arietta favoured. She'd have to look tidy, not wear jeans without non-designer rips in them, and remember to put on a bra.

Yuck, not to be considered.

Nor was the idea of seeing two people loved-up when her loved-up-ness was zilch. A big fat do-not-go-there zero. She'd sworn off men for the duration. Being dropped with no warning had hurt too much. Even if she'd found out afterwards he was a two-timing, two-faced rat fink.

The idea of a wedding was anathema to her. Especially that one.

She stared at the card again.

It had to be a joke. Was a bloke in tighty-whities going to jump out from behind the front door, take her photo and shout gotcha? She hoped not. Her current attire of a pair of leggings that had seen better days with a large bleach mark down one leg like an exclamation mark and a scarlet uni sweatshirt that had once read '*writers do it the right way*', and since faded to a dark pink — with splotches of something unmentionable — wasn't the sort of look she wanted captured for posterity.

Arietta dropped the card onto her desk, just missed her cold cup of coffee — she had been carried away with her writing and forgotten all about it — and caused three pencils and a toffee to rattle off the surface and onto the floor.

Request the pleasure indeed. Pull the other one. That was called rubbing her nose in it, big-time — or it would have been if she'd been bothered. Which, she ruminated, she wasn't. Ten years was a long time to get over the non-event of a short and not-so-sweet romance, and a barely begun friendship. Strange how it mattered to other people, though.

Nevertheless, why the invite? Just to show what they'd got up to? Perhaps, but seriously, she was *not* bothered. Life was too short, and she had a book to write.

"Hey, what's this?" Thomas, her twin and, as she often said, the annoying ten-minute-older half of their twinship, came into her study unnoticed. He picked up the discarded card and whistled. "Whew… Posh place. Who do you know who can afford to get hitched there?"

"I don't, not really." Arietta plucked the card out of his fingers and dropped it back on her desk. This time the corner dipped into her coffee mug. "Someone's being funny — not. It's a snarky attempt to rub my nose in something. It won't work." She might have been upset — for all of half an hour — at the time, but she could honestly say she had not given the two people concerned a thought in the past years. In fact, she could probably pass them by in the street and not recognise either of them. "I don't give a monkey's these days. Over, done with, and the proverbial T-shirt burnt almost immediately." She flicked her finger at the now getting-soggier-by-the second card. "Overkill."

Thomas tutted at her handling of the card. "You can't treat it like that. I bet you need to take it with you to get into the place. Think how downmarket you'll look with it covered in coffee stains." He took it out and wiped it on his T-shirt. "Mind you, November… Maybe it's winter rates and cheaper?"

Arietta shrugged. "No idea. Knowing the bloke, it could well have a lot to do with it, but then I'd bet he's not dipping his hands in his pockets anyway. Not big on sharing his coffers. Or he wasn't. It's a long time since I knew 'em." She pointed to Thomas' T-shirt. "You'll need to rinse that or it'll stain." Gah, she was conscious she sounded like their gran. She'd be suggesting a blue bag—whatever that was—next.

"The card?" Thomas, an up-and-coming actor and well on the way to becoming the teenagers' latest, or next, heartthrob, perched on the edge of her desk and swung his legs. As ever, his jeans were ripped in places no jeans should be and still be worn, and his T-shirt with a hole under one armpit was a hand-me-down from when their dad had gone to concerts and had been three stones lighter. In faded black it proclaimed 'Iron Maiden'.

"No, twerp, your shirt."

He winked and she growled. He held his hand up in the universal peace gesture.

"Just makes it look distinguished." He plucked at the faded material. "Actually, could you tell it was stained? It looks part of the pattern to me. I guess if it was still proper black you'd not see it at all."

Arietta shrugged. "If that's what you think." The T-shirt was ready for the ragbag anyway. "Who am I to argue."

She saved her work on her laptop and pushed her chair back from her desk. From past experience, she accepted she would get no more written until Thomas had gone home, and as he announced he was stopping for lunch, that wouldn't be any time soon. "What would your fans think if they saw you now?"

"I'm retro cool?" Thomas hooted with laughter. "The shirt's not a problem, it's my car mending one." He housed his elderly MG in Arietta's garage and tinkered with it whenever he visited. "I do have another one with me. And it's not even one of Dad's, just plain boring blue." He picked up the card again.

"You've got to go, you know. Apart from seeing how the other half live, or whatever, it will do you good to get out and about again. I worry."

"Nope, and what do you worry about? I'm fine."

"Hmm." Thomas tapped the card on the corner of the desk. "If you call sitting here writing for ninety percent of your time, not socialising, and ignoring your friends fine, I don't."

"Honestly what a load of cobblers," Arietta said defensively. "I do get out, and I do mix. I've got lots of friends and I do see them."

"Nope," Thomas corrected her. "Who you rarely see. Not since… Okay." He held his hands up in a 'peace' gesture. "I won't mention it again, but that arsehole isn't worth your thoughts."

"And I don't give him any," Arietta assured him. But it stung to be so gullible. Stu with his, '*Oh I'm away for work*'. "I don't know about him being a good screw salesman, but it seems he was a great one for screwing. Ach." She dusted her hands together. "I'm just a bit wary now. Okay?"

Thomas nodded. "If you say so, no problem. But I can sense a mystery. C'mon, spill. What's with the Harriet bit?"

Brothers. How on earth had she thought she could put him off? He was like a truffle hound on the scent of truffles. Arietta pushed him off her desk as she walked to the door then turned to look at him with exasperation and affection.

"The people concerned never ever bothered to get my name right. It annoyed me then, it doesn't now. It's not a problem, for either of us. Any of it. What do you want for lunch, or are you off before then?"

"Here's your hat?" Thomas said wryly as he followed her into the kitchen. "It's not eleven o'clock yet. I can smell a good story when I see it."

Of course he could.

"Mixed metaphors, love."

"So?" He put every ounce of incredulity possible into that one word. "Stop trying to change the subject. Come on, tell your lovely brother all about it. I'm a good listener, and I promise not to share it…unless it's juicy and I can get one of the ghastly rags that dog me for an interview to print it for mega millions. Then all deals are off. I can retire on the money, and lotus eat." He opened his eyes wide and blinked theatrically. "Er, what does that mean? It sounds uncomfortable."

"Idiot." It was just as well she loved him.

"That's me. Look, on a serious note, this is one fancy deal," he said earnestly. "I've heard it's at least two to three tho' a guest, and that's without a meal, bed or booze."

"Two or three thousand pounds?" Arietta said, aghast. "What for?"

"A seat in the chapel, exclusive use of the place—the chapel, not the whole kit and caboodle. There's cottages to rent in the grounds, and if someone's got in first, tough luck—and a bun fight I guess." Thomas stared at her. "Without the buns. At *the* venue of the decade, and I mean *the*. Where the oh-so-beautiful go to be seen and talked about and are prepared to pay the big bucks. No press, or at least not without prior notice and invitation. The rooms start at five k a night, and that's for a shoebox. You can however add many noughts on for a suite or a cottage."

"Sounds pretentious." Arietta observed. "And you know all this how?"

"Because Rob Toleman, a fellow actor, enquired about renting one for his parents' golden wedding and his mum told him if he wanted to waste his money, would he waste it on flying lessons for her instead."

"What about his dad?" Arietta asked, fascinated by the insight into the life of someone Thomas associated with. As an up-and-coming actor he was, as he said, *"happy rubbing shoulders with the good and great, but not quite on a par yet"*. "What did he do?"

"Bought his mum the lessons and gave his dad his dream."

"Which was?"

"An allotment." He paused for effect. "With a shed, a bench, a coffee maker, comfy chair, radio, iPad and a generator. And Netflix."

"Oh I love it." That sounded amazing. Sometimes Arietta wished she had somewhere like that — well, she wasn't bothered about Netflix or any streaming gubbins. As long as no one except her knew where the allotment was. Why did people assume because you were at home you weren't doing anything important? She'd lost count of the number of times someone assumed she'd do whatever, because *"you've nothing on"*. However, as she rarely told people what she did, she guessed she only had herself to blame. Goodness knew what they thought she lived on. A private income? A sugar daddy? One day she'd have to try to find out. "Were they pleased?"

"Oh yes, and back to the subject in question." Thomas waggled his finger at her. "There has got to be a good reason why you don't want to go. Apart from being anti-social and anti-weddings, and not over that arsehole Stu, I sense a mystery."

He *was* like a truffle hound on the scent.

"I am so over him," Arietta said indignantly. The note she'd got that morning had been for her information only. Thank goodness she'd thrown it in the shredder. Why did some people enjoy being bitchy?

There was no answer to that.

"Earth to Arietta."

She jumped. She'd forgotten she was having a conversation with Thomas

"This is me, you're talking to, love," Thomas said. "He who knows you as well as he knows himself. Well, almost. The sod hurt you, and you wouldn't let me hurt him back."

"Yes, okay, he did, but that was then, now I'm just wary and off men. Present company apart…as long as you stop this interfering."

"Stopped," Thomas said hastily. "But spill the deets over why the invitation and why the antipathy."

"No mystery," Arietta said, resigned to telling him everything — almost everything — as she spooned coffee into her stovetop coffee maker and slid it onto the hot plate of her Aga. "Just someone trying to be superior, and I'd guess they think they're rubbing my nose in it. Which they aren't, but I bet my next royalty cheque they wouldn't believe that even if I swore it on oath."

"I need more." Thomas sat on top of the work surface, as close to the Aga as he could without burning. "Lots more. What's better than coffee and gossip?"

Arietta rolled her eyes. It didn't matter how many times she complained about his preferred seat, he just grinned and carried on doing it. One day he'd burn his bum and it would be his own fault.

"Bride or groom?" he asked as he began to juggle the salt and pepper pots. "As I have no idea what it's all about it *is* still a mystery to me" — he began to sing *It's a Mystery* in a very tuneful voice—"spill the beans. Who?"

"Both, sort of, but I suspect it's the bride." Arietta grabbed the condiment set before all the contents ended up on the floor and put them down out of his reach. Then she handed him a cup of coffee and sighed. "She was a bit of a bitch, and that's doing bitches a disservice. Ditto if I said a cow, to cows."

Thomas raised his eyebrows and rolled his eyes. "Ooh…you're not usually spiteful. Tell me more, sister mine."

It was Arietta's turn to roll her eyes. "Oh all right, Mr Nosy. Let's sit in the conservatory and I'll give you chapter and verse."

"Done." He jumped down and tweaked Arietta's nose. "Let's go."

"Anyone would think it's the story of the century and it's really not," Arietta said as they settled in the sun-warmed room. She watched two robins eyeing each other up with suspicion and smiled. Her garden wasn't large but she loved it. This room and her study both overlooked the lawn, pond and bird table. Contrary to popular belief, she was never distracted from work by the view. It gave her inspiration. Many a hero in the historical romantic crime stories she wrote had had his complicated love life resolved as she'd stared out of the window.

Thomas coughed ostentatiously. "Earth to Ari."

"Don't call me that," she said automatically. He always made it sound as if he'd deliberately dropped the "H". "Okay, well, you remember when I first went to St Andrews, to uni? I shared a flat with four other people?"

Thomas nodded. "Yeah, you, Jan, Daisy, Helen and someone I don't remember. Long hair she tossed around at every opportunity and over-plump lips. Do you think she'd had them done? She definitely needed her roots done."

"Miaow."

Thomas laughed. "Got the claws out," he agreed. "She had to be a cat to upset you. What was her name again? I can't keep calling her trout lips."

"Kristin, who called herself Krystal, and regarding her lips, who knows? Her roots, yup, always two-tone but not by style. Several years older and evidently she'd swanned around, 'trying to find herself' — that's a direct quote by the way — before she chose to go to uni. She wasn't with us for many weeks. She got a feller, got fed up of actually having to work and got a better offer from Daddy. Went to live the life of a…well, a well-heeled lady in London, I guess."

"It's *her* wedding?"

Arietta nodded. Thomas whistled. "And you've kept in touch?"

"Oh no, never heard from her since she left." Which Arietta decided was a plus. "Weird or what?"

"Then why now?" Thomas sounded as puzzled as she felt. "'Weird or what' is about right."

"Ah, that's the rest of the story." Arietta sipped some coffee then put the cup down. It must had been her mood because the best Kenyan blend tasted like cardboard. Soggy, cheap cardboard. That was annoying. She was limiting the amount of full strength, full flavour, full-on caffeine coffee she drank every day, so for one not to be up to par didn't seem fair.

"You remember for a few weeks back then, in the first few weeks of my first year, I said I was sort of seeing a bloke?" she asked. "He was a post grad. I wasn't sure about him, but was prepared to give him a chance? He had… I dunno, something about him that was appealing. Up to a point, I guess. He had an appalling taste in socks. Anyway, we had a barney and I told him to sling his hook? You were in Spain filming that TV series where you played an alien, so all my angst was by phone and email?"

"Oh yeah," Thomas said fervently. "When I got back all fired-up and ready to kick ass, you told me to calm down, it was well over and done with. I've never seen you so...so disgusted, I guess. You never did say why, though, and I was too much of a gentleman to pry."

Arietta laughed. "Get it right, love. You were too much involved with that pretty blonde who called you Tommy. Or was it the one who lisped and called you Th...hom...uth and kept sending you pouty kisses?" She mimed blowing him a kiss with her bottom lip stuck out. "And cwoowtie pie."

"Susie and Loretta," Thomas commented with a reminiscent smirk. "I'd forgotten them. Ah, to be young and have stamina. Actually, it was neither then. They came, they went, I was gutted. Until it was Maybelle Fortune. Lovely Maybelle. She married a vicar and has six kids at the last count. Even one named Thomas. Lives in Cumbria. I get a Christmas card every year. And stop changing the subject."

"I wasn't," Arietta said indignantly. "Well, not very much," she added with honesty. "And it's boring, the old, old, story. I met him in my first few days at uni. He tried to monopolise me and didn't take kindly to me not letting him. Then, after only a couple of weeks, he wanted to have sex. I didn't. Too much, too soon. I mean, you and the parents had drummed into me...be sure, and I wasn't. We were having a heated discussion about it in the communal lounge when Kristin walked in and said, well, if I didn't want sex with him, she did." She smiled at the memory as Thomas let out a long whistle. "Not good." With hindsight it was humorous, but it hadn't been at the time. Kristin had sent her a malicious smirk as she had spoken. It had been obvious by her snarky comments she'd been smitten by the guy and most annoyed he'd chosen Arietta to ask out.

"Oh…my… And?"

"He said, 'last chance, babe', to me. I said not interested, too much too soon, and I didn't realise he was that desperate, so he shrugged, said my loss." She snorted. "I said not really, plenty more fish in the sea, less needy, not much of a loss.

"He said I was well named—he'd thought my initials were HRC and said it was short for hah-archaic. Then he said to Kristin, 'yeah, why not'.

"She said to me, 'All's fair in sex and war' and they walked out of the room together. I laughed loudly, well, it was laugh or throw things and I wasn't stooping to that. Not wanting to be around to hear anything—the walls weren't that thick and we already knew she was a screamer—I went down to the union."

Thomas spluttered his coffee. "Oh my a…" He shook his head in mock sorrow. "Look what I missed. Luckily."

"You better believe it. Anyway, I met up with the others, had a good slag-off fest and lots of dodgy cocktails. Eventually we meandered back, slightly mellow, shall we say, and her room was empty. Just a toothbrush and a packet of contraceptive pills on the bathroom floor. Mega oops there, we reckoned. Even so, that was the last we saw of her in the flat. We were told she'd changed halls. For a while after that you'd see the pair of them arm in arm, or tonsils against tonsils all over the place. The term ended, and then… No one saw her again. Nor him."

"But it's over, what, fourteen years since then," Thomas pointed out. "*Nothing* since then?"

"Not a lot. I did hear third or twentieth hand about six or seven years ago that he was working for her father, who has a multi-million-pound company recycling rags, and that she was modelling."

"The rags?" Thomas said and almost fell over as he snorted. "I'd love to see it."

Arietta punched him. "Idiot. I never saw her name mentioned anywhere afterwards, so who knows. Anyway that's it. A non-story. I don't half know how to pick 'em."

"I don't get it." Thomas ignored her woe is me remark, picked up two pencils and began to juggle with them. "Why has she suddenly decided to ask you to her wedding?"

"I'm guessing that's got a lot to do with her groom," Arietta said and sniggered. "All those years and..." She did the 'da...da...dah daaah' out loud.

"You mean?" Thomas smiled, very wickedly. "*You mean...*"

Arietta nodded. "Whatever the pair of them have been up to in the meantime, the bloke I ditched is the groom to be."

Thomas howled. "Ohh, the cat she is. You have to go, you can*not* miss it. Don't you have a handsome, hot-as-hell bloke tucked away? Someone to make her drool? Someone you can ask to be your partner?"

Arietta rolled her eyes. "Nope." Droolworthy men in her orbit were few and far between, as in zilch, none she wasn't related to. "The only one of those is you. Stop grinning, you sod, I was going to add allegedly, though I can't see it myself and frankly you're too well-known for anyone not to know you're my brother. Plus you'd be mobbed and I'd be stuck in the corner as Ari-no-mates." She couldn't stand the thought of Kristin's smirk if she turned up alone. "I'll send my apologies and say I'm at some writer's convention in Ulan Bator or somewhere." That sounded sort of plausible, and she had a mate who could mug up some tweets if need be.

"Tut, tut." Thomas shook his head in mock sorrow. "What is that our dear mama always says about liar, liar, pants on fire?"

"She also says if you have to lie, do a big one," Arietta pointed out. "And I'm doing that. Mega big. Though I might say Hong Kong and go visit Jan. She's still out there."

"Ah, the lovely Jan. Still refusing to admit I'm the love of her life?" Thomas patted his heart. "Gutted, I am."

"'Fraid so." Arietta looked at him curiously, struck by the wry note in his voice. "Would you like to be?"

"Gutted? Nah. The rest? Who knows," Thomas said in what Arietta decided was a cryptic manner. "Dammit. I really wanted to find out what Pannerburn Castle was like, even if it's second-hand. You're cruel, love."

"That's me." She didn't mention his change of subject. On the odd occasion that Jan and Thomas were in the same vicinity, sparks flew, and Arietta had long wondered why, made her own conclusions and decided never to interfere. "When you get your Oscar, you'll just have to treat yourself," Arietta said, unmoved by his 'woe is me, poor deprived male' expression. He was a bloody good actor and used that at his convenience. "Or just be brass-necked and go and have a look around. It's only on the other side of the loch. Not far as the crow flies." Although a lot longer by road. "Now make yourself comfy with the paper or something while I write my sorry, but thank you note and sort out something to eat for lunch."

"I'll need to slip into the village and buy a paper." Thomas patted his pocket. "Wallet in place. You write your scaredy-cat note and I'll pop it into the post box for you. Anything else you need?"

"Nope." Arietta nipped back into the study, found an appropriate card and scribed her apologies. She handed it to Thomas with a flourish. "Are you happy with my pâté and stuff for lunch?"

"Well, duh. Look, my last attempt. Are you sure you're not letting what happened with them and that bloody Stu cloud your judgement? I mean, you should go and say sod 'em all."

"I shouldn't go and be miserable. Which I would be. To say nothing of bankrupt and not able to feed you when you visit. Now are you going to give it a miss and give over, shut up and let it be and stop for lunch, or have me throw a hissy fit and chuck you out?

"Shutting up. Lunch, please."

"Great. It'll be ready when you get back. Here you go." She handed him an envelope. "I've even found a stamp for it."

Chapter Two

Several days later, that, Arietta thought, was that. It was a pity because after she'd researched Pannerburn Castle, she hadn't been able to help a pang of regret that she wasn't going to experience some of its hospitality, but such was life. The price of a room, even when it wasn't for such an event as the wedding she'd been invited to, would wipe out a large chunk of her hard-earned royalties, and, if she were honest, she had better things to spend her money on. As the central heating boiler was making alarming noises, she had a feeling that was going to be one of them.

Resolutely, she put the whole thing out of her mind and concentrated on rescuing her Regency heroine from the clutches of a white slaver without recourse to screaming for help—or the hero. As ever, once she started to write, she was oblivious to anything else.

The roar of something loud and close by made her jump, and a line of *xcvbnm,**#fbn* appeared on her manuscript. Arietta swore, deleted it, pressed Save and got up just as the doorbell rang. She wasn't expecting a visitor, it wasn't bin day, and as far as she knew she had no parcels due. Probably someone lost. There weren't many weeks when someone didn't knock and ask if she was the local bed and breakfast—not a chance, she hated fry-ups in the morning—were they on the road to the town—no—and on one occasion, Pannerburn Castle. The answer to that was, not unless your car is an amphibious vehicle. Arietta wondered what this visitor would want.

She pulled the front door open to see a body next to a kick-ass motorbike. In the mandatory leathers and a crash helmet with "Hot rods and hot bods" inscribed on it, the rider looked lean, mean and dangerous. Arietta put her hand to one side and fumbled for the spray can of coloured water she kept handy just in case she needed it. As all self-defence sprays were illegal in the UK it was, she reckoned, as good as anything. She had one of those shrill noise-making gadgets as well, but living where she did doubted anyone would be able to hear it. Plus, she was of the opinion a sharp dig with her nails into somewhere vulnerable would give her time to run or slam the door, lock it and call the police before any would-be assailant recovered.

He turned to walk up the path to the door. To say the cock-of-the-walk male strut was menacing was an understatement. Arietta panicked and slammed the door in his face just as he reached his hand out to…to what?

She had no intention of discovering that.

Arietta leant on the door, her chest heaving and her pulse racing. Who should she contact?

Thomas?

He was miles away, but hopefully would tell her what to do.

The doorbell rang as she began to thumb in Thomas' number. She missed a digit and swore. Why the hell hadn't she just gone into the recent calls directory?

Because I'm flustered.

"Arietta, look out of your window and you'll see I'm not a threat."

He knows my name?

"Go upstairs if you think it's safer. I'm no danger to you, but I realise I might look like one."

Might? Understatement of the century.

Arietta checked the bolt was across and the chain on before she headed upstairs to the landing window, which overlooked the front doorstep. She opened it cautiously and peered out. Not too far, just enough to see what—or who—was below.

The guy looked upwards. "Hi."

She nodded warily. "Hi."

Whoever he was bowed—*dramatic or what?*—and removed his headgear to reveal a shock of copper-coloured curls to his shoulders. He—it was definitely a he—shook his head so the curls danced all over the place and nodded. "Hi again."

Arietta blinked.

Oh...my...it isn't...is it? Him? On my doorstep? Of course not. Stand-in copycat lookalikes were really excellent these days. However, why? It wasn't her birthday, no one had intimated she needed a whatever-o-gram, so what was going on?

"Arietta Clare, I presume?" The said hot bod grinned, and his deep green eyes crinkled up at the edges. Contact lenses could do an amazing job. However...talk about drool central. "Nice to meet you at last. You are everything I was told you are, and more."

It *was* his voice. What did he mean by *'at last'*, and *'everything'*?

Recognisable, even though with the overlong hair and lack of a beard it wasn't easy. "And you are?" No way was she going to presume he *was* who she thought he was. And if he was, why was he there? "Who has said what, why and when?"

That's enough who, why, what, when and was to confuse anyone.

He smiled. One of those if you could bottle it you'd make a fortune smiles.

"Let me introduce myself. Moss Kirby, at your service."

If she was a lesser person she'd have done the ogle and swoon stuff. As it was, she bit her lip to stop herself gawping. Fangirling was so not her thing.

Liar.

Of course it was him. No one else could get that voice off pat. Arietta blinked and swallowed as she did her best not to make sheep's eyes at him too obviously. Now he'd said who he was, her mind went haywire and all her cool, calm, collected common sense went with it.

Moss Kirby. Known to everyone as Amos Kirby — hot bod and drooled over by thousands? For me? Oh, I wish. Not a lookalike, the real him. Be still my beating heart, down girl and anything else deflating. And he's pleased to meet me at last? She sensed a mystery and had no idea what it was.

"Arietta Clare, as you already know." *And sorry, mate, there is no chance I'm at your service. Off men. Especially drop-dead gorgeous ones with a reputation.* "Er, I might sound a bit dim, why are you here? Really here." That was the million-dollar question. "No messing, and oh why 'at last'?"

"Because I've seen your photo and I'm intrigued, and according to your brother, you've got a wedding to go to and you are without a partner. I offered my services, he said thank you. I'm your partner. Your wedding date."

Arietta stared at him blankly. "Pardon?" She'd had no idea she was due to get married, or to whom. *Have I got engaged and no one thought to tell me? To him?* It wasn't April the first, so what was going on?

More to the point, what was Thomas up to?

"Your date for the wedding. At Pannerburn Castle. According to a mutual, er, friend, some plonker and a non-friend getting hitched and you need a partner."

Ah, that sort of date. Thank goodness she hadn't blurted her thoughts out!

"It's months away."

"I know." He grinned. "Gives us plenty of time."

She wished he wouldn't smile like that. It made him oh-so personable and she couldn't cope with it *and* discover why he thought they were going to a wedding together.

"Time?" she queried, mentally rolling her eyes at her pathetic responses. Couldn't she do any better? "Around twelve-thirty."

He gave her a thumbs-up. "Good one. We really need to get to know each other first."

"We can't, it's already twelve-thirty."

He narrowed his eyes in what her mum called a man's patently impatient look. The one where they are long-suffering as you act the idiot. Which was, she allowed, fair comment.

"You have an answer for everything?" He sounded amused, not annoyed. "Love it."

"Hardly. Anyway, Thomas got it wrong, and I'm sorry he troubled you. I'm not going to the wedding, so we really don't need to get to know each other for it," Arietta said shortly, belatedly entertained that for one moment she had thought he was asking when *her* wedding was to be held. She needed to get her mind out of the cellar she'd left her heroine in, and to the matter in hand. Or in front of her. "Thanks for offering, though." She'd remembered her manners. "Now is there anything else?"

Damn. That could be a leading question.

He waggled his finger. "Well, your non-appearance would make your acceptance look a tad foolish, won't it?"

What? Arietta went hot and cold. Her what? "I didn't..." She hadn't, but someone may well have. Arietta groaned. "I might have guessed. I swear one day I'll crown my brother... Why on earth did I trust him to post my apologies?" she asked rhetorically. "He's annoying, meddlesome, a pain in the..." She took a deep breath. "Sorry. He shouldn't have made you part of his stupid plans. Sorry you were bothered. I'll just ignore the date and not go. Apart from the fact I don't want to go, as in really do not want to go, I'd have nowhere to stay." She wasn't going to admit she didn't have x number of pounds to spend on a broom cupboard for the night, which was probably all she'd be able to afford. "It's really kind of you to offer, but I wouldn't want to put you out."

He grinned. "Sorry? Hmm, I'm not sorry. Be assured you need me and no one puts me out unless I'm agreeable. Er, one thing, though. Do we have to have this conversation like this? I saw a woman in the village staring very suspiciously at me and Mike, that's the bike, when I checked which way to come. Maybe it would be better conducted in less shouty tones?"

"Oh shit." Arietta went hot and cold. He had to be on the level surely? After all, it sounded so like her brother to do something outrageous like that.

As if her thoughts transferred straight to him, her phone pinged with a message from Thomas.

It is Moss, I did ask him to come.

"Be right down," she said hastily, and took the stairs two at a time to let him in.

"Sorry," Arietta said breathlessly as he followed her inside and she shut the door behind him. "Can't be too careful. You were saying?"

"When Thom told me about the thing I said straight off—if you were short of a partner to give me first refusal. Like I said, you intr—your intransigence made me wonder why."

What had he been going to say? Arietta was damn sure intransigence wasn't it.

"Thomas seems to have said rather a lot," Arietta remarked dryly. "Considering I gave him a refusal to post. Anything else?"

"He did tell me that, but he also mentioned he was of the opinion you should go and what was the rest…ah, 'sod 'em all'. With that in mind, he'd taken it upon himself to say you would attend. It didn't seem to bother him any, said no one would ever know it wasn't you who'd replied. Except you, of course. I never knew Thom was such a good forger."

Evidently Thomas has used his talents again. The last time—to her knowledge—it had been to copy their mum's signature to allow him a week off school to go for an audition. Their mum had known nothing about until it was all over—he'd got the part and she'd had to okay it.

"Sorry." Sheesh, would she ever stop apologising? "He's a meddling so-and-so, and really shouldn't have involved you." Arietta grimaced. "I'll have words with him."

The guy smiled. "Okay, enough of the sorry. As for Thomas involving me? Oh he really should. Therefore, as he did…" His voice lowered to the octave that sent shivers down every woman's spine—in the nicest possible way. "We'll have fun."

Yeah and I'm a banana.

"Amos Kirby, star of stage and screen and the recipient of naked girl photos, knickers and goodness knows what else, and all those other clichés, accompanying me, as my partner to my not-really-mates' wedding?" Arietta asked sceptically. "No one would believe it. Anyway, I'll resend my apologies. Say I got the date mixed up. They think so little of me, they'll believe it."

He patted her shoulder. "Oh ye of little faith. Want to bet on it? Any of it? You'll look a right eejit if you do that. Why reinforce someone's stupid opinions? Show them how ridiculous they are."

It was true, which didn't make it any better. Arietta groaned. "I'll kill my brother. Why did he stick his nose into it?"

"He loves you," Moss said. "He was worried because, in his words, the snotty little gits have no regard for others. I must admit, I didn't think they'd stoop so low, which just shows how little I really know them, if you get my meaning. I'm at a loose end, and I'd enjoy doing it, if for no other reason than to rub their snotty little gitty noses into the ground and show you're a better person than either of them. I've met Tarquin, he's a close friend of someone I know and boy does he think a lot of himself. I'd love to see him squirm a bit. Or a lot. When I first met him he was a repulsive creature. Better now but oh-so boring... I do wonder about Kristin's taste at times, but then, as she's grown up I guess her taste has changed." Not necessarily for the better, his tone inferred.

"You know them?" Arietta asked. That could be a problem.

"Slightly...or let's say a bit and a bit more but...."
Clear as mud.

"So we'll go together." He made it sound as if it was settled.

Arietta decided it was time to be forceful and explain he'd got it wrong. She would not be coerced into doing the opposite to what she wanted, whatever her twin thought was for the best. It was her life, not his. She hadn't interfered with the tangled relationship — or non-relationship — between him and Jan, so he could just keep his nose out of her life, thank you very much.

"I'm not going, it doesn't matter," she said shortly. Gah, she was beginning to sound like a stuck record. "Thomas needs to mind his own business."

Moss did the crinkle-eyed grin again. Really it should be labelled Dangerous, Avoid At All Costs. "He worries. He says as his twin you are his business. As his friend, what worries him is my business. He's been a rock to me, and you could say I owe him, big-time. As I fancy you..." He stopped and cleared his throat. "You need a...a what?" he went on glibly. Too glibly, Arietta decided, but kept her peace to see what he came up with next.

"Someone with you," he said. "I'm your man. Amos to Mum when she's mad with me, and to all and sundry as my 'work name'. Moss to my friends, especially my close friends. Like you from now on."

Oh how I wish. Actually she didn't. The last thing she wanted was to be classed as someone's arm candy or whatever. Not that she fitted into the arm candy classification. Arietta was perfectly happy with her five-foot-ten, thin-as-a-lath, not-much-boobage figure, but she could imagine what some people would say if she were linked to such a bloke as Moss Kirby.

"With you as a…a what? Friend, partner…"

"Lover. Or," he amended, as she blinked and laughed, "wanna-be lover at least. No idea why you're laughing, though."

"Oh, come on. You and me?" Arietta waved a hand at herself. "I'm not in the partner-of-the-famous category."

"Snob."

"I am not," Arietta said indignantly. "I'm a realist."

"Nope." He shook his head and the curls did their dance and bob thing again. "A snob. S…N…O…B. I think you would fill the position of my lover, the woman I'm besotted with, admirably." He gave her a smouldering look and his green eyes appeared to sparkle. "You, only you, my love. For now and for eternity. Shall we kiss on it and ride off into the sunset for ever after?"

"Very good," Arietta said admiringly. "You smoulder beautifully. But you forgot to add something about my beauteous eyes, or amazing— Well, no, not that."

For a second she could have sworn her remark hurt him, but before she had time to think about it, he blinked and laughed.

"I can do better if need be. Smooth talk and …" He made quote marks. "You know. Act all lovey dovey and gooey. Go on, live dangerously, say yes. I'd love to do it and, better still, I'm an actor. Evidently I excel at…what is it Thom said? 'Playing the hot-as-Hades lover'." He rolled his eyes and hooted with laughter. "By the end of five minutes they'll all believe I'm madly in love with you, and you're the one holding back."

I wish.

"What did Thomas do as your rock, or shouldn't I ask?" Rude, and an abrupt change of subject, but hey ho, if you didn't ask, you certainly didn't get. Anyway, Arietta reasoned, she was nosy, wanted to know and it might, just might, help her understand what had motivated him to come and offer to help, even if it wasn't wanted. He hadn't known that.

"Ask away," Moss said cheerfully. "He held my hand, metaphorically speaking, when my life went arse-up. I was well on the way to chucking it all in because one of my fans got a bit too chummy in a stalkerish way, then put about lies and scurrilous gossip which people were only too happy to believe. Thom told me not to be a twit. That it wasn't my fault and I'd need to get harder in my attitude in dealing with that sort of crap." He smiled reminiscently. "Brought me to my senses and gave me what for when I needed it. He's done it more than once. This is a chance to show certain people, we're not Billy No-Mates, repay Thom and help you."

"That sounds like him."

"I owe him big-time. That apart, the you and me scenario? It'll work."

"Sure of yourself, aren't you?" She wished she could believe him.

He shrugged. "I've learnt not to sell myself short. So should you."

Sometimes she could strangle her brother, best intentions and all.

"I'm not the actor in the family." Arietta was aware she sounded pathetic and sorry for herself. *Pitiful, pull the panties up.* "I can't act at all. I used to be the mushroom, or a statue, in the school plays. A non-speaking, not-moving part. No talent. Can't act."

"That's the beauty of it," Moss assured her. "You won't need to. I'll do it all, acting or otherwise. You just hold on to my arm, and if anyone asks something you don't like, either smile enigmatically or look down your nose at their impertinence. I'll do the rest."

Arietta shook her head. He made it all sound so believable, but she knew herself. "I'd fail. Or freeze."

"You wouldn't, you know. I wouldn't let you. Oh, go on," he coaxed. "It'll be fun. Apart from anything else, Tacky Tarq needs to be shown he's not the be all and end all of everything, even if Kristin thinks he is."

Arietta spluttered. "Tacky Tarq, oh I love it. We called him Tarq the Tosser. Afterwards."

"We?"

"My flatmates and me. Apart from Kristin-Krystal, the bride-to-be, of course. The flatmate who chose him and not uni. Evidently she thought he was beddable. Seems she still does. No accounting for taste."

"So, any of those flatmates…" Moss said in a strange voice that she didn't understand. "You still in touch?"

Arietta nodded. "All of them apart from Kristin." She wondered if any of the others had received an invitation and made a note to ask. She'd been so engrossed in getting her latest book finished that they'd not been in touch for a while. Luckily they knew her and accepted that.

"What would your flatmates say you should do?"

Did he sound relieved? She had no idea and didn't think it was something she could ask. Nevertheless, it intrigued her.

She sighed. "Go for it."

Moss raised one eyebrow. "So?"

How the hell he managed that without screwing up his face and appearing ridiculous she had no idea, but wished she did. It was such a handy trick.

"Are you up for it?"

Arietta made her a split-second decision. "Okay. If you think we can pull it off, you're on."

* * * *

It was one thing to say okay, another to accept just what she'd let herself be talked into. More than once Arietta started a "can't do this" text, only to berate herself for being a wimp and deleting the words. If nothing else she'd get to see Pannerburn Castle, which she reasoned could perhaps work as somewhere she could use in one of her books. Not as it was now, but as she could imagine it had been two hundred years earlier. Poetic licence was a wonderful thing. Idly she wondered if there were any cellars that could pass as a dungeon or two. Not that it was likely she'd get a chance to find out.

Arietta pondered the subject and decided she wasn't actually interested enough to find out, and she really didn't want to go to the wedding. She'd send Moss a note saying she'd changed her mind but thank you anyway.

When it came down to it, she really wasn't up for a posh wedding, having to wear shoes that would no doubt pinch and watching two people she didn't care for go all sheep-eyed over each other. Taking their vows and plighting their troth when she knew just how easily vows could be, and were, broken.

Time to woman up and make a stand.

Which was exactly what she would have done except she realised she'd forgotten to get Moss' phone number. He'd said he'd be away for a week or so then call by. They had arranged a day and a time. It seemed daft for him to have to come to her house to be told she'd changed her mind.

However, the daftness looked as if it would have to go ahead. Arietta had phoned her twin to ask for the number.

Thomas had refused. *"We thought you might renege,"* he'd said. *"Which is why you don't have it, and I'm not sharing. If you're going to be chicken and bloody rude, you can tell him face to face. I never knew I had such a coward for a sister."*

"I'm not a…" Arietta had discovered she was talking to herself. Thomas had disconnected. *Oh boy. Another apology to make.* She'd need to start a list at this rate. The day before she'd snapped at the postie when he'd rung the doorbell to ask for a letter he'd put through her letterbox by mistake. It was for someone half a mile away and had got mixed up with hers. It was lucky he'd realised and saved her a trip into the village, but he'd broken her train of thought, and it had taken her ages to get to the point where she had been.

Damn. And damn her brother for saying what he had.

She was *not* a coward, just cautious. "Life is too short to do stuff you really do not want to do," Arietta said out loud as she picked up a dishcloth and wiped a smear she'd missed from a plate. "Sod him." Now she was going to have to explain it all to Moss, and apologise about her change of heart and the fact that she'd dragged him from wherever he could have been just to tell him that. No doubt he'd be annoyed, and she couldn't blame him.

Meanwhile she had edits on her latest book to do and send back and really couldn't get in the right frame of mind. As her editor had asked for a bit more love interest, she was even less inclined to get stuck in. Writing about sex, even sex of the two-hundred-years-ago variety, when it was a dim and distant memory, was not in her top ten list of things she wanted to do.

Poor Lady Amelia was in for a hard time. Arietta decided the woman would lead the bloke on, drop him and save herself from being murdered. Then she could forget about people in love, weddings and sex.

She hoped.

* * * *

She didn't have a chance. Everything she read, watched or heard seemed to be about happily ever after. Even the daily news had a bloody wedding on it.

And if it wasn't marriage it was divorce. Arietta switched the evening news off with a groan of annoyance and took herself off for a walk towards the village. The local shop stayed open until nine, so she would nip in and buy some chocolate.

She was munching her way through a honeycomb bar when someone shouted her name.

"Arietta, wait up."

Arietta turned to see probably her best friend in the village, Maggie, waving.

"Hey, you! I hollered, but you didn't hear me," Maggie said breathlessly as she jogged to where Arietta waited. "In the throes?"

"Nope, wool-gathering. Want a bar?" She waved the wrapper. "It was a pack of four."

"Prefer a gin." Maggie grinned. "Fancy joining me in the pub garden for a swift one? My darling husband is at the footie and I'm bored of my own company. I was actually going to walk past yours and see if I could see you and coax you out."

Arietta made up her mind. She had nothing to do that couldn't wait—except the edits, and she'd get stuck in the following day. Maybe she could sound out Maggie's opinion over the wedding? "Why not?"

"Great! Come on, I'll shout you for one." Maggie led the way across the green. "Grab a table near the midge eater."

Arietta laughed, did as she was bid, as well as spraying herself liberally with bug repellent. She handed the can to Maggie once that lady had returned with their drinks and settled on the opposite side of the table. "Want some?"

Maggie grinned. "Whew ta, hon. I forgot any." She used the spray in much the same way Arietta had. "Thought I'd outrun the buggers. So as in the words of one of our favourite TV shows, what's occurin'?"

Arietta laughed. What a good opening. "Loads. Are you ready to be my muse or whatever?"

Maggie opened her eyes wide. "Ohhh, a muse. Bring it on." She put two packets of crisps on the table. "I have my muse hat here all ready and waiting. What am I to muse about?"

"It's not a muse exactly," Arietta said as Maggie opened the crisps and gestured to them. She took one and ate it as she considered how best to explain. "I want to pick your brain."

"Difficult," Maggie said with a grin. "Not sure it's working after the day I've had. Anyhow, have a go and good luck."

"Right, well in a nutshell, I've been invited to a posh wedding of a very brief time together ex and a girl I knew for an equally brief time at uni, if you follow that?"

Maggie nodded. "Yeah, you've the same sort of convoluted way of putting things as me."

"Great. Well, I've not spoken to them since then so that's what, about fourteen or so years ago. No idea why they sent it really. After all, I couldn't care less what they're up to."

"Ohhh, do you think they think you do?"

Arietta shrugged. "No idea, I mean I've rarely thought about them. Lots of water under the bridge. Anyway, I decided I'd send my apologies, except my meddling brother decided I needed to get over them, Stu and out in the world again — his words — and forged my signature on an acceptance. I am over them, it was a very short-lived acquaintance, and over Stu, and I get out just fine. When I want to."

"Stu was a plonker who deserved castrating," Maggie said explosively. "Even I thought how lovely he was at first, and I'm the least susceptible person in the world. How were you to know he would turn into a two-timing slimy evil toad? He fooled the lot of us. Hell, even our dear vicar's wife thought he was a lovely personable young man with impeccable manners. Just goes to show."

She didn't elaborate on what it showed, for which Arietta was glad. The sorry saga of Stu was best swept under the carpet. *There's a title for a chapter in a romcom if ever there was one.*

"Are you going then? By yourself or…?" Maggie left the question dangling.

Arietta sighed. "It looks like it, maybe, probably. Oh hell I don't know." She didn't want to admit that Moss was only going with her because Thomas had asked him to. That was way too pathetic. "With a friend, if I go, but I really resent time away, new clothes and so on to go to a wedding I don't want to attend at a place where, after I've paid to stay there, I'll need to live on bread and jam for a month." She realised she and Moss had got round to discussing her accommodation. "Even with so-called 'preferential wedding rates'. I prefer to keep my arm and a leg. Shows they live in a world I don't."

"Airbnb? Nearby caravan site?" Maggie suggested. "Where is it anyway?"

"Pannerburn Castle."

Maggie whistled. "Oh my... Bread and jam for a month? More likely six, at least. Why not go, don't have a drink and come home?"

"Or why just not go and save myself all the angst?"

"Thomas was right." Maggie shook her head. "You need to go and show them you don't care. Is your partner a hot bloke? You know, one who can go all gooey-eyed over you and show them that they're the losers, not you."

Arietta giggled. "Not sure about the gooey-eyed bit, but yes, he is very personable."

"For personable, I'll read hot. You're going. And introduce me to Mr Personable next time he's about. Want another G and T?"

"Why not, my shout this time."

Chapter Three

A picture in the Sunday paper of Moss with his arms round a very glamorous woman in an almost-there dress captioned, "Amos Kirby out on the town with Selina Readon, his glamorous co-star," didn't improve Arietta's already fluctuating state of mind. He'd told her he was going to be busy promoting the film he'd not long finished and would see her the following weekend, but no mention had been made of his name linked elsewhere. Contrarily, Arietta wondered how on earth he expected to pull off their so-called romance if he was with someone else. She stomped around the house, wished she had a budgie so she could use the paper to line its cage, and once more swore off men. A short paragraph the next day saying the couple had been at a charity film showing hadn't helped a lot. He hadn't even mentioned he was going to anything like that.

And not invited her?

That brought Arietta up short. Why on earth should he? As it appeared there was a totally innocuous reason for the photo, she decided she either had to ignore it and accept things like that were part and parcel of almost-but-not-quite being involved with a celebrity or spend half her life wondering what he was or was not up to and becoming a distrustful, unlovable, misogynist female.

She opted for the former and hoped, if they did do the whole we-are-a-couple thing, that she would learn to accept it.

Meanwhile she had a book to write, and she had best get on with it.

As usual, that helped to put things into perspective, and by the time Moss turned up the following week, she'd talked herself into a much more resolute and amicable frame of mind.

* * * *

"To pull it off, as you say, we better learn a bit more about each other." Moss sat in Arietta's garden and glared at the midges, which danced over the lawns and would make it impossible to be outside once the sun went down. "Who invented midges and why?" he asked as he swatted at a nigh-on-invisible insect. "Damned things."

Arietta passed him the spray. She'd already got the midge-eating machine on but it didn't seem to matter how many were drawn to it, the same number weren't. Sitting in the garden was always a juggling act, deciding how long to stick it out and when you gave up and had to go inside. Even with a long-sleeved top and trousers, there was too much uncovered flesh for the midges to home in on. Moss in his cut-off jeans and short-sleeved T-shirt must appear like dinner, lunch and breakfast all rolled into one to them.

"Midges are one of the nasties of the world," she said as he sprayed himself liberally. "You missed a bit on your neck." She pointed to the appropriate spot and moved her hand away smartly as he hit the nozzle on the can. "They're sent to try us, and my goodness they do. But then, without them I'd spend every one of the few nice days we get outside and miss my deadlines, so it's catch-22."

Moss chuckled as he covered the bit she'd pointed out with repellent. "So their reason for being is to send procrastinating authors hot-footing to their computers and actors to a comfy chair and a beer? Sounds fair enough to me."

"So it seems. And our aim is to stop them biting us and committing suicide in the wine. In the pond, yeah, go for it, but in the wine? I can get protein elsewhere, thank you very much." She laughed. "The number of times I've sat outside covered in clothes and repellent, holding a beer mat over my wine glass, determined to stop out because allegedly it's summer. Just because we get long-light nights doesn't mean the midges stay away. I'm sick of hearing about people down south with their barbecues and friends in the garden till ten. It's not worth it here — you pay for it in the end. Usually with a bite map of Australia on you somewhere because the buggers found a spot you missed, or you had a hole in your sock. Now I've got the time-to-retreat-act down to a fine art. Any minute now."

Moss slapped his arms. "Damn, one got by the barricade. I've had enough. Time to go in?"

She nodded. "Yep."

"Discussion to follow." He picked up their glasses of wine. "After you."

Would the discussion include why there had been that picture of him and Selina Readon arm in arm?

At least it wasn't tonsil to tonsil.

* * * *

The discussion was something Arietta wasn't looking forward to. Whenever she thought of it, her mind circled back to the fact that if she didn't go to the wedding, they wouldn't need to have the conversation. She admitted that as an essentially a private person, talking about herself was hard. Thomas was the gregarious twin, not her. However, she understood it had to be done if they were going to carry their charade off. It had been hard enough trying to find a few days when Moss could make it to her part of Scotland so they could chat in private and be sure to get their stories straight for later. Thomas had crowed when she'd told him she'd given in and would be happy to say he'd introduced them. Not exactly true, but she'd reasoned the best she could do at present. The story to be put about was that when he and Moss had turned up at Arietta's for a couple of days of peace and quiet, Moss had been immediately smitten.

Arietta was glad it was Moss smitten and not the other way around. She wasn't sure she could carry that off. Fancied yes, but… "Do you really think people will believe us?" she said as they settled indoors. "I mean, why on earth would someone like you fanc—" She broke off as Moss put his hand over her mouth.

"Enough already. If you say that once more, I *will* shake you," he said in an exasperated voice. "Why shouldn't I? Grief, woman, have you such a low opinion of yourself?"

Arietta hadn't thought of it like that. "Well, no but…" She sighed. "I guess I'm just worried that somehow, someone will show it as it is."

"Yes, someone will. Us." Moss took hold of her hand. "Why do you find it so hard to accept I do like you? Don't you like me?" He did a hangdog look. "Not even a little bit?"

Arietta shook her head. "Oh, man, you do that poor me even better than Thomas and he's a master at the 'woe is me I'm so hard done by stuff'. Look, you're a well-known person. Oscar nominated, Oscar winner and all that. Everybody knows everything about you. You learn lines for a living. You'll remember what I tell you. I'm just me, and I'm sure not to remember something important. I don't go to posh dos all glammed up."

He looked wary then laughed. "Aha, now I know why I thought I detected frost. The not so lovely in real life Selina?"

Arietta felt a fool. "It's nothing to do with me really, is it, but I admit it was a bit of a shock to see that picture in the paper."

"What you didn't see was her very possessive boyfriend on the other side of her, who stood back while the photo was taken and reclaimed her damned quick after. Publicity for the film. Out of interest, if I had asked you, would you have gone with me?"

"What?" she said, astonished by the question and ignoring the brief flutter of her heart. Of course she wouldn't...or would she have? "No, of course not."

Hurt flashed across his face in a manner she'd noticed before when she'd been so dismissive of his life. *Dammit.* "It's a bit too soon for that," Arietta added as diplomatically as she could. "I'd be all fingers and thumbs and say the wrong thing. Scary thought."

He laughed. "Like what? All we really need to get clear is how we met, where we met and when we met. We would have sorted that out beforehand and hey presto. All would have been well. We can start practising now and you can come with me if I get a nomination for something. You never know, we might not need to act by then, we might be a loverlee couple," he finished in a sing-song voice. "Us. Until then, we'll practice for the wedding."

"It's easy to say." Arietta sighed. She could undoubtedly let herself more than just like Moss. It was the aftermath that worried her. She couldn't see any way two people with such different lifestyles could coexist, and she'd had enough of unrequited... Not love, but consideration? Loyalty? Whatever it was, she was all for a quieter life for a while.

"It's easy to do as well." Moss rubbed his hands up and down her arms. Such a simple thing to do, but so personal. Arietta was disappointed when he stopped.

"Look, any new-together couple don't know everything about each other," Moss added. "You learn things as you go along. If you forget, you ask again. Simple. But think on this. You write, you remember what you've written, yes?"

She nodded. "Most of the time, but I make notes as well." *Lots of notes.*

"So imagine this as part of a book. Neither of us need to be word perfect."

"My books do," Arietta said with a smirk. "Or they'd be one-starred and get horrible write-ups."

He twitched his lips. "Well, this is the first read over then. Where you hope everything is going well and you've not edited it. We'll be at the confident-that-we-like-each-other stage but wondering if there's more. Enjoying discovering each other's foibles and so on. Well, you are. I'm damned sure there's much more. However, I'm prepared not to rush you."

"You what??" She hadn't expected that.

He winked. "Maybe we could discover, er, be discovering if there is a spark or two between us? Both in our roles and in real life. When you're ready to believe me. So anyway, let's start. Introduced by Thom. When was he last around before he found your invite?"

Arietta considered. "About a month before, I think. He said the pair of you had just finished a film and you both had a few weeks off."

"Yeah, we actually came up to Scotland. You were on a deadline so I went off to do some wild camping for a few days while he popped in, and as he said, annoyed you, fed you coffee and bullied you to eat. Then we met up again and headed back down south."

"I remember." She'd wanted to shake Thomas on more than one occasion as he'd bullied her into stopping typing and eating whatever he'd prepared. However, she'd admitted later, it had been the best thing that could have happened. Fed and watered, she'd got renewed energy and had finished on target. "I got the manuscript sent off with a day to spare. He said he was going to do a low-key film set in the Channel Islands, which is where he is now, and you're... Damn, I don't think he said what you're going to do."

"That's because he didn't know." Moss stretched his legs out. "All very hush-hush, and several months overdue, but I guess the news will be out soon. I'm doing a TV series set in...drum roll...Scotland. Which fits in perfectly for us. Due to the leading lady breaking her arm, it doesn't start for a few months, but I like to learn the lie of the land. Do you have a spare room I can rent?"

"A sp... You mean it's around here?" That she hadn't bargained for. "You'll be local?" Arietta wasn't sure how she felt about that. Good for their story but...

He nodded. "Yup. On the loch. Twelve weeks' solid filming, starting late summer. Well, solid except I've said the wedding weekend I'm not around. Which, if we had started when we should have would have been when we finished, if you get my meaning. Lucky for them I told my agent I needed some time free, so my next film isn't due to start until the new year." He twirled an imaginary moustache and leered. "Perfect for us."

Arietta spluttered. "You are incorrigible." She didn't mention his declaration about the fact he thought he more than liked her. She'd think about that later. "You know you've almost got me believing in this romance. So we met where? Here?"

He nodded. "Seems plausible, don't you think? Did anyone see Thom when he was up?"

"Nope, friends know to steer clear when I'm on deadline." *And I'm a solitary sod, really, especially at that time of the month when snarling comes more naturally than a smile.* She decided to keep that to herself. "Apart from Thomas, who is a law unto himself." She grinned. The 'do not come near me this week or for however long' came in handy sometimes. She always caught up with her friends when a deadline had passed. "Otherwise, I had a gorgeous week all on my lonesome."

"Perfect. So no one would know if there was only you here, you and Thom, Thom, you and me, or just me and you. Unless you mentioned it."

Arietta cast her mind back. "Nope, no one, because I was adamant I had a deadline. It's just as well some certain people don't understand how few deadlines I actually have. There's some who always get told the deadline story if Thom is about or they would be moaning I'd not invited them round so they could fangirl. I do wonder how old some of them are, or what their IQ is. I mean, seriously." She shook her head. "Married women acting as if they're silly knicker-throwing teens."

"Honestly?" Moss asked with interest. "Er…where?"

She shook her head at him.

He laughed. "Poor Thom, he was the one to insist I soon learn how to dodge anything like that. I don't blame him for keeping a low profile. I had one friend of my mum's, years ago, who kept hinting she'd love to 'show me the ropes'. And emphasised ropes. I declined for every reason you could think of and then some. In the end I had to ask my mum to do something."

"Did she?"

Moss nodded. "Yeah, said I had a morality clause in my contract. Or she told me she said that, but by the way the woman gave me a wide berth the next time, I've a feeling that wasn't all she said. Anyway, whatever it was, it worked. It was all fine and dandy until the stalkerish episode I told you about. I've no idea how I would have coped with that if it hadn't been for Thom's support and suggestions, even if we didn't go with the more outrageous of them. Before you ask, I'm not sharing them. Very much in the dodgy spectrum. In the end we used the morality bit, and added I'd be penniless and on the dole when the film ended. A bit far-fetched but Thom showed her an, *ahem*…document purporting to say that."

"I love it! It'd be the same for either of you, I guess. Thomas doesn't come here for anything but peace, and goes into hermit mode, and after that horror I'd reckon you'd be the same."

"Oh yes," Moss said and shuddered. "There's a time and a place for everything. I've been thinking, and at the risk of sounding up myself, it works even better if we say Thom and I were both here for a while, then me by myself for the last three or four days?" He glanced sideways at her. "And we discovered how close we are and want to be even closer? Yes?"

Why on earth not? Maybe it is time to live dangerously.

"Yes." She returned his high five with vigour. Perhaps they might pull it all off. Maybe—as long as she didn't screw up.

"So on to the next." Moss gestured at the wine. "Can I top us up?" They'd only had a small glass each. Arietta nodded. As she rarely drank alone, it was good to sit with someone and savour the merlot.

"Okay." Moss sorted the drinks and put the bottle back down. "Mini condensed Amos Kirby life story. Loved drama in my teens, did a lot of amateur stuff. Kept me out of mischief—mainly, though I did once almost get caught in the props cupboard with— Okay, enough of that." He coughed. "Don't want to give you the wrong idea."

"Never," Arietta said gravely, then spoiled it as she sniggered. "Good visual, though."

"Thanks for that, love."

"Love?"

"Practising, and stop distracting me. I can't get the poor girl's horrified expression as we heard the door open out of my mind. Or the slap on the face I got as the door closed behind whoever it was. Sad thing, I hadn't even managed to get to half first base, let alone first. The joys of youth, and all that. So where was I?"

"In the prop cupboard?" Arietta suggested. "With a sore face and an angry girl, who I must add, went in willingly I assume, so why was she so incensed? Surely she didn't think you were going to play tiddlywinks or count backcloths?"

"True enough," Moss said. "I learnt my lesson, though. Don't choose anywhere you might be discovered."

Arietta rolled her eyes. "I bet. With a twin brother I learnt a lot about how the male thought process goes. Apart from thinking with your gonads not your brain, it's now or I might miss my chance until, all of a sudden, it's now let's plot properly. Yes?"

"Yes, okay, we are fickle and lead with a part of our anatomy that prefers to act first."

She laughed.

Moss tutted. "Enough, woman, let me concentrate."

Arietta firmed her lips—to stop herself laughing again—folded her arms and inclined her head. He rolled his eyes.

"Okay, Early thirties, left school after I got my first bit role, got a bigger bit role so no uni, though I was going to do history at Durham," Moss went on. "Still might someday. Been mainly employed since, so very lucky, though I have done the what-almost-seems-mandatory waiting on tables, and also served in a chip shop. Both of which I enjoyed. My batter is second to none. Okay, I like it anyway," he added as Arietta rolled her eyes. "I make great scraps as well. Or do you call them scranchuns or batter bits?"

"Bits, or scraps. but one of my uni mates used to call them scrumps. I know what you mean anyway."

"Great. So, Mum and Dad are alive and living in Franschhoek, South Africa. Loving their retirement. Two elder sisters, both married. Donna the eldest, just about to hit the big four-oh and doesn't care. Married to Frank, has two boys, and lives in Portugal. Marian, two years older than me, married to Chris and living not far from Mum and Dad, is steadfastly refusing to have any kids. Says two nephews are enough kids in her vicinity. Not that that makes sense as Portugal and South Africa aren't exactly on the other's doorstep, but I think I know what she means. Each to their own."

Would he like kids? Arietta had no intention of asking.

"What else?" Moss continued. "I'm thirty-three, single, solvent, hale and healthy. I did think I might be in love once, a long while ago, but it turned out she was, in her words, 'slumming' while the rich boyfriend was away. When he returned a few weeks later 'bye, bye, Moss' and that was the end of us. Hurt at the time, lots of consequences, one who...but...not relevant at the moment, maybe later." He sighed. "That's life. I got over it soon enough, which shows it wasn't serious after all. Also taught me to be cautious."

One who? What else had he been going to say? Arietta considered pushing him and decided it wouldn't be right. Not yet.

"I bet. Guess we all go through that stage to some degree or another." She certainly had. *In spades.*

"Guess so. Anyway, I love seafood and fish in any shape or form, except jellied eels. Give me real ale every time, no fizzy lager stuff, and my secret vice is prawn-flavoured crisps. Hate pork and detest fruit with meat. Fruit is fruit, meat is meat, and in my mind, never the twain should merge. Note I didn't say never *meet*." He rolled his eyes and Arietta laughed.

"Yeah, a bit cringeworthy." She opened her laptop. "Hold on."

"What are you doing?" Moss asked curiously. "What should I hold on to?"

"Ha-ha. Funny, very funny." Arietta rolled her eyes. "I'm writing it down like a plot," she explained as she typed furiously, hit a wrong key, cussed, pressed delete and typed what she meant. "I'll get rid of it soon, don't worry. I'm taking your advice and treating it like a plot for a book. And if it isn't all true, it would make a darned good plot as well. This way, though, it's more likely to stick in my brain. As long as I don't accidentally think it's a real plot and you find your life story as my next book."

Moss roared with laughter. "It's all true, I promise, but I love your style. You could always disguise me somehow, give me a double chin and a wart or three."

"Nah, too stereotypical for a baddie. Make you a smooth-talker and —" She broke off as she decided that to say a hot lover would be one sentence too far. "And anyway, I don't want lots of Moss fans dissing me."

"Fair enough, and I like the fact you think I've got fans. Sometimes I do wonder, especially when I get crap written about me on social media. Okay, I try to ignore it, but occasionally it stings."

She hadn't realised he could be vulnerable as well. It helped her think she just might have made the right decisions about agreeing to go to the wedding with him. For if she were honest, to send her regrets now would look weird, and cause a lot of speculation she didn't want.

"Your turn," Moss said.

"Just a sec. Right, think I've got it all." Arietta pressed Save and shut her laptop. She'd reread it all later. "I don't know how much Thomas has told you?" She wasn't sure where to start. Did he really want to know how old she was when she walked or how Thomas had broken her arm by sitting on her? Had Thomas mentioned her habit of eating jelly babies headfirst, then legs and finally the torso?

"Pretend he's told me nothing, it'll be easier," Moss suggested. "Just tell me what you'd share with a new maybe-lover and add a bit more. After all, what Thom would tell me would be nothing like you'd say."

"True." Why hadn't she thought of that? "Our mum and dad live about an hour's drive from here, — still in the same house they bought when they got married. That's when they aren't, as Mum puts it, gadding about. They travel a lot. One brother, my annoying, ten-minutes-older twin who you know oh-so well. So, thirty-one and three-quarters, single and solvent, own this house as my godmother left it to me. Thomas was peeved as she left him a motorbike, three dozen chickens and a sewing machine. Non-vintage. Aunt Mairi, as I called her, was loaded, and left the rest to a home for ageing whippets. Not that that isn't worthy, but as Thomas said the motorbike needed a MOT, and the chickens were past laying."

"Was she his godmother too?"

Arietta shook her head. "Nope, and his godmother is alive and well, and says she'll leave me some chickens and a clapped-out mini to even us up. He got the better deal, I could do with another sewing machine. Mine is great at scrambling the thread." She chuckled. "Actually, on second thought, scrub that, it's probably my crap sewing skills that mangle the cotton and not the machine's fault. Mind you, a new one, not one from the ark would be good. Preferably one for idiots."

Moss smirked. "Mine left me a book of sayings. Horrid things like 'cleanliness is next to godliness' and 'a tidy house is a tidy mind'. The tidy house she left me was anything but. Run down, falling down and not a penny to spend on it. She thought actors were all up to no good and said that in her will, plus the declaration she wasn't going to give me money to waste. Presumably she thought the house wasn't worth it. When I saw the state it was in I agreed with her. Sorry, go on."

She tucked that snippet in the back of her mind and hoped she'd remember it. "Not a lot more really. Thomas broke my arm by sitting on it when I wouldn't make him a cuppa. Mum went ape, Dad drove me to hospital, and Thomas had to make my breakfast every day for six weeks and carry my rucksack to and from school for a couple of months. As it was bright pink and covered with patches of pop stars, I reckon it was penance enough."

Moss roared with laughter. "Poor Thom. Yeah, I reckon that was punishment and more. Did his street cred survive?"

"Duh, of course. Eventually he did the 'I'm male enough to embrace my female side' stuff, but it took a while for his sense of humour to resurface. After school St Andrews Uni, where I met Tacky Tarq and Kristin. Didn't know them not really, even though she shared with us and he spent some time with me." That was a neat way of putting it, she thought.

"Didn't work?" Moss asked with what Arietta decided was considerable constraint.

Arietta shook her head. "Nah, we wanted different things. Anyway, I got a degree in English, left and worked at a few non-memorable jobs. Some I enjoyed, like tourist officer and library assistant, some I didn't, like bookshop manager. Too many books and no time to read them. Then I decided to try and write and after a few 'no thank you, sorry, not for us' replies and a few more 'heard nothing' non-replies, got published. The readers of my little genre seem to like me."

Plus, with the house all paid for she could afford to live from her earnings—just. Not all writers earned mega bucks, but she didn't intend to share that. It might sound as if she wanted Moss to contribute.

"Food?" Moss prompted.

"Always."

"Oh good." He rolled his eyes. "Expand, and not our waistlines."

Arietta sniggered. "Er, let me see. Love chocolate, coffee and wine, hate liver, kidney and cheese."

"Cheese, that's it, the love affair is over." Moss roared with laughter. "I love it, the stronger the better. On second thoughts, nope, it's on. It means I get twice as much cheese. Between us we can always find something to eat. Now about that room?"

He was like a dog with a bone.

"Do you really need it?" she asked, suspicious it was a ploy, though she had no idea what for. "Honestly? Wouldn't a hotel be better?"

"It really wouldn't and I really do. I have to sleep somewhere," Moss said reasonably. "I'd rather it here with all the home comforts than in an impersonal hotel. Meals with no gravy, fancy bits and bobs that I can't identify, and just some jus dribbled over everything soon lose their appeal. As does shop talk every night. Plus, it will add credence to our story if I'm here."

Arietta sighed. It was all getting rather complicated. "Well…"

"Pretty please, Ettie Betty."

She glared. "What did you call me?"

Moss winked. "I thought it could be my lover-like name for you. I could make it Etta-Betta if you'd prefer?"

"Not if you value your body as it is." She'd had some weird nicknames but that one was new. And unacceptable. "Anything less lover-like I have no idea." Apart from fat-bum, and she had no intention of sharing that thought.

"Ouch." Moss made a show of covering his groin. "What then?"

"Oh grief. Ari, or Etta, I guess." She'd never liked her name shortened. "Never unless you have to, please. It leads to stupid jokes like 'Ari up, and Etta move on', which actually isn't funny. Nor is Arc or Arcy, which some twit thought might be good for me at uni."

"Definitely not Arcy... Fair enough to the rest, petal, my love. How's that?" He beamed as if he'd handed her first prize for something special, but spoiled it as he winked and grinned. "Good, eh?"

"Complicated. Okay, you win, dearest. Or is that sweet cheeks?" How had she never realised banter was fun? "Lollipop, cupcake, precious?"

He paled in an overdramatic manner. "Ow, woman. Dearest, or my love will do admirably. Sweet cheeks is a bit too sugary."

She agreed with that. "Right, where were we?"

"A room?" Moss prompted. "After all, I have to live somewhere."

"Don't you have a home?" Arietta asked absently, forgetting he was looking for somewhere near where he was going to film, and that it was all a way of getting to know each other. It seemed an awful lot of faff for a wedding she didn't want to go to. It would be so much easier to send her apologies.

But then there would be no reason to meet with Moss. And if she were honest, she enjoyed their time together. As long as it stayed casual and there was no pressure for anything else. She wasn't up for that yet.

"Yeah, but I'd rather be here."

Chapter Four

Arietta blinked. She'd been so deep in thought she'd forgotten what she'd asked him. Ah, yes, a home. "Why's that? What's wrong with it? Where is it anyway?" She'd noticed he hadn't told her where it was.

"Apart from I want to be with you? It's had cows in it."

"Cows?" Had she wandered into a different universe? "You keep cows in your house?"

"Not me and not anymore, but it was a cowshed."

"Surely you've had it converted, cleaned and so on?" It sounded intriguing. She loved how creative some people could be. Not, she guessed, that he'd done it all himself.

He nodded. "Of course, they moved to brand new, all-mooing, all-dancing quarters, but their presence sort of lingers. I keep finding presents, especially in the garden."

"Good for the roses. So what else?"

"Tadpoles," he said mournfully.

"Tadpoles?"

Moss nodded. "In the pool."

"What's wrong with that?" Arietta asked, mystified. "Frogs breed in pools."

"Not in a swimming pool."

The conversation was becoming more surreal by the minute. "Right... Why?"

"They wanted a new environment and who am I to deny them that?" Moss asked. "But it's damned inconvenient if you want a swim. You could swallow one, and that wouldn't be good for you or them. Then there's the local fishermen of course."

"Fishing for tadpoles?" She really was confused now.

"No, don't be daft." He gave her a sorrowful look, which he spoiled by winking. "Trout. They use my drive as a short cut down to the river, which is all fine and dandy, I don't mind generally. The fishermen, not the trout. However, that's no good for us to get to know each other on the quiet."

"Why not for us, us?"

He did his innocent expression. "They fish at the oddest hours. They know who's around when, where and who with. You think women gossip? You should hear our fishermen. And of course you get the tales of the ones that get away...and then the winks. We'd have people offering to sell us trout or tadpoles, apologising for mud on the path, or water spilled on the doormat. Eavesdropping to see what we were up to, did we need any help and who washes the car for us? I thought that was the whole idea, we need to be together, with a bit of solitude. We can't do it there very easily, and anyway I know your office is all set up here. You'd need to sort one out at Bannock Cottage."

Arietta's mind was reeling. It was too much to take in at once. Plus, she still had no idea where this Bannock Cottage was.

"Now tell me the truth," she demanded. "I like your fairy tales, but not about this."

"Okay, spoilsport," he grumbled. "There *are* fishermen around but…yes, not relevant. Or the tadpoles and cows. What really happened was I had workmen in to install a new bathroom and somehow they managed to flood the place. Damp house, can't use the electricity until it dries out and at least two rooms will need replastering. It's a bloody nuisance as I've got to move a hell of a lot of stuff out, because the place isn't secure at the moment. Harassed is an understatement. Plus the film is near here and I do not want to go into a hotel. I'd end up having to find somewhere to rent and…well, it seemed like a good idea at the time. Saves me hiding from people or trying to find the energy to cook and… Shit, that sounds as if I mean I'd want you to cook. That's not it and—enough, gonna shut up now, except to say if you want to ask Thom if he thinks it's a good idea, go ahead."

It sounded complicated and horrendous and surely no one could be that inventive on the spur of the moment. Plus, she had no intention of involving her twin. He'd just tell her what a good bloke Moss was, as he had when she'd rung to ask him what he was playing with regards to the wedding. He had added, *"I'd trust him with my life, and yours."*

"Okay you can have the spare room." She gave in. It was much simpler than trying to discover more. "There's only a double bed, not a super king, and no I am not giving mine up." That was non-negotiable. Arietta loved her bed. "Sorry, the room is a bit short of storage space at the moment, we'll need to sort something out. This is with the proviso that if I'm working to a deadline, or in the throws, spelt t-h-r-o-w-s, as I'm liable to throw things, as Thomas calls it, you fend for yourself. I don't cook then, unless it's nukeable in the microwave. Okay?"

He nodded. "Okay, show me my new home from home."

* * * *

After all their discussions, Arietta then found herself without visitors — or house guests for a while — as Thomas wasn't around and Moss ended up in New York for a week. Even at such short acquaintance, she had found out that there were weekends he had other commitments and could neither pop by nor call. She didn't ask what those commitments were, although of course she wanted to know. He'd mentioned he wasn't married nor had a significant other, and she'd accepted that.

He flew to South Africa for a whirlwind visit to see his parents to, as he put it, sow the seed he thought he had found someone special. "*They know I'd tell them if I had and so they'd think something was dodgy about it all if they found out some other way. I can always tell them we couldn't make it work if I need to, later, and garner sympathy and Sauvignon.*"

"It makes me sound like a horrible person," Arietta said as he popped in on his way to a meeting somewhere unspecified. "As if I'm a gold digger, or a groupie. Why couldn't you just keep it quiet for now?"

"Because when I have time in between projects, I either go there or to the Algarve, unless someone or something important takes precedence. As in you, and now. We're a close family, we tell each other a lot." He winked. "Not everything, but a lot, and if I didn't mention I'd found someone I...well, you know, the phone lines and FaceTime app would be red-hot, and questions asked. Therefore I popped over, gave them a brief—very brief—outline as in 'my good mate Thom's sister, not been seeing each other long, so keeping it quiet', etcetera, etcetera. Then I said I was coming back to see you. Which I did. And here I am. Er, got anything to nibble? I've not eaten since a dodgy airline breakfast."

Arietta shook her head and sighed. "What is it with you actors and food?"

"We eat when we can. A lot of the time it's long hours, no food. Any of your pâté lurking around? It's very moreish."

Arietta sighed as she stood up. "My pâté does not lurk."

He grinned.

Arietta couldn't help but return it. "I must have known you'd be here today. I made some this morning." Moss had been incredibly appreciative about her smoked salmon pâté and eaten his way through enough for four on his previous visit.

"Great stuff. Um, mushroom soup as well?" he said hopefully. "I meant to go into everybody's favourite food store and get us some treats but the car park queues were awful so I just headed here. I'll go another day, I promise."

"And get mobbed?" Arietta asked him. "I'll go, you give me a list."

He grinned and kissed her cheek. "Great idea. I'll give you the list and a credit card."

* * * *

Several weeks later, Arietta stood by the open freezer door and debated between a homemade curry, prepared in one of her zealous 'I must eat better' phases and frozen for nights when she was too tired to think about cooking, or a shop-bought paella — also frozen. Neither appealed. She decided she'd have an omelette instead.

Three eggs, a wizened mushroom and a sad-looking tomato reminded her she would need to go shopping before Moss turned up in a few days' time. Her pantry, fridge and freezer were all looking a bit sparse. Thomas had done one of his 'pop in, eat enough for three and run' sessions the day before. As ever, after one of his visits it looked like she'd had a Scout troop around for a meal. One who'd been wild camping for a fortnight and not foraged enough to last more than three days, max. The freezer was half empty and denuded of what she'd call treats. How anyone could eat a large tub of ice cream in one sitting, after a full meal, like Thomas often did, and wasn't sick, she had no idea. It was a wonder she even had the makings of an omelette after his inroads in her cupboard and fridge-freezer. She took another look at the wizened mushroom, decided it was hard enough to crumble cheese and threw it in the compost tub. Surely there must be something else in the freezer she fancied?

Which did nothing to solve the problem, if that was what it was, of Moss and his impending stay. How many times over the past weeks, when he'd been filming or promoting the series and not been around, had she picked up the phone to tell him it was all off only to put the instrument down again. She really didn't want to share her house *or* let another man into her life in any way, but couldn't think of a manner to say so and still be polite. Why did it bother her so much? If she was honest, it was the fact that given not very much, Arietta knew fine well she could fall for him and that, she decided, was not sensible. They were both too driven and focussed to be amenable to giving way to someone else. Or, she allowed, *she* was, and from what Moss let drop, she suspected he was no different.

Except... She sighed. Except for the things he'd done that touched her and she suspected made her ever more susceptible to his charm.

The times he'd surprised her and appeared on her doorstep on odd occasions with dinner or lunch or supper and demanded to know more about her, to make, he said, everything more real. When he'd called in, filled her freezer with ready meals, kissed her, told her not to forget him, left, then messaged her every evening to say 'time to stop writing and eat'. Those moments had made her more aware of him than ever.

There was the occasion he'd flown up from London to have a picnic in the rain. They'd sat under umbrellas, eaten chicken salad and drank champagne. An hour later he'd left. That visit had been noticed, and she'd fended off several nosy comments. One from the vicar's wife, when she'd dropped off the parish magazine, had almost made Arietta choke on her chocolate. Josephine Lovell had asked if her friend was that bloke from that series about aliens that the vicar was hooked on. The blue one.

As Arietta hadn't seen said series—she couldn't even watch Dr Who without hiding behind her fingers—she could answer quite honestly that she had no idea. But as it was one of her friend's mates she doubted it. It was only later that she remembered the alien Thomas had played and that she could have mentioned that. However that might have given the woman even more ideas. Luckily her phone had rung and she'd excused herself to answer it before the questioning became more intense. It had been, she said to Moss later on when they spoke, a close call. They decided to say he was called Geordie, the name of one of the characters he'd been years before and a diminutive of George, his middle name, and stick to the friend of a friend story for the time being. They could, Moss said, say later that as it had been very early in their relationship they hadn't wanted to 'go public' too soon.

He performed as a lover — or almost-lover — to perfection. The almost bit had begun to irritate her. Was it all play-acting? Did he not fancy her? Was she so un-fanciable?

Maybe, or maybe not, but she acknowledged she *was* damn contrary.

More than once Arietta had tried to renege and he'd laughed and clucked 'chicken' before he'd filled her with additional information about what he called 'the real Moss', and she'd ended up even more hooked.

After he'd mentioned his normal childhood and acting lessons, he'd added his elder sisters made sure he was grounded, and never got above himself. That he and Thomas were proper friends who played squash whenever possible and went to watch Newcastle United incognito. His mum was a schoolteacher and his dad had been a train driver and now worked for a winery. He, his dad and his brothers-in-law all got on well, and accepted that woman's word was law.

Arietta had rolled her eyes. *"I'll hold you to that."*

She thought about Moss' explanations, which he'd shared over various conversations, as she rummaged even further into the depths of the freezer. It looked like apart from the rejected curry and paella, it was fish fingers or something that appeared to be mushy peas — or mush anyway. The label had peeled off, or more likely, she allowed, she'd forgotten to write on the bag what the contents were. Neither the fish fingers nor the mystery bag appealed to her. However, as her tummy was making loud protesting noises, Arietta thought she'd better eat something. Toast? Did she have some bread without mould on it?

A loud rumble — not from her stomach, but from the lane outside — broke into her reverie. It wasn't a motorbike rumble, more like a van of some sort. She closed the freezer door on whatever might — or might not — be dinner and went to be nosy, by dint of peering through the hall window.

A white van was reversing up her drive. No writing on the sides so not a major delivery firm or rental. Who did she know with such a vehicle?

No one.

A mystery.

As far as Arietta knew, she didn't have any parcel due to be delivered. If it had happened to be someone looking for directions, they would have parked in the lane, and if it were burglars they'd be on plums. The only things of value in her house were her laptop — and she'd backed that up on to a hard drive when she'd finished writing for the day — and her godmother's pearls. Which she'd hidden so well when she'd gone on holiday she had no idea where they were. Not that she was worried. She never wore them and they'd turn up eventually. Last time she'd hidden them, she'd found them three months later in the pantry, behind ten tins of rice pudding. The tins were Thomas' —she hated tinned rice pudding. It had to be made from scratch or not at all.

All of which, she realised, was nothing to do with why the van had parked in her driveway.

The door opened and a familiar tall, copper-headed figure got out and walked towards the cottage.

She might have known.

Arietta opened the front door and gasped as Moss swung her around in a circle before he kissed her soundly.

"Hi, Ari, my love. Have you missed me?"

She blinked and did her best to unscramble her brain. "Like measles. Hi, Moss…um, Geordie, my whatever. Er…sorry, did you say you were coming today?" Surely she couldn't have forgotten that?

Moss shook his head. "Nope, I took a chance you'd be in. Thom said he thought you would. I've bought a few bits and bobs while I had a free day. Once we start the actual filming it will be manic, and anything I don't have I'll have to do without. My life won't be mine. Anyway, I thought it might make it easier to decide where everything needs to go and what else is needed, and then I can throw myself on your mercy and beg you to help me get it." He paused. "Whatever *it* is."

Men. "What would you have done if I was out?" It would have looked a bit dodgy if he'd sat —or worse, slept —in the van. Not that she had many neighbours, but Arietta could well imagine one of them becoming suspicious and ringing the police. That would look good in the papers. 'Film star caught napping!' "Could have been awkward if someone asked what the hell you were up to. You know, like casing the joint."

Moss shuddered. "I made sure that wouldn't happen. Thom lent me his spare key. You forgot to give me one." He grinned. "Author in the throes, eh?"

"Damn." She'd meant to and not got around to it. Was not doing so a Freudian slip of the 'if he doesn't have a key he won't come' kind? "Yeah, sorry. Though I had arranged to be here when you were due. And I did find a key. I put it on the window ledge in the spare room, and I've emptied the wardrobe and cupboards. But if I'd come home and found a white van on my drive I'd have called the police. "

"Which is why, my love, I texted you. I'm judging by your expression you didn't see it?"

"Oh shit. Where the hell did I leave my phone?" It was something she had a habit of putting down and forgetting. Which as she rarely had the sound on caused no end of trouble.

"Thom did say to email you as well, but I don't have your email addy, and I forgot to ask him for it." There was no accusation in his tone, more an amused acceptance.

"Crap girlfriend, aren't I?" She smiled and shook her head. "Sorry, but today was research day and I do tend to get carried away. Remind me to give you it."

"Your research?" He ducked as Arietta mock punched him.

"Smart-ass. You know what I mean."

He grinned the sort of grin designed to make some women go weak at the knees. Just as well she'd decided she wasn't going to be that sort of woman.

And if I believed that, someone would have a bridge to sell me, and my middle name would be gullible.

"I do and I couldn't resist. Bet you're starving after all that research. Never fear, Moss is here and I've brought dinner with me," Moss said. "Pizza or curry, your choice. And yes, I did get your pizza without cheese."

She hugged him. "Star." Her tummy rumbled and Moss laughed.

"Saved by the friendly delivery man?"

"Too true. I've examined the freezer and it was two-year-old fish fingers, a homemade curry of unknown contents or date, a few other bits and bobs, or something unnamed and by the look of it inedible. Can we eat first? Then I'll help you empty the van." She hadn't realised how hungry she was. "Or I might expire on the drive between the rose bushes and the van's back wheels. That would give the neighbours something to talk about."

Moss did a very over-the-top look around. "So many of them looking as well. Ouch, not to be thought of. Pizza?"

"Pizza," Arietta agreed. "And you'd be surprised who sees what in the country."

Moss got out his sunglasses. "Do I need these?"

"Doubtful, it looks like rain. Now lead me to the food." It sounded perfect.

He bowed. "Your wish and all that jazz. I hope you're happy with my choice of accompaniments."

Moss' idea of a pizza, no cheese, was to get almost every other topping imaginable.

"Though, as Thomas says, it's really loaded pita bread, but hey, it works for me." Arietta finished her fourth slice and wiped her mouth on her napkin. "Inelegant, but I'm stuffed."

"Good." Moss polished off the last piece of his own and looked thoughtfully at the two slices left on Arietta's plate. "Nope, can't do it, I'm full as well."

"I didn't offer you it," Arietta pointed out. "I'll have it for breakfast."

"Cold?"

"Is there any other way?" she asked.

He shook his head and grinned. "I'll be generous and let you have it."

"How thoughtful of you," Arietta said dryly.

"I know," Moss replied in a complacent tone. "Right. You do whatever you have to, and I'll even wash up before unloading."

"Leave it, it's only a couple of plates." She pushed her chair back from the table and stood up. "I'm caught up for now, and today's work is saved and backed up. Let's get that van emptied. How's the house?" He hadn't said a lot except he was letting the insurance company deal with everything.

"They made a start on it yesterday, with a lot of head scratching and questions about stuff they asked me to answer ages ago. This lot was stored on set overnight, which meant a lot of moaning till I moved it. I suspect that was one reason for the immediate offer of the van from the film crew. They like their storage space for themselves."

"When do you have to get it back?"

He grinned. "Monday. I'm not needed until then, when we're starting on some bits and bobs. After that, life gets hectic, and I become short tempered and bloody-minded until we get into things. So here I am, and I'm throwing myself on your mercy and putting the next part of our plan into action. It was a bugger everything was delayed for a week or so, but in one way it works in our favour now. It got me the chance to put the 'I'm stopping with someone special stuff' into action. I reckon they're taking bets as to where I've gone. Mind you, it might only be for a few weeks, because then we're filming too far away to make it tenable, so I reckon we ought to make the most of it."

"Get the van keys and let's get the stuff inside before it rains," Arietta said, resigned to the fact her life was about to be turned upside down. She'd store the *only a few weeks* away in her mind to think about if everything got a bit too much. For now, she'd had no option but to go with the flow. "The forecast is naff, and as old Peter next door said when he went past earlier, his bunions were playing up awfy bad and if that didnae say a wee bitty rain he hae nae idea what did."

"Neighbour?" Moss raised one eyebrow as he scanned the fields that surrounded her house. "He lives in a burrow and his surname is rabbit?"

Arietta sniggered. "Neighbour as in three fields over and round the bend in the lane, not in the mind. He's saner and more with it than anyone else I know. His house was originally a pigsty, now it's a cute wee cottage." She manoeuvred the heavy doorstop in the shape of a thistle into place to wedge the door open. "His son farms the place and Peter oversees, as in, according to Dougie the son, meddles wherever possible. The farmhands have learnt to say 'yes of course' and ignore him."

"Sounds a right character," Moss commented as he flung open the back doors of the van. "Do I need to do the steely-eyed look and tell him you're mine?"

"Hardly, he's eighty-odd, been married to Jacobina for sixty of those years and still loved-up." Arietta peered in and reeled. Did he have all of his possessions with him? It was jam-packed. "'Struth, Moss, how long did you say your house was out of bounds for? I'll need an extra room for this lot."

"Nah, some of it can go in the garage." He lifted a mountain bike out and leant it on a convenient bush. "I only bought the important stuff, the rest is in *my* garage. Soon get it all sorted, you'll see. I reckon the place will be ready in three, four weeks but you know insurance companies, builders…"

"Yes, well. What do you need with seven pairs of trainers and three boxes of books?" she asked as he passed the footwear to her and hefted the boxes in his arms. "You can only wear one pair at once and read one book at a time."

"You sound like my mum, who thinks one pair of anything is enough. As for Donna…" He grinned, obviously amused. "She'd be asking where the rest is. Books, though, how many books do *you* have?" He put the boxes on the floor of his room.

"That's not the point," Arietta said defensively. "I live here."

"So do I, for now." He straightened and stretched so his T-shirt crept up and showed an admirable washboard-flat stomach. "Seriously, they're ones I hate leaving in an empty house. Some first editions and some old favourites that are now out of print. I do read them over and over when I can. Trainers because they all work for different things. Leisure, jogging, squash…" He rolled his shoulders and groaned. "Getting old, I need to do some exercise. We could follow the boot camp workout I do, if you fancy. Though I might need another pair—"

"Okay, I get it," Arietta said hastily. She didn't need chapter and verse. "I'll find you a bookcase and a shoe rack and pass on the boot camp. I'm not a fan of self-torture."

"Chicken."

"Cluck cluck and remember who your landlady is."

"Yes, miss. Sorry, miss." Moss got on his knees and clasped his hands together in front of his face. "Please forgive me..."

She sniggered. "As long as you do the dirty stuff. And take the bins out."

"Hard taskmaster. However..." Moss stood up and lifted her off her feet. "Ohhh, dirty stuff. Elucidate."

"Your trainers for one."

"Not dirty," he protested, albeit with a smirk on his face. "Just well lived in."

"If you say so, now put me down, you eejit, and let's hurry. It looks like it'll rain any minute."

"Half hour tops," Moss said as he passed Arietta the first box.

By the time the van was emptied, the rain had started and she was ready for a shower and a glass of wine. Moss kissed her cheek. "You're a star. You have your shower, I'll open the wine."

* * * *

"Do you know some woman, around fifty, dark brown hair and a beaky nose?" Moss asked after he'd also showered and they were sitting in the lounge and watching the swarms of midges through the window. "Awful dress sense, though I suppose that might be down to what I like and what she does. Had a mop of a dog on a lead and a loud hectoring voice."

"Josephine Lovell, the vicar's wife," Arietta said resignedly. "The dog is called Milton. What did Josephine do?"

"Waved me down, told me this was a dead end, a private road, so I would be trespassing. Was I lost, where was I heading for and could she help me. I told her yes I knew, no such thing as trespass in Scotland, no I wasn't and why did she want to know and I needed no help. Then I revved the engine, she took a jump back, slipped and landed on her bum and said I was intimidating her. I managed not to say the boot was on the other foot, and merely asked if she was lost? She gibbered a bit, then rambled on about how familiar I looked. Which, as I don't usually wear my hair this long, drive in sunnies on a cloudy day or drive a white van, was a bit disconcerting. At least she didn't say I *sounded* familiar. I was using a Geordie accent."

"That's Josephine. She's the village gossip and has to know everything. Most people can't find out how to get out of her clutches unscathed. I reckon if anyone wanted to play away around here they'd have no chance. Did she ask you if you played a blue alien as well?"

"She did. Does she have a penchant for them? She was most disgruntled when I asked why.

"She would be." Arietta got up and wandered around the room, suddenly restless. Everything seemed to be rushing ahead at an alarming pace, and it unsettled her. All she wanted was a quiet life. It didn't seem she was going to have it for the foreseeable future. "She asked me the same thing after your first visit. I said you were a friend of a friend. I suppose we better sort out a story for you being here."

"Why?" Moss asked. "It's no one's business but ours."

"Have you ever lived in a village?"

He shook his head. "Not a villagy village, no. Near one, in one that was more of small town, but as a fully paid-up full-time member of that society I was away a lot, so, then, no."

"If you had, you'd not ask that," Arietta said. "Most of the time it's a good thing that people care about each other. Like when I had the flu and the postie realised she hadn't seen me and shouted through the letterbox to ask if I was okay. Then brought my messages for me."

"Messages?" Moss queried. "You've lost me."

"Sorry, shopping. Scottish word. Like a jag for a jab and so on, and Jai for the letter Jay."

Moss looked bemused but nodded. "Ri...ight."

Arietta sniggered. "It's okay, I'll translate when need be. So the postie—postman, well postwoman, actually—keeps an eye on people and houses as she goes around her route. I tend to see her and wave, as it's the least intrusive way of showing I'm okay."

"I love it," Moss said sincerely. "But why do we need a story?"

"Do you really want a queue at the gate?" Arietta asked. Moss blanched and she nodded. "Exactly. I might not get out and about a lot—my choice—but when I do I hear things. And evidently you're high up on the list of blokes who would be the best to spend a night with." Arietta grinned. She wouldn't add that she'd found it hard to appear blank and uninterested and only just managed to act not really interested... "Guess who's in the top three?"

"Me?"

She nodded. "Yup, along with someone called Rock Cafferty and Colin Firth. The queues would be endless."

"Did you take part in making up the list?" Moss asked in a speculative voice and put on a hopeful expression. "You've realised it?"

Arietta laughed. "Nope, nothing to do with me."

He sighed and patted his chest. "Ah well, I can live in hope. What next then?"

"Someone will recognise you if you're about, and I doubt you want to stay indoors all the time when you're here?"

Moss shuddered. "You're right there, babe. But d'ya think I'll be seen as an actor bloke here, like? When I'm just a mate of a mate from uni who is working as a gofer on some fillum thing?"

The accent was pure Geordie, and so unlike his normal voice that Arietta blinked. "Okay, now I know why they pay you the big bucks, but can you keep it up?"

"Why, ae, man."

"Then, Geordie, let's see how it goes."

"Gan on. Any cake left?"

"For someone as fit as you, you can't half pack it away." Arietta headed for the kitchen and the cake tin. She'd have to bake again the next day and make twice as much as normal at that rate.

"I need to keep my strength up, a growing lad."

"Out as well as up, at this rate." Arietta picked up the last of the fruitcake she'd baked the day before and returned to the lounge. "Here you go. Lots of calories in every bite."

"I'll run it off. As Geordie Armstrong, gofer to the stars. And I'll bake next time. I make a mean banana bread."

"I'll add bananas to the shopping list."

"Great stuff. Shall we go and shop tomorrow? In the village?" Moss said. "We might as well start as we mean to go on. I'm your lodger, and they'll see me around and about. Then I'll become part of the scenery."

With a physique like his, and the commanding presence he unconsciously projected, Arietta doubted that.

"I'll make a list."

Chapter Five

"That was fun." Moss shouldered the rucksack he'd unearthed from his wardrobe and took one of the shopping bags from Arietta. He'd insisted they walk to, as he said, get Arietta outside, and to smell the daisies. "I loved the way your friend did her best not to appear nosy, and quizzed you about me at the same time."

Arietta grinned. "Maggie said you were a bit of all right, and when you went to choose the bananas asked if your accent send shivers down my spine." She hadn't meant to share that, but somehow it didn't seem natural to keep it to herself. Maggie had also added, with an audacious wink, that if he was the friend she was going to the wedding with, to remember the expression 'with benefits' and pack some condoms. Arietta almost blurted out that she'd already checked she had some and that they were in date. That brought her up short. She'd been determined not to let Moss get under her skin, hadn't she? She'd been going to be friendly but stay distant.

That hasn't lasted long. Arietta made a mental note to be careful how she acted and what she said. He was a temporary house guest, a pretend lover-to-be, and once his own house was habitable or he needed to head north for the film he'd be off and she'd get her spare room back. Then after the wedding they would go their separate ways, life could go back to normal and she could resume her usual habits.

Why did that not sound as appealing as she'd thought it would?

"Anyway, I did the wide-eyed 'you what' look and then said very confidently that I'd never noticed as my mate at uni had the same accent," Arietta continued in a hurry. She wasn't going to say anything to make it appear as if she were interested in him. "Then I added I'd be sure to listen more carefully what you answered when I asked if you wanted mash or jacket with your dinner. She said I was hopeless, I said afraid so, and she said if only she was single. But not one word about Amos Kirby."

"Great stuff." Moss nodded to Josephine Lovell, who stood and stared at them from the other side of the road. "Morning. Nice day, isn't it?"

Josephine dropped her dog's lead, picked it up and cleared her throat. "Er, yes. You didn't say you knew Arietta."

"Nope." Moss sketched a wave and turned to Ari. "Nor did you. Ha'way, love, shall we gan on?"

"Bye, Josephine." For once Arietta wasn't bothered about seeming rude. As her brother often said, *'give back what you get'* …

Or, less subtly, Karma will up and bite you in the bum. Judging by Josephine's astounded look, Karma had just done that.

"How awful we are," Arietta said as they turned down the track to the cottage. "It was very rude. Why do I not feel repentful? Is that even a word? You know what I mean."

"She doesn't deserve your repentance," Moss replied. "Full or not. Now if she'd been polite it would be different, but she wasn't. I'm guessing she uses her status as the vicar's wife to bulldoze everyone into doing what she wants. Wouldn't matter if her spouse was the vicar, the doctor or the bin man, she'd use it to her advantage somehow. Yes?"

Arietta thought about it. "That's about right. She'd love for Lionel to be higher up in the church so she could really lord it over us." Her choice of words hit her and she sniggered as Moss bit back a snort of laughter. "Maybe not the correct expression, but you get the gist."

"I get it. Why, though? I mean, whatever your family, husband or partner is doesn't define you," Moss said. "Does it?"

"Not in my book, but Josephine thinks differently. From what I gather…" She slanted a glance of mischief towards Moss. "And I'm not really in on all the gossip, so this is goodness knows how many hands, she's a younger child of a minor member of the aristocracy. According to someone who knows her family, they lived the rich life for years, never worried about money, did exactly as they chose. Papa lost his money in the Lloyd's crash in the early nineties so boy, was the new life they had to lead a shock to the system. Up until then she'd lived a hunting, shooting, fishing existence and suddenly, poof, Papa was downsizing. The result being Papa and then the rest of the family all had a chip on their shoulder, at the way their lives had changed. They were, it was rumoured, told they would have to, shock, horror, work for a living." She rolled her eyes and Moss chuckled.

"Oh my, what next?"

"Josephine grabbed Lionel before he had a chance to say amen, and her brother, Jonathon, took himself off to Canada where, as far as I know, he met a bloke, and they live in Alberta. Her younger sister, Jacqueline, was already married and was living the high life with her banker husband. Still is. Josephine thought the church better than any other profession or vocation and tries to tell everyone that at every opportunity. And stick her nose in everywhere as well. She's well-meaning but just hectors and lectures so everyone closes in and ignores her good bits."

"Unhappy lady," Moss observed. "Even so, I'm still not taking any nonsense from her. Let her wonder. We've got enough to worry about what with bloody midges, whether my Geordie accent will hold up — it will — and whether you're going to get your book sent away before your deadline — you better. On which note, I'll cook, you write and we'll have an assignation in the sunroom at six."

Which seemed to set the pace of their relationship, or whatever it was. Arietta wasn't certain. It remained friendly and unthreatening, which was what she wanted...wasn't it?

She wasn't sure anymore.

Whoever was least tired — usually her — cooked, and the other set the table. On the nights Moss knew he'd be late, Arietta left a casserole or some homemade soup in the bottom, warming oven of the Aga. Both things Moss admitted he could eat at any time and all year long, they were easy to make and keep warm. On the odd day he wasn't needed or was home early, Moss cooked and they ate the sort of food that had to be thought about. As it wasn't her cooking, Arietta appreciated how nice it was. She would have been happy with beans on toast if need be, but admitted Tournedos Rossini, Seafood Risotto or Surf and Turf, all Moss' favourites to cook, were preferable.

Over time, Arietta realised, it had become the norm to grab his linen bin and wash his boxers and shirts with her undies and blouses. She told him each night if it was lights or darks for the wash the following day and found the appropriate clothing at the top of his dirty linen. He stripped and remade his own bed and even did his own ironing. In general, he was the perfect houseguest.

Almost.

Apart from the little fact that he never stepped out of line and never showed if he now thought of her as anything other than Thomas' sister and his landlady. Which might be a bit of a problem at the blasted wedding, the date of which was growing ever closer. Why, when at first he'd appeared eager to put their friendship on a closer level, did she now feel he had changed his mind?

She wasn't going to ask. She wasn't that needy.

One evening as they sat either side of the kitchen table, doing the daily crossword and waiting for a steak pie to cook, Moss looked over at her.

"Arietta, I have to ask. Do you think you might in time fancy me a wee bit, or am I barking up the wrong tree and you think I'm minging?"

She blinked. Choked on the mouthful of wine she was drinking and suffered him patting her back. "Of course you're not rotten or nasty," she said when she got her breath back and was able to speak coherently. "I thought *you* didn't fancy me. You've been so distant lately, I thought the fancying bit was all part of the act, so you weren't going to do anything about it."

"Damn." He hit his forehead. "Talk about crossed wires. *I* thought any advances, or whatever you want to call them, wouldn't be appreciated. Maybe we set a new rule, as in 'ask, don't worry'?"

"That sounds good to me," Arietta said. She ignored the warning in her mind that said no entanglement, no sex, no complicating things. "I tell you, it's been hard."

"Don't I know it," Moss said. "You agree we move on to stage two?"

She nodded. Whatever that was.

"Then let's start by going to the pub. Geordie could do with a night out. I'll take wor lass and we'll gan pubbin, eh?"

* * * *

It was quiz night and the pub was packed. Arietta hovered in the doorway, undecided whether to turn tail or dive in. However it seemed Moss was made of sterner stuff. "Come on," he said in a low voice. "No cluckin' chickens, let's go astound people. Look, isn't that Maggie who has the good taste to fancy me over there beckoning us? That's a great place to start, and there's seats."

Arietta followed his pointing finger to where Maggie was indeed pointing to two empty chairs. "Are you okay with that? We'll be full-on view for nosiness."

"Get it over and done with, then it's finished. I'll just be your mate Geordie for now. Red or white?"

If he thought that would be it, she had a bridge to sell him. However, Maggie and Doug were good friends and they could talk things over with them sooner rather than later if Moss was willing. "Ah, oh, white, and crisps maybe?"

"Gotcha. Go grab the seats."

Arietta nodded and threaded her way between tables and an assortment of chairs and stools to the back wall where Maggie and her husband, Doug, had bagged a table that had two empty chairs next to it.

"Wow, great you're here," Maggie said as Arietta took off her jacket and draped it over the back of her chair. "We were worried sick we'd be stuck with Josephine and Lionel, who tend to come in at the last minute. We hate it. JoJo shouts everyone down without raising her voice, if you get me."

Arietta nodded. "With spades. She'll kill you if she hears you calling her that, Maggie. Sounds like a budgie."

Doug spluttered into his beer. "Pretty Joey, pretty Joey," he said in a sing-song voice.

Maggie nudged him. "Give over. You'll get us into bother."

"Lordy, no more," Arietta said, heartfelt. "We've both had a run-in with her lately. She seems to have become worse. Either that or my Josephine tolerance levels are lower.

"Thanks," she said to Moss as he handed her a glass of wine, put a pint of beer on the table and sat on the spare seat. "This is..." Her mind went blank and she fabricated a hasty cough. What had they decided to call him? She gave Moss an agonised look, which thankfully he clearly understood. He gave an infinitesimal nod.

"Hi, I'm Geordie Armstrong." The north-east England accent sounded so natural. "A mate of Arietta's. How ya daein?" He nodded amiably as Maggie introduced herself and Doug.

"We were glad you came when you did. JoJo and LiLo have just come in," the irrepressible Maggie said as Doug rolled his eyes. "Spoil the evening with them as co-quizzers."

"My wife is not known for her subtlety. Tell it as you see it, Mags."

"I do," Maggie said as Arietta spluttered.

"LiLo? Grief, Maggie, do not let that gem out in the open," she remarked. "Though he can look a bit squashed and deflated at times."

"And puffed up at others," Maggie said. "Anyway, they're on the other side of the room. I was praying we'd not be stuck with them again. If you'd said you were coming I could have told them the seats were reserved for you."

"We only made our minds up at the last minute," Arietta said. "Geordie got back early. He's, as he puts it, a gofer on that film they're doing over by the loch." She thought she'd got that tidbit over nicely. "He isn't needed at work tomorrow so we thought why not. I've got to a point in my book where I can take a break and not lose my thread, and so…here we are. I'd forgotten it was quiz night, though." Actually she hadn't known it was quiz night, let alone forgotten it, but there was no need to share that information. "Not sure how good we'll be." She sipped her wine. "Who do we pay our entry to?"

"It's done," Moss said. "I was asked if we were taking part when I got the drinks. Given pencils and quiz sheets, though they're a bit screwed-up in my pocket." He fished out the two pencils with the pub's logo on them and several sheets of crumpled paper also decorated with the logo, plus that day's date stamped on them. "I was told very firmly that no proper pencils and sheets, no can take part. Do they have a problem with cheating or something? It was all said with a gimlet stare." He blinked. "That sounds impossible, but you know what I mean."

"Evidently many years ago a team from another village came on meat draw night, didn't pay their entry fee, won and took away half a cow. Scandal and almost riots," Maggie said. "So now it's so regimented you almost expect to have your pockets checked for a book of common quiz question answers. If there is such a thing."

Moss laughed as a microphone screeched and someone tapped it. "Here we go."

Doug groaned and stood up. "This is where I head to the bar so my wife can't thump me for being facetious. I take a while to get into a quiz. Same all round?"

"Doug, I've hardly started," Arietta said. "I'll pass, thanks all the same."

"He just wants to make sure they don't run out of his favourite beer," Maggie said as the quizmaster told them to get ready. "It's happened twice, and for a real ale aficionado to be told it was lager or lager is like me being told no favourite chocolate, only stuff that..." She stopped as the quizmaster *ahem-ed*. "Ooops, that's me told."

Arietta grinned. That was Maggie. They might not meet up every week, but she was probably Arietta's closest friend around. One who wouldn't pry, but who would certainly be interested in Moss and what was going on. She was also the one person Arietta thought she could confide in if needed and who didn't really deserve to be lied to. That was something to ponder over.

Halfway through the quiz there was a break for raffle tickets to be sold, pork pies to be eaten and general gossip to be exchanged. Arietta noticed the other two's attention had been taken by someone on the next table, and nudged Moss. He bent his head so his breath feathered over her cheek.

"What's up?"

"I feel rotten lying to Maggie and Doug," she muttered. "It tastes wrong."

Moss shrugged. "Then don't."

"You don't mind?"

He kissed her cheek as Maggie turned back to them. "Nope. I've coped for years. As long as you're okay with it, it's fine by me. How and when is up to you."

Arietta thought furiously. "Tomorrow night at ours?"

He squeezed her hand. "Go for it."

"Hey, you two, want me to go away?" Maggie said. "I can go and powder my nose again."

"Ninny. Nope, we were just wondering if you and Doug fancy coming round to us for a drink tomorrow night," Arietta said. "We've got something we'd like to tell you and no, Maggie, not that, I know the way your mind works." She hadn't thought how her words could be interpreted. "No worries if you can't make it."

"Oh we can," Maggie said instantly. "Can't we, hon?" She appealed to Doug, who had also turned back to the table.

"Whatever you say," Doug agreed then raised one eyebrow. "What have I agreed to?"

"Drinks with Arietta and Geordie tomorrow at theirs."

"I'll have some decent beer, I promise," Moss said. "As well as whatever the ladies drink."

"Nice one, look forward to it." The microphone screeched again and Doug lifted his glass. "Ah, here we go, time to show my lack of knowledge regarding all things films and musicals."

* * * *

They didn't come first, but they weren't last either, and as they walked back down the lane arm in arm, Arietta mused that it had been a good evening. The thought that they would own up to her friends just who Moss was, was good, and she was glad they had made that decision. What would happen then she had no idea.

"I can see the cogs whirring," Moss said. "What's up?"

She sighed. "Wondering if I'm a pain in the you-know-what. Am I overreacting? Under? Not? Why? How did we get into all this? Do you really mind? Wh...*ooft*." Moss had shut her up in the best way possible.

It was as well the lane didn't have much traffic using it, as Arietta dimly realised they were standing in the middle of the road, oblivious to who or what might come along.

When Moss finally raised his head, they were both breathless. Arietta pushed her hair off her face and took a long deep breath. "I never ever do stuff like this in public. One look from you and..."

"And wow," Moss said unevenly. "Hardly public, though, unless you count someone's cat and the owl in the oak tree, but I get what you mean. I'm amazed there's not some hotshot photographer lurking in the rhododendrons ready to grab a photo and make a few bob."

Arietta shuddered and glanced around anxiously. "Really?"

"No, don't worry." Moss hugged her. "Not at this time of night anyway, and I don't think anyone knows I'm here. Even the bossman only has my mobile number and an assurance I can get back within an hour if need be. So no one really knows where I am. Except you, me and that sparrow makes three."

"They will tomorrow. Do you think we shouldn't tell Maggie and Doug? Make up something that we wanted to share?"

"I hardly think they'll go rushing to the daily 'dish the dirt' rag, do you?"

"Nope, nothing less than the *Times* for them. And that's only because they like doing the crossword together."

"Well then, sorted." Moss urged her down the lane again until the gate of the cottage came into view. "Race you. Last one in makes the coffee." He began to move.

"Oy, cheat." Arietta followed him then smiled. She knew a gap in the hedge and thought Moss didn't.

She was correct, he didn't, and she got to the front door a scant second before him

"You're the cheat," he panted. "Not fair."

"Not raining, though, and you do make better coffee."

Moss looked her up and down as she inserted the key in the lock. "Arietta Clare, are you trying to butter me up by any chance?"

She fluttered her eyelashes and he laughed. "Well?"

"By every chance. Am I succeeding?"

"Hmm."

She opened the door and he followed her inside. Kicked the door shut with a slam that made them both wince then pulled her close. "Every time, love. Every time."

* * * *

"I knew something was going on," Maggie said as she and Doug sat with Arietta and Moss in the conservatory overlooking the cottage's garden, the midges having driven them inside even before they started their drinks. "Mainly because you look sort of different, he looks besotted and you jumped every time one of us called him Geordie. Then when the quizmaster said he hoped we were all up on Amos Kirby films the pair of you shared a secret smile. Not that I thought Moss was Amos, but that if he was working on an Amos Kirby film then you might have some inside gen. Well, you do, but you didn't use it. Or did you? I mean, we didn't win, and we did get that question wrong, or were you trying to not show you knew or what?"

Doug put his hand over his wife's mouth. "Maggie, my love, we got it wrong because you insisted you knew the answer and no one dared argue."

"I still think I was right," Maggie said. "I'm sure I saw him…er, you…or— Hell, this is complicated, say that you—his—whatever's—walk-on part was at primary school, but the answer was secondary school, and as you didn't argue, I kept my mouth shut."

"First time then," Doug commented, and ducked the mock punch Maggie swung at him.

"Rotter."

"You were right," Moss said. "But it's not that well-known, and I could hardly jump up and say you're wrong and prove it without saying who I was. It'll come out sooner or later, but we'd prefer it to be later so we can get to know each other better before we're in the goldfish bowl."

"We didn't want to lie to you two, though," Arietta added. *Hell on wheels, I hope I don't look besotted. I am not besotted. I won't let myself be. Been there, done that...* Well, not quite, but she had no intention of ever doing so. "And we will come clean one day." *If we're still an almost-but-not-really couple and it gets about...* How she prayed it wouldn't. After the Stu debacle she hadn't been able to stand all the sympathy—and pseudo-sympathy—when it had got out they were together no more. "But you know what this village is like. We've both had the Lovell grilling."

"I get you," Maggie said. "To say nothing of the gate brigade. That's some of the mums that meet their kids at the school gate," she explained to Moss. "They'd be doing the shelfie selfie."

"Maggie, what are you like?" Arietta said with a giggle. "Honestly."

"Well they would," Maggie said reasonably. "Look how they are with Thomas when they see him. Ooohhh, can I have a picture to put on my shelf...and every social media site you can think of."

"That's true enough," Arietta agreed. "Poor Thomas, last time he came home he brought enough food for a fortnight so he didn't have to brave the village and he was only here a week. Scary stuff." She remembered just in time the story she and Moss had concocted about how they met. "When he and Moss came he gave Moss such detailed instructions on where was safe and where wasn't, I did the shopping and Moss stayed in."

"No wonder you were adamant about your deadline." Maggie laughed as Arietta started. "I know some of the deadline times aren't that at all, but I'd never share that fact. Those who know you write accept that, those who don't know don't hear it and just think you're a bit of a loner who doesn't like her personal space invaded. Or that you've got something to hide, because how else would you live. The something to hide has varied from winning the lottery, a rich divorcee or a professional gambler, to the more mundane Daddy has money, you have a sugar daddy, or you're on the dole because of some illness or another. Creative are us locals."

Moss laughed. "Bit more exciting than the truth?"

"Until they realise it's you, or Thomas here. Then it'd be mayhem."

Arietta shuddered. "I'll encourage the gambler story, I think. I can just see me at a green table saying twist or stick in a deep fifty a day cigarette-riddled voice with rings of smoke spiralling upwards. Except I don't smoke."

"It would more than likely all be online these days," Moss added as he put a plate of canapés on the table. "And puffing on a cancer stick indoors is banned."

"Ah well," Arietta said as the others laughed. "Maybe I'll say I'm living off my immoral earnings." She nudged the plate towards Maggie. "After you."

"I'd love to see dear Josephine's face when she hears that," Maggie said as she chose a mushroom vol-au-vent. "My favourite. Who's going to start the rumour?"

* * * *

"Bet she does," Arietta said once they'd waved Maggie and Doug goodbye. "She's a sod for a bit of excitement. I remember when one of the school gate brigade had a new patio put down and her husband wasn't around for a while. Maggie was in hysterics when someone suggested maybe he was under the patio. She had about twenty reasons as to why he'd been done away with. All hilarious and if shared could have caused ructions and have had her sued for slander. I'm not sure who was the most disappointed when three days later he reappeared and eventually it was discovered he'd been in hospital for an operation on his piles. The patio story was much more fun."

Moss locked the door. "I bet. Reminds me of the time one of my teachers got called out of class to see the cops in the head's study. We had him guilty of everything from littering to murder. Turned out he'd reported his bike stolen and they'd found it. What a let-down." He yawned. "Sorry, long days catching up with me."

"Then sleep in and get up when you feel like it."

* * * *

Arietta waved in an absent-minded manner as Moss gestured driving, pointed to his watch, indicated eight and pointed at her before he mimed sleeping. She nodded, knowing he meant he'd be back by eight in the morning—they had started night filming while the weather was as they wanted—and telling her not to get up for him. He did it every time, even though Arietta told him over and over she was usually awake by six and writing by half past. He merely asked her to humour him. "I worry you're not getting enough sleep."

She watched the car go up the lane and turned her attention back to the phone. "Sorry, I missed that bit," she said. "Say again, Thomas. Mum and Dad want what?"

"You and Moss and me and…me to go for a pre-Christmas Christmas evening."

What's with you and pause and say you again? I smell a mystery. She knew there was no point asking what he had been about to say. If he wanted to share he would have.

"Er, well." What could she say? "Okay." She kept her fingers crossed as she spoke. It would or wouldn't happen, there was no point worrying about it. "How do they know about Moss and me?"

There was silence.

"Big mouth," she said. "Why did you tell them?"

"Come on, Arietta, something had to be said before they found out some other way," Thomas said reasonably. "You couldn't let them see it in a gossip rag, or in a photo of that wedding now could you? I just said it was early days and knowing you, you were keeping quiet until you were sure it was going to last. And as I don't have a better half, significant or otherwise, if you do both go it takes some of the heat off me and the when am I going to settle down crap."

She could see his point but wished he hadn't.

"You're a menace," Arietta said, resigned to the fact she'd have to put it to Moss and see what he said. "When are they suggesting?"

"That's the beauty of it, the Sunday after the wedding. You could combine the two."

"Like going to the dentist? Get it all over at once?" If it had to be done it made sense in a strange sort of way. "I'll see what Moss says."

After that conversation, Arietta couldn't settle to writing. An hour later, she shut her laptop down and stood up. She might as well go for a walk before it got dark, wander into the village and see if the shop had anything she fancied for dinner.

The evening was balmy, and with enough of a breeze to hopefully keep the midges at bay. Even so she made sure she was covered in repellent, and with a self-conscious grin at her actions tucked a midge net into her tote. She'd rather appear ridiculous than be bitten.

The village shop was deserted apart from one old man buying tobacco—or trying to. He wasn't best pleased they didn't have his favourite type in and said so in no uncertain manner before he stomped out. Dinny, the teenage daughter of the shop's owner, was at the till. She rolled her eyes as Arietta put a bag of frozen chips, a rump steak and a packet of peas on the counter.

"I've telt him mony a time we dinna hae it, we'll nae get it, but he disna listen. That Jockie McColl, he'll n'ere be telt eh?" She grinned. "Do you like my dialect for the uni end-of-semester hall party? I've been practising by listening to old radio shows and my mum has been trying to remember how her grandpa spoke. Minging was every other word. Evidently he was from the islands and spoke only the Gaelic until he went to school. I'm trying to get it spot on, but I keep forgetting words. The joys of uni. We're a right mixed lot in my halls. I love it."

"Excellent, for trying, hold on." Arietta mentally translated Dinny's words. "Got it. You don't stock his baccy, never will, but he doesn't listen."

"Yup, the old bugger, sorry, blighter, thinks if he keeps hectoring, oops, sorry, Mum says he's just asking forcefully, we'll get it in. But one pack lasts him ages and Mum reckons any other we had would probably go stale before he was ready for more. So he stomps in and out on a regular basis and just gets his son to buy it for him in town. Don't know why he keeps coming and bothering us."

"Probably gets him out of the house?" Arietta suggested. "I've heard his daughter who lives with him is a bit er…determined to get her own way and rules the roost."

"Could be." Dinny—short for Dineen—rang up Arietta's purchases. "She was a sister in the Royal Infirmary years ago and he was grumbling about her and her hospital corners one day. Not sure what he meant."

Arietta grinned. "A way of making beds where you tuck the sheets in tightly."

"That'd be it, he said he felt he was in his shroud and demanded a duvet." Dinny snorted as Arietta chucked. "He's a one all right. Told me he was happy escorting Mrs Ross to the dances and the bingo but left her at the door when they got home. He didn't want another woman in his life, he'd got enough trouble as it was with his daughter. Then coughed, spat discreetly, and said relationships needed too much work and at his age he was retired." She hooted with laughter. "Talking about relationships, what's all this about you and some hot bod who's working on the film up the lochside?"

The change of direction flummoxed Arietta for a second. "Work…ah, you mean Geordie." Thank goodness she remembered his 'name'. "He's a friend of a friend who may or may not be important one day."

Dinny nodded gravely. "Ah, one of them. A bit like my Fergus. Getting on fine for now, but who knows next month."

"That sums it up perfectly," Arietta replied. It was true, with Moss as himself *and* the mythical Geordie. "Early days." She put her purchases in her tote. "Right, ta, that's my dinner sorted. See you."

Chapter Six

She sketched a wave and headed out, only to try to sidestep Josephine, who was marching towards her and rummaging in her bag rather than being aware of her surroundings.

"Watch where you're going, why don't you?" Josephine snapped as she headed towards the shop doorway. She passed by too closely and her shoulder hit Arietta hard on the upper arm.

Arietta stopped dead. She hadn't been the one who was unobservant. Usually she would have let the comment go and say something non-committal, but for some reason she had no intention of doing so then. "I was," she said cheerfully. "You seemed somewhat preoccupied, though. Hello, Josephine. What's up?"

"What?" Josephine looked at her and plumped down so hard on the wooden bench outside the shop it probably jarred her teeth. She gave one great sob and hiccupped. "It's Maynard."

That was her son. A bit wet in Arietta's opinion, but Josephine doted on him.

"He and Dorothea have separated. She's gone to Glasgow because she's not gay."

Arietta blinked. Had she heard that correctly? What had Glasgow got to do with it? "Why Glasgow?"

"I told you," Josephine said crossly. "Listen."

"No," Arietta said through gritted teeth. Honest, Josephine could be annoying at times. Scrub that, *most* of the time. "You said because she's not gay. What has not being gay, or being gay for that matter, got to do with Glasgow?"

Josephine stared at her, obviously uncomprehending. "Nothing. She's just gone there. She's got herself a flat by the river."

The way Josephine said that, Arietta thought anyone would have come to the conclusion that Dorothea had done something illegal. Arietta did her best not to show any reaction. Whatever she did would no doubt be taken the wrong way. Idly she began to plot a scene in her next book with someone remarkably like Josephine as the overbearing matriarch of an aristocratic family, who was murdered by —

"Arietta?" Josephine said peremptorily. "Are you listening? Poor Maynard is distraught. He thought they were so happy and now she's saying she wants gaiety in her life and he's not gay enough. He wasn't giving her it. How can we cope with that? The shame."

"I don't see why you have to," Arietta said bluntly. Did Josephine understand how her words could be interpreted? "It's Maynard and Dorothea's problem, not yours."

Josephine scowled. "Don't be so unfeeling. He's our son, of course we have to do something. How can she treat him like this? He doesn't even know how to make coffee. What should I do?"

Oh, Lor'. It was becoming more like a family farce with every sentence.

Show him how to make coffee and man up? Maybe not. Arietta took a deep breath. *Just go for it and duck.*

"Josephine, at the risk of sounding like a busybody, I'd say keep out of it. It's up to them what they do next, and you might just make things worse." Arietta thought there wasn't a lot of *might* in it. Josephine's way of going at things like a bull in a china shop was enough to put anyone's back up. "And watch how you phrase things. Your words could be easily misconstrued."

Josephine went red. "That's disgusting. I would never be so rude."

"I know that, and you know that, but others might not," Arietta said gently. "You asked for my advice, I gave it. Whether you pay any attention or not is up to you." She smiled and patted Josephine on the shoulder. "I wish you good luck whatever you decide. Better be off, I've a cake in the oven." She hadn't, but as Josephine was acknowledged as one of the best bakers for miles round, Arietta guessed that would be an acceptable reason for leaving in undue haste. "Take care." She headed towards her house, leaving Josephine still sitting on the seat.

She needed a gin.

* * * *

A month later, Arietta stared at her not-really-empty spare room and blinked. It still had a lot of Moss' stuff in it, including his books, but it was less cluttered and sadly a lot dustier. She'd not got round to sorting that out yet. She was aware of a weird sense that something—or someone—was missing in her life. It was somewhat disconcerting, as she was usually used to a solitary life and had trouble accounting for how, in such a short space of time, he'd become part of that life. Almost, although she would never admit it out loud, a vital part. She picked up a missed sock from next to the window and put it in a drawer. It had been half hidden by the curtains, and Arietta thought it had probably fallen off the dressing table as he packed. At least it was clean.

She'd become accustomed to having Moss around when he wasn't filming, and the empty house felt alien. They split the cooking, argued amicably about books and had even managed a few walks around the nearest loch. Now she had to remember to cook, had no one to argue with and no inclination to walk alone. Thomas was abroad for a month or two and apart from the odd email asking if she was eating and how was the book getting on, she had heard nothing. The one time he'd tried to FaceTime she'd been in the loo and had missed him. When she'd tried to call back he hadn't answered. It had turned out *he'd* been in the loo.

With Moss, Arietta had learnt when not to chat, to let him have ten minutes to, as he called it, 'come to' after a hard day, and when he needed chatter, inane or not. She'd discovered he was attuned to her moods as well, and blessed him when he'd come in, kissed her cheek and left her to finish whatever she was doing. Sometimes to put a cup of coffee next to her, other moments to make himself scarce, and she'd find him in the garden with a beer and a book if the weather was nice, or in the lounge if it wasn't.

He'd agreed they'd go to her parents' pre-Christmas Christmas and had asked what he should buy them, had loved the idea of a present for a quid, and the questions to add to the quiz.

He even ironed. Said it was a nice non-thinking job.

Arietta admitted how much she liked him, about and not just for the ironing

However, Moss had left three days earlier to spend the next however long on a loch further north. He'd grumbled good-naturedly as he packed the bare essentials, asked and got affirmation if he could leave the rest of his belongings that he'd arrived with. As he'd put it the alleged three weeks — but God knows how long in reality — stay for filming was a pain, and not strictly necessary. It could have worked just as well closer by, but then as he'd said, he was "*neither calling the shots nor putting up the money, so he'd go and get on with it*". They were, he'd added, "*well on time with everything so far, so no doubt if things went wrong it would be when he wasn't stopping with Arietta.*"

He'd texted every day, and managed a phone call the night before, where he'd given her some wicked verbal sketches of their location and what was going on there.

"*So she screamed, the spider scuttled away as if it had been stabbed or whatever, and the guy sharing the bed with her lit a fag and ignored her histrionics,*" he'd said in a deadpan voice. "*She threatened to quit, the bloke asked if she wanted him to write her leaving letter, and I kept well out of it. But now we're not on time of course. Up shit creek without a paddle is striking. But never fear, our wedding is on. Only a few weeks to go.*"

Ari had spluttered, "*I hope no one is around or they'll get the wrong idea. And check your calendar, it's more than a few." Thank goodness.* She still wasn't looking forward to it.

"Who says it's wrong?" he'd asked in such a pseudo-innocent voice she'd been hard-pressed not to chuckle. *"Be good, darling. Miss me loads and I'll see you soon."*

"Moss, you…"

"Bye, bye, love, got to go."

The phone line had gone dead before she'd thought of a suitable retort.

Damn him.

The rest of the week it had been texts every day. The one time he'd tried to phone, she'd been on her way to town to look for a hat—a hat of all things. She hated them. *And* he'd phoned when she was in the one place she got no phone reception. Of course when she'd tried to ring back, she'd got voicemail.

She'd got the hat, even though it had seemed a waste of money for the few hours she'd wear it, and had treated herself to a pair of shoes and a ruinously expensive rip me off and have your wicked way with me bra and undies set. Which was stupid, as she wasn't spending all that money to have the stuff ripped off. In passion or whatever. Nevertheless, she had it all stowed in the tiny box room, laughingly called a bedroom, next to the one Moss occupied. Along with her suitcase, in preparation for the wedding weekend. At least if the maids saw it at the hotel she'd look the part… That made her wonder at her stupidity. The part for what? Arietta shook her head at her conflicting ideas and went to make a cuppa.

Moss was due to visit a few days later. He'd got, he told Arietta, an opportunity to have the weekend off as they were filming something where he wouldn't be needed, and he'd grabbed the chance to have some Moss-and-Arietta time.

"Two whole days and three nights off," he crowed in triumph. "Almost unheard of, but I'm not knocking it. Can we have a lazy weekend? Do not a lot and just chill?"

That sounded good to her and she said so. "Perfect, I'm bug-eyed at all the research I've done and I can't think of anything better." She had almost finished checking what she needed to make notes on, so a visit would be most welcome. "I've been reading up on newspapers in Regency times. The problem is I got ever so distracted and instead of checking up on murders most horrific and the devils who killed people—that's a quote by the way—I ended up reading about a rampaging elephant and wondering if my baddie could be trampled to death." She drew breath as Moss laughed.

"A perfect way to say good riddance to bad rubbish," he said. "More realistic than pecked to bits by ducks?"

"I reckon so. I'll cook on Friday. I'll enjoy it."

"Are you sure?" Moss asked. He sounded dubious. "Seems a bit rotten to let you slave over a hot stove when you've been busy. I could bring in a takeaway?"

"Tempting, but there's no need," Arietta answered. "I've got a stocked freezer thanks to Maggie, who went to the wholesalers and went mad, and I actually fancy cooking something proper with nice ingredients. Any preferences?"

"Ah, now," he drawled. "Not sure my preferences would be cookable."

Arietta spluttered. "Yes, well…and on that note I'll say you'll get what you're given."

"Oh, I *do* hope so."
He was incorrigible.

* * * *

By Friday morning Arietta was all caught up and metaphorically twiddling her thumbs. The house was tidy, beds made, lounge vacuumed for the first time in weeks and she'd even dusted. She hardly recognised the place. She'd prepared a fish curry, one of Moss' favourites, another of veg and some dhal. Remembered to buy naan bread and poppadums and had even had a go at making frozen fruit yoghurt, something she was pleased with. If Moss didn't like it she'd eat the lot with pleasure. After all that frenetic activity, the rest of the day stretched out empty in front of her. She didn't want to start writing or she'd get too involved and not be ready when Moss arrived. The same applied to the next book in her to be read pile.

After wandering aimlessly around the garden and pulling up two flowers instead of weeds, she swore and in disgust went indoors to wash her hands. *What next?*

In a light bulb moment, she remembered the local craft and farmers market was on that day and the last time she'd gone someone had had some fabulous wicker baskets for sale. A new linen bin was on her list of things she needed now—like a new electric toothbrush, as hers died a few days before for no apparent reason—rather than later. Like some very expensive pans for her Aga cooker and a new air fryer.

She'd left her well-loved wicker linen basket outside earlier in the week gone for a bath and returned to the garden to discover there was a heavy shower and the basket was a casualty. Soggy, twisted, unravelling and very much the worse for wear — or for the rain. As she'd had it since she'd gone to university, it hadn't owed her anything, and it was time to go mad and purchase another one. With a swift glance through the window at the weather — it had a look of 'shall I or shan't I rain' about it — she grabbed a waterproof tote bag and a thin raincoat with a hood. If it did rain, an umbrella would just get in the way and she'd spend more time making sure she didn't put someone's eye out than browsing for bargains.

The main car park at the place the market was held had, as ever, a 'full up' sign, and Arietta headed for the overflow spaces a few hundred yards further away. She had no intentions of joining those who thought it was worth taking a chance to see if someone had driven away and left an empty space. Even if they had it would be sod's law the space in question would be a tight fit, even for her car. Or someone would pip her to it. It wasn't worth the time, effort or loss of temper to find out. Arietta discovered a spot with no cars around — though she would bet her next royalty payment that however many empty spaces there would be later, someone would have parked close enough to her to make it hard to get in or drive away. That seemed to be another law of car parks.

The rain had held off and the sun was trying to come out. Arietta put her coat in her bag and headed towards the brightly covered stalls. With a bit of luck she'd find her linen bin and some other goodies. She was in a mood to shop.

There was a short queue to get through the gate to the area cordoned off next to the loch, where the stalls were set up. People chatted as they waited to give a donation to charity and entered the area. Arietta loved the idea that local charities could benefit and no one had to give more than they could afford. There was even a notice saying, 'Entry is free but if you wish to donate please do'. She did.

Once she was through the entrance—a gateway decorated with paper flowers and balloons—Arietta headed for the wicker stall. If she found something she liked, she would pay for it and ask the stallholder to keep it safe until she was ready to leave. To her joy, the exact type of washing basket she had thought about was on the stall, and at a price she considered very reasonable. That, along with some new tablemats, a set of quirky napkin rings—goodness knew when she'd use them, she tended to have paper serviettes that would look daft in them—and a rug for the garden were purchased and left behind the counter with her name written on the packaging. Now she could wander and buy at whim. As long as the whim wasn't too extravagant or stupid.

She walked past a clock in the shape of a gnome, which was next to a fish slice that had a carved fish handle with a tail that could take out the eye of the unwary. Laughed at two people dressed as mermaids who were doing the stand still and don't move a thing until someone dropped some money into their pot then waggled their tails to say thank you. She put a two-pound coin in—all the change she had—and was rewarded with very energetic waggling.

That cheered her up and she didn't hesitate very long as she grabbed a pair of new-to-you Levi's 501s from her favourite pre-loved clothing stall, eyed up and bought some hand-painted egg cups and a milk jug to match from the stall next door. She did dither over some fine as to be almost see-through mugs. Although she was a sucker for fine china, she was equally as good at breaking it. Nevertheless, the six matching mugs were carefully wrapped in newspaper and bubble wrap and put into her tote bag. There was only one of her, so in theory that gave her five spares. She chuckled to herself at her tenuous reason for purchasing so many.

A few minutes later at a nearby stall she saw some linen napkins and bought them. They'd fit perfectly in her newly purchased napkin rings. All she'd need then was a chance to use them. Would Moss be happy sitting at the dining table and using a linen napkin instead of their usual kitchen bench and kitchen roll in lieu of serviettes?

Soon she might have a chance to find out. Arietta added two candlesticks and a set of candles to the rest of her goodies. She could never resist the scented ones, and these were vanilla, her favourite apart from Christmas scents.

Her feet ached and she looked longingly at the long wooden seats, which were set so you could see over the loch. They were full. With a sigh, Arietta changed her mind about sitting and staring at the view. She decided to queue for a coffee and drink it 'on the hoof'. It would taste the same.

Ten minutes later she was headed back to the wickerwork stall, the coffee in one hand and a homemade sausage roll in the other, when a glimpse of a profile stopped her in her tracks.

It looked like Moss.

With the same copper curls and about the right height, the guy had on a battered leather jacket that could have been the twin of the one Moss owned.

Why would he be there?

Calm down. No doubt so do thousands of other guys, especially if they ride motorbikes or are of a certain age. Didn't they say everyone had a double somewhere? This was more than likely Moss'.

Or was it?

Surely it couldn't be him? He had said he was busy until later, when he would head to her house. Even so, she couldn't help but wonder, and on the spur of the moment decided to get closer for a better look.

Arietta dodged three women deciding—or, it seemed, unable to decide—on earrings, and a lady with a dog in a tie-dyed jacket who blocked the walkway between stalls. Manoeuvred around a couple choosing tomatoes who disagreed loudly over firm or ripe, Green Beefsteak, whatever they were, or Roma, and tried to follow the man in question without showing she was.

She knocked into a boy on a skateboard who wobbled, grabbed her arm to steady himself, accidentally brushed the side of her boob and blushed the colour of the tomatoes she'd just passed. It was a close-run thing who was the most apologetic. At least half a dozen people turned to see what had happened, and Arietta decided she could never be an undercover agent.

The bloke didn't pay any attention, though, thank goodness—she'd hate to be caught staring at a stranger. He ignored the chatter and mayhem behind him and headed for the water's edge, where he joined a young girl of around thirteen or fourteen who wore a jacket similar to his and leant on the railings as she idly threw bread into the water. He said something and the girl nodded, flung her arms around his neck then slid one arm into his and urged him towards an ice cream stall, talking and gesticulating as she did. He laughed, nodded and walked away with her, totally at ease, as he said something and the girl's reply of "Daad," was heard clearly across the intervening yards.

Daad? Arietta's head spun and she grabbed onto the nearest thing she could find — a tall woman in a waxed jacket, who looked at her in concern. "I say, are you all right? You've gone grey and you look as if you can't see very well. Should I call a doctor?"

Oh, Lord. That was the last thing she needed. "No, sorry I forgot to eat breakfast and I need food, I just went a bit lightheaded," Arietta improvised rapidly. "I'm off to get another coffee and a big sticky bun. But thank you, and I'm sorry I grabbed you like that. You must have wondered what the hell was going on."

The woman smiled. "I did wonder if it was a novel way of pickpocketing for a sec. Then I worried you were going to die on me."

"Oh glory, sorry again." How mortifying. "I hope no dying in my immediate future. It's my fault for not remembering the market was on and rushing out when I did. I'll make a note not to be so daft in the future."

"Good idea." The woman glanced at her watch and yelped. "Almost time to get Tamara and Ronan from nursery. Glad you're okay." They nodded to each other and went off in different directions, the lady almost running, Arietta at a more leisurely pace.

As she reached the queue for the cake stall, she saw the guy and the teen again as they stood next to a stall of scarves and accessories. She half turned away, but not so much that she couldn't study them clearly. The guy so did look like Moss. Even though she'd already had the double take you never knew where or when you'd meet your doppelganger moment, Arietta was taken aback. *Seriously. Enough already. Just mention it to Moss when I see him, and we can laugh about it.*

As long as it *wasn't* him.

The young girl pointed to a scarf. Her voice rang out clearly. "Don't you think that would suit Mum?"

He nodded. "Matches her eyes."

It was red and gold.

"Daad." The teen giggled. "Bet you wouldn't say that to her face." They moved so the side of the stall was between them and Arietta.

"Lord, no."

Due to the depth of feeling he put into the word, Arietta could imagine the shiver or eye-rolling that accompanied it.

"I bet not. Come on, Dad, should I buy it? We did promise Mum we wouldn't be too late back."

"Yes, buy it, and we'll head home, and be in your mum's good books. Do you have enough money?"

Arietta had got to the head of the queue, and by the time she'd made her purchases, paid for them and turned away, the other two had gone.

Judging by the conversation she'd overheard, it wasn't Moss she'd noticed. Nevertheless, the incident left her unsettled. She had it bad if she saw him everywhere.

Somewhere nearby a clock chimed a half hour. Arietta glanced at her watch and decided it was time to collect the rest of her purchases and head home.

* * * *

Of course there was a tailback to get out of the car park. It was just her luck. However, there was no point in getting antsy so Arietta turned on the radio, drummed her fingers in time with the music and sat patiently as three lanes of traffic from different directions filtered into one line that led to the road proper. She never could understand why people got so worked up about stuff like that. It didn't make the queue move any faster and just got you all hot and bothered for no reason. Plus it probably did nothing for your blood pressure. She slipped a mint into her mouth and happily crunched it.

The car in front of her reached the head of their string of traffic and moved off. Arietta waited as a car from each of the other lanes left then edged forward. Just as she manoeuvred into position to be the next to leave, she caught a glimpse of a red Ferrari out of the corner of her eye.

Nice.

She had to hope whoever drove it had parked well away from idiots. It was the sort of car that shouted 'scrape me'! The sort of car she was unlikely ever to drive in, let alone own, even if she won the lottery. She'd had a list of must-do and must-have with that imaginary winnings, and a car that ate money via the petrol pumps wasn't on it. A lovely car, but not a lot of use on the lanes and narrow, twisting roads near to her cottage. It would bottom out on the lumps and bumps.

Halfway home the Ferrari overtook her with a throaty roar and as it got to the next T-junction headed down the road that led to the nearest town. Arietta turned in the opposite direction.

* * * *

An hour later, the curry was all ready to be reheated, the rice waiting next to the rice cooker ready to be switched on and everything else under control. She'd unpacked her purchases, put them where she wanted them for now, though no doubt that would alter, changed her going-out trousers and smartish blouse for a floaty skirt and a T-shirt and headed outside. The sky had cleared and the sun was out. It wasn't hot, but a good warm temperature where, with little or no wind, you could sit outside and enjoy it before the midges took over. As much as Arietta enjoyed summer — when they actually had weather that was at all summerlike, not a given in Scotland — she longed for September, when the midges began to go and you could enjoy walking by the river in an evening without being bitten. For now, though, she'd enjoy the chance to sit outside as she waited for Moss.

It was unusual that Moss hadn't texted or phoned to see if she needed anything, but she reasoned she had said she was going to cook and everything was under control. She *didn't* need anything, except him there. The wine was chilling, she had beer in the fridge and lemon and ice cubes for the gin, or fizzy water. *All options covered.*

Conscious of the fact that for some unknown reason she was antsy, Arietta deadheaded a few roses, watered some pots and wondered what next. She headed inside, picked up the daily paper, went back out again and began to tackle the crossword to take her mind off Moss' non-appearance. As ever, once she got started she was oblivious to most things and another half an hour had passed before she realised she was stuck on the last four clues, Moss still hadn't turned up, and it was a lot later than his usual arrival time.

Arietta put the paper down in disgust. There was a new crossword compiler and she hadn't sussed out his way of thinking yet. She'd read a book instead.

Her tummy rumbled and she put her hand over it. Should she eat her dinner and save his or just have a snack?

A delve into the fridge decided her. She'd snack, because if for any reason he didn't turn up, the curry would save. Armed with some homemade pâté and just a couple of crackers, Arietta made herself a small gin and tonic and, feeling slightly fraudulent—she rarely drank gin alone—headed back to her favourite garden chair. With a bit of luck, she would get another forty or so minutes outside before the midges drove her in. She left the paper on the table and picked up a book by a new-to-her author in the hope it would engage her interest.

It didn't.

The characters were one-dimensional, the author appeared to have a love of certain words and started almost every sentence of dialogue with 'so', and as far as she could tell she had a good idea who the murderer was by page ten, with no inclination to read on to discover if she was correct. It was destined for the charity shop. She might not like it but that wasn't to say someone else wouldn't.

Ten minutes later, just as she finished her snack, there was a throaty, grumbling roar in the lane.

A bit like the sound of the Ferrari she'd noticed earlier. Arietta imagined whoever was driving it had mistaken the lane for the road they wanted. Hopefully they were well-insured, had navigated around the potholes and hadn't lost too much paint or half of their exhaust on the way from the village. She expected to hear it drive past then five minutes later return as it had discovered the lane ended a few fields down. Therefore she was surprised to hear it stop and two doors slam.

Damn and blast. Now she'd need to dredge up her local knowledge or hunt out a map on her phone. Why did people ignore the no-through road sign? It wasn't there for fun or to fool you.

Arietta dusted the crumbs from her lap and stood up, ready to head inside and to the front door. Where had she put the key?

She didn't have to worry. Footsteps sounded on the gravel path that edged the house. Someone who understood that very often people in the countryside ignored front doors as they were inconveniently placed for the everyday movements indoors? When Arietta was a child the room at the front of the house — the lounge — was only occupied on a Sunday afternoon or when the vicar came to call. Everyday living took place in the kitchen or a smaller room next to it. And these days the vicar rarely called and would use the back door anyway. As Doug, who had an ordained cousin, said, the back door was usually nearer the kettle and the cake tin. Gregory, his relative, put on two stones in his first year as a parish priest.

She would swear the guy and the young girl she'd noticed at the market came into view, hand in hand and with different expressions.

He looked worried. She appeared sceptical.

Both looked nervous.

It was Moss.

'Dad'?

She felt sick. *Dad? Moss* was *Dad.*

Chapter Seven

"You weren't answering your phone. I've left several messages, including one about dinner."

What? "Ah…" Where was it? "I plugged it in to charge a couple of hours or so ago, it was with me until then," Arietta said shortly. The last thing she wanted to do was get involved in small talk or feel wrong-footed. Why did she ever listen to men or let them into her life? Because it seemed as soon as she did, they hurt her. Lied and prevaricated and did the dirty.

Hell, she felt dirty. Dirty and betrayed. It didn't matter the relationship was all a pretence, she'd been beginning to warm to him. Trust him. And now this.

Moss narrowed his eyes as if he could read her thoughts. "I'm certain I tried before that."

"Doesn't seem like it and I've no idea where I put it, sorry. I wasn't expecting calls." *Hoping, though. What am I like, I need a pouch and a lanyard for it.* Which sounded most uncomfortable. "I didn't hear it ring once I was home, sorry." *Stop saying sorry.*

"Or your landline," Moss added flatly. "I was worried. I couldn't get in touch with you."

"Fault on the line," Arietta said shortly. His blame-her attitude was beginning to irritate her. "Due to be fixed next week." Oh how she'd have liked to have added, 'So why were you only going to ring last hour or so? What was wrong with earlier?' However, after a swift glance to the enthralled teen next to him, she decided against it. Whatever their dirty linen was going to be, she had no intention of airing it in public, even if the said public was obviously related to one of them.

"I needed to speak with you," Moss said. Had he been going to tell her before they turned up that he had someone with him and who it was? Arietta wondered uneasily. Would it have made the situation any better? Probably not. It was a bit late in the day to say 'oh by the way, I forgot to mention it, but...' She was conscious she was hurt by his lack of openness.

"Dad *was* worried," the teen added. "So we came to see if you were okay."

Dad... Yeah... What was she supposed to say or do? Arietta did her best not to act as if the bottom had fallen out of her world at his duplicity. No significant other indeed. Did an ex or not an ex—that was somewhat unclear—whatever and a daughter not count? Instead, she did her utmost to achieve a non-accusing, subtly enquiring and non-threatening expression. She wasn't sure she achieved it. By the expression on Moss' face, he didn't think she had either.

Moss cleared his throat. The teen had a faintly worried expression, as if she was certain that whatever would be said would bear little resemblance to the truth.

Well, it seemed it hadn't in the past so why should it now? Damn her phone. *I wonder where I've put it?* She glanced enquiringly at Moss, her hands clenched and hidden in her pockets. *What next?*

"What did you want to speak about?" she asked in as pleasant a tone as she could muster. "I'm all ears."

His expression showed he doubted that.

"Ah, Arietta, this is Audie." Moss paused, and when Arietta didn't respond, he sighed. "My daughter. Audie, this is Arietta. The lady your mother is certain does not exist."

What? Whatever she had expected to hear, it wasn't that. What had she got to do with Audie's mother and *why* did it matter if she existed or not? What part did the mother play in Moss' life? *So many questions and not a one answered.* Arietta opened her mouth to ask, however good manners came to the fore instead and she held her hand out. "Hello." 'Pleased to meet you' stuck in her throat and she left it unsaid. "Why does your mother think I don't exist?" *Who is your mother? Are your parents still involved in a more than share-a-daughter way? Why didn't I know any of this?*

Audie shrugged. "She reckoned Dad made you up so he didn't look like a Billy No-Mates or find an excuse not to go to her wedding. She's finally decided to take the plunge and wants Dad there to show there's no ill feeling. Which there's no reason for there to be. Though why she prefers her husband-to-be over Dad I have no idea, but then I'm not Mum."

What wedding am I going to and no one has told me about? Hold on, her wedding, not Moss' and her wedding? Or are they retaking their vows and he's here to say hi and goodbye? No, that doesn't make sense. Actually, none of it does. Argh, enough already. The little bubble of doubt and worry began to grow. Now she wanted to give him a piece of her mind, but not in front of his daughter. Arietta's temper began to simmer and she had to fight the urge not to tap her foot. Not a good sign.

"Audie, language," Moss warned. "I've got nothing to do with it. I'm your dad, no more, no less. Anyway, I thought you liked him?"

Well that partly sorts that question out. One down and a million to go.

"Well, duh, I do, what's not to like? But honestly, Dad, he's so...so wet, *you* know that. A right numpty. He doesn't even like *watching* golf, let alone playing it. As for swimming or tennis or —"

It was Moss' turn to roll his eyes. "Enough, hon. Nor do a lot of people. He's...okay," Moss finished.

"But wet? A numpty? Okay a nice one but..." The teen rolled her eyes. "Honest, he so is. And before you say anything, Dad, I know he loves Mum, and she loves him and they're loved-up and you know they don't exclude me and all that, but he's still wet."

"I plead the fifth, or anything which won't incriminate me. Now, no more, or I might start using your full name." He grinned and ruffled Audie's hair. "Should I?"

"No." Audie giggled. "Daad, my hair... First it got all blown about and now you've messed it up again. Gah, men. You have no idea, do you?"

Moss looked quizzical then grinned. "Poor useless creatures we are, says the man who conquered a ponytail when you were three and plaits two years later."

"Neither of which I have now," Audie pointed out.

"Irrelevant." She put her hands on Moss' sides and began to tickle him.

He laughed. "Enough, you hoyden. Or I'll say M—"

"Noooooooo." Audie shook her head and dropped her hands to cuddle him around the waist instead. "I'll be good." She wrinkled her nose as Moss raised his eyebrows. "Okay, I'll try to be good," she amended. "Can't promise, though."

"Try works."

Arietta could sense and see how close father and daughter were. One point in his favour, versus a hell of a lot against. Sadly, the one point for didn't help the way she felt betrayed.

"As for my name," Audie went on, "do not even think about it. Not unless you want me to tell everyone about the time you got your toe stuck up—"

Stuck up? Arietta's mind boggled. *Stuck up where? Or what to? Or… Stop it now.*

Moss put his hand over his daughter's mouth and she giggled behind his palm. "Okay, truce," he said as he grinned at her. "Right, so now you've seen Arietta exists we'd better get you back to your mum." He turned to Arietta. "I'll be back when I can. Sorry about supper and so on. Hope you can do something with it?"

What else could she do but nod and say, "I'm sure I will." Add 'oh yes, put it in the bin, or over your head, you sod'? After which, change the locks and diss him on social media? It was just as well she wasn't so vindictive. Or she thought she wasn't. It had never been put to the test before. And what the hell did '*so on*' mean? Help with the washing up? Share a nightcap? Go one step further? She stopped her thoughts from getting even more outrageous and concentrated on what Audie was saying.

Audie looked disappointed. "I thought we'd stop for a while so I can get to know your…"

She blushed as Moss uttered a warning, "Audie..." in a low voice.

"Sorry. Friend. Your friend. Okay, well, nice to have met you, Arietta. I'm glad you're real. I can reassure Mum that Dad won't be all on his lonesome or have what Gran would call a bimbo with him. You are coming to the wedding, aren't you?"

Arietta opened her mouth to refute the statement and add something caustic like 'not even if you smear me with honey and put me next to an ant hill', saw the hopeful expression on Audie's face and laughed reluctantly. Audie was so frank and patently honest you couldn't take offence at anything she said. Moss appeared relieved. He should not be, she decided. She might have no argument with his daughter but he was a different thing entirely. Arietta didn't have many grudges, but when she did, she held on to them.

"Of course she is," Moss said hastily when Arietta didn't answer. "Got the hat already. For a wedding she's going to and taking me."

Got the... Today is the first time I've heard I'm off to another wedding, and it seems my hat is doubling up? It began to sound as if Moss had more than a few explanations to share.

"Can I see?" Audie asked eagerly. "I've got to wear an Alice band sort of thing. It's horrible. I'll look like a nerd in it. It's so not me."

"You'll look lovely, I'm sure," Arietta said diplomatically. *Disappear, the pair of you. Just clear off and let me throw things.* "It goes with the whole bridesmaid thing, doesn't it?"

Audie shrugged. "Nerdiness? Go...gosh, I hope not. I love hats, though. I had to take mine off so it didn't blow away today. It's pink and purple felt and so cool.

Dad got it for me in Australia last year. So can I see yours? Please? We've got time, haven't we, Dad?"

Moss smiled as he gave a sidelong glance to a silent Arietta. "I guess so. If Arietta doesn't mind showing you."

Oh I so do, you bastard, and you know it. Why the hell could he not see how miffed she was? Or could he and he just thought she was in a snit and would get over it soon? If that was it, he was in for a surprise. Arietta decided she could now hold a grudge, big-time, for longer.

"Will you?" Audie said. "Please."

It appeared she was outnumbered. "Come on then," she said, resigned to the fact she wasn't going to get rid of her visitors anytime soon. "Your dad can wait here." She turned to Moss, who immediately looked wary. "The paper's on the kitchen table. Three down and seven across have me stuck. You know where the coffee is kept, feel free to make yourself a cup. It's this way, Audie."

"Are you mad at my dad?" Audie asked as Arietta led the way upstairs.

How to answer that diplomatically? "No, why?"

Audie sighed as she followed Arietta up the stairs. "Well, you seem so. Is it cos he didn't let us meet?"

No, because he didn't acknowledge your existence.

"Not at all." Arietta opened the box-room door and ushered Audie inside. "I can understand that." *Actually, that I can, the fact I didn't know you existed is a bit harder to swallow. I mean, even 'I've got a daughter, she lives with her mum, we weren't married' would have been something.* "After all your dad and I are still getting to know each other. If he and I didn't work out and you and I did, it could make it hard if your dad and I split up. Gah, that sounds complicated. I expect he didn't want to upset you with a woman in his life."

Audie giggled. "I get what you mean. I've not ever met one of his ladies, or floozies, as Gran calls them. She's never really rated Dad and thinks the sun shines out of Mum's fiancé. I'm the other way round, you know? Well I would be, wouldn't I? He's my dad."

"Exactly, that's as it should be."

"I don't think my gran totally gets that, but that's her problem." Audie sounded a lot older than Arietta thought she was. "Don't get me wrong, I'm not thinking Mum and Dad should get together, that would never work, even they say so. As Mum put it, theirs was a short-lived, explosive relationship which resulted in me, about whom she discovered after they'd split up and she'd gone back to my soon-to-be stepdad. They'd had a row or something I guess. Never been bothered enough to ask."

The consequences one who… Ah. Now she understood that cryptic statement. It didn't make her hurt any less, though.

"Mum's beloved is okay, honestly, but I cannot rate him as a dad type," Audie went on. "Not my kind of a dad type anyway. I mean, he won't eat ice cream unless it's in a bowl and he has a spoon. I suggested we go out for a burger one day and you'd have thought I suggested we ate worms. Weird. But Mum loves him and he loves her and there's nothing wrong with him except he's boring. Never ever wears odd socks, I mean, how insane is that?" She pointed her toes to show one green-clad foot and one in orange and purple stripes.

"And you have another pair just like it at home?"

Audie broke into gales of laughter. "See, I knew you'd get it. No wonder Dad likes you. When you meet him, I bet you think the soon-to-be stepdad is a boring weirdo as well."

Arietta nodded as she took her hat out of its box. The bloke was getting more interesting by the second, and more than reminded her of someone. She was also wondering who on earth Audie's mother could be. "Okay, what do you think? Marks out of ten." She put the lace and feather concoction on her head and struck a pose. "Dress is in the wardrobe, shoes under it. No, your dad hasn't seen it, and yes, I'm still undecided if it will do."

"Oh it so will do. It's fab. Mum will be green with envy. As for steppie-to-be, he'll just ogle."

Steppie-to-be. What a mouthful?

"Is that what you call him?"

Audie laughed. "I call him Popsie. It sends him demented. Says it makes him sound like an American female of the fifties. He's not that old, but knows all bizarre things like that. I'll probably call him by one of his names later, but for now it's a game and he knows it. Can I see your dress as well? Have you got it?"

"Yep. So your stepdad-to-be, one of his names?" Was it so wrong to quiz the girl? Probably, but at that moment Arietta couldn't give a damn. "Has he got lots?"

"Yeah, so I need to decide which one." She didn't say any more and Arietta chose to change the subject.

She put her hat back in its box and re-swathed it in yards of tissue paper. "There you go. I think I'll have to show you the rest another time."

"Oh, okay." Audie sounded disappointed. "Love the hat, though. It's so cool. Now why can't I have something like that to wear?"

"Because you're not in your thirties," Arietta suggested, "and you don't want to look old before your time?"

Audie giggled. "There is that. Well, thank you for showing me, and I'll look forward to seeing the dress if Dad brings me again. You would let him wouldn't you? I mean, whether you and Dad stay together or not, you will be at Mum's wedding with him surely, and I'd love to see the dress before then. Oh yeah, and with those shoes. I adore them, I'm a shoe-aholic"

"I'll see what I can do," Arietta said diplomatically — and not quite truthfully. "We better go back to your dad."

Audie sighed. "Yeah, men have no patience, do they?"

"Not a lot." Arietta led the way downstairs. "That's why they need women."

"Oh yes, my mum says that as well."

Moss looked up — warily — as they went back to the kitchen. "What's the verdict?"

"It's gorgeous," Audie said. "Cool and groovy."

"She's been watching old 60s programmes," Moss said. "So we get groovy, fab and hey, man a lot. It'll be a headband and a cowbell next."

"I have those." Audie giggled. "They were Granny's. She said it was the best time of her life. Do you think it was cos she hadn't met Grandpa?"

Moss looked heavenwards. "Daughter mine, do not go there. That's my parents we're wondering about. Say thank you and goodbye to Arietta. We best get going." He waited until Audie had done as he asked and gave Arietta a very wary hug. "I'll call you."

She nodded and did her best not to tense up. "Fine. Drive safely." She ignored his chagrined expression. It was all down to him, not her. And she was entitled to hold a grudge.

"Bye, Arietta, so-oo nice to meet you," Audie carolled. "See you again so…so I can inspect the rest."

Arietta laughed. "Okay." What else could she say? 'No chance' to Audie and 'sod off, you bastard' to Moss? Not with Audie there, but she could think it. And did.

Moss bent his head, hesitated and kissed her cheek. "We need to talk, and I promise we will," he said softly into her ear so Audie couldn't hear. "I'm sorry about all this."

What could she say? "Of course." Arietta cleared her throat and raised her voice. "Nice to meet you, Audie. Drive safely, Moss."

Arietta waited until she'd waved them off before she went indoors, back kicked the door shut and threw a cushion at the window. Then remembered she needed to find her phone. She discovered it in the kitchen, blank and uninformative under a tea towel. Its battery was, as she'd suspected, flat. She jiggled the connection, blew on it, hoped that would help and plugged it in while she dealt with the rest of the unwanted meal.

What next? A new phone? She hoped not. She'd get to work with a cotton bud or cocktail stick first. The amount of fluff that came out of a tiny aperture amazed her. No wonder the connection was dodgy. With a bit of luck, it would be better from then on.

She scrolled through her messages and voicemails. Moss had rung and left several of them. Apologising for not being able to come for dinner or be with her that night and would explain it all once he saw her.

Bummer. Guess I need to grovel and apologise as well.

She burst into tears.

Five minutes later she blew her nose, sniffed and thought about the last few hours. She detested a watering pot, and there she was trying her best to be one. *Enough already*. As her gran used to say, worst things happened at sea. Apart from that, it was ridiculous. Arietta reckoned she had cried more in the last few months than in the last twenty-five years. And that included Thomas breaking her arm.

It needed to stop, right there and then. She washed her face and found a crochet hook and some wool. She'd been meaning to crochet a blanket for age. Now was the time to start. With rubbish on the TV, a glass of wine and a sneaky bar of chocolate poised ready on the coffee table, she was sorted.

She'd think about what had happened that day when she was less likely to throw things.

It wasn't so simple. Arietta discovered she couldn't turn her emotions on and off like a tap. Her mind wouldn't let her. How ever much she tried to think of anything other than Moss had a daughter he hadn't told her about, she kept coming back to that, and the hurt would rear up and hit her all over again.

What was it with her and blokes? Did she appear to be the sort of person they could walk all over and get away with it? She wouldn't have said so before but now she was beginning to wonder. She glanced down at her crochet and swore. Halfway along the row she'd changed stitches for no apparent reason, and the result was wobbly and out of sync with the rest of the pattern. Arietta swore, put it down with disgust and went to have a bath.

An hour or so later, the evening stretched out in front of her. She made a sandwich, took one bite and threw it in the bin.

Four hours after that with no message from Moss, she made her mind up and with her phone fully charged she dialled a number.

"Hi... Want a visitor?"

Half an hour later she'd packed a bag, locked the house up and set out. If Moss did turn up he'd be in for a surprise.

Petty maybe, but she wasn't going to hang around just in case and she needed some love and fuss.

Sixty miles down the road she turned into the drive of an old Victorian villa and stopped the car next to a mud-splattered four-by-four. As she turned her car's engine off, the front door of the house opened and her double, albeit a couple of decades older, came out.

Arietta exited the car, keys in hand, burst into tears and flung her arms around her mother.

Jessie Clare rocked on her heels, held on fast and threw Arietta's car keys to her husband, who patted his daughter's shoulder and headed to the car.

"Kettle's on," Jessie said. "Comfy chair awaits, got plenty of gin, crisps, chocolate and tissues. Ready to rant, rail, commiserate or tell you to build a bridge and get over it, whatever is appropriate. Anything else?"

"Oh, Mum, I do love you both." Arietta sniffed, fished a tissue out of her pocket—luckily clean—and blew her nose. "I'm probably overreacting, but I feel let down."

"Overreact?" Jessie did a big wide-eyes look. "You? She who punched her brother and loosened one of his front teeth when he threw a slug, a dead slug mind you, into the bin, overreacting? Never." She urged Arietta towards the house. "Come on, let's go in and you can have a misery fest for half an hour. Have you eaten?" she asked, practical as ever.

"Nope, it would have choked me. But be proud, I didn't bin it and I oh-so wanted to. The bastard," Arietta added. "Why be so duplicitous? Did he think I would go to the gossip rags? Did he?" she asked fiercely. "Did he really think that of me?"

"As I have no idea what you are talking about, I have absolutely no clue," her mum replied. "You can tell me what you can once we're indoors and sitting comfortably.

"Then I'll begin?" Arietta gave a watery giggle. "Fair enough." Her tummy rumbled. "Oops, sorry, it seems I *am* hungry now."

"Just as well I've got shepherd's pie in the oven then. No, don't get up, I'll bring it in and we'll eat off trays."

Arietta obediently sank back into the chair again. "Ohh, comfort food, I like it. With Brussels?"

Her mum sighed. "Even though they're out of season, yes, with Brussels. I wouldn't dare not."

Thank goodness for mums.

* * * *

A couple of hours later, Arietta sat back, replete and sipped her gin. "I feel better for that. I needed it, and I'm sort of cool, calm and collected and ready to talk."

Her mum had insisted they eat before anything to do with Arietta's state of mind was discussed. It had been the right thing to do. Arietta was conscious now she was relaxed she ought to check her phone or ring Moss. She had a quick look at the screen. Six missed calls and ten, no, *twelve* texts.

Oops again.

"Mum, I need to send a text. Then I'll spill the beans."

Her mum nodded. "Okay, I'll make some coffee. Do you want Dad here or not?"

"Might as well. Just confess it all at once." Arietta waited until her mum had left the room and thought for a second before she sent a brief 'away for a few days. Speak later' message. That would do for now. She turned her phone off again as her parents entered.

"Okay?" her mum asked as she put a tray with the insulated coffee jug, mugs and milk down on a side table. "All sorted?"

"Think so. Right... This is confidential, not to be shared. Promise?"

Both her parents nodded.

"Do I need to say cut my throat hope to die? Down a whisky?" her dad asked. "Is it a shock horror sort of story? Do I need to go and duff someone up? If so, I'll need more than a couple of drams." As far as Arietta knew, the biggest crime her dad had ever committed was waving a banner at Faslane Naval Base denouncing nuclear weapons. Even then he'd done no more than wave it, and not thumped anyone over the head or threatened to do so. He was a peace lover through and through and, as he often said, "*amazed to have gone to Woodstock in 1969 and survived to tell the tales*". Her mum, almost a decade younger, usually just rolled her eyes and said she envied him.

So did Arietta. She'd watched the film, listened to the music and reckoned she'd been born forty years too late.

Jessie bemoaned the fact she had to do Knebworth Festival with her brother, but luckily once she'd met Tam, Arietta's dad, they'd gone to at least two festivals a year together, including Live Aid.

"So shock horror or a mild oh dear, how sad never mind or do?" her dad prompted. "I want to get into the correct frame of mind."

"Depends on how you look at it if you think it's shock horror or not," Arietta said as Tam stirred the embers in the grate into a cheerful blaze and they all settled down. The fire wasn't really necessary but it made for a peaceful, cheerful setting and she needed that. A comfort, like her dinner had been. "It's about Moss."

"I think we guessed that," her mum said. "Seeing as you'd told us you were spending the weekend with him and you're here instead. Is it over, love?"

Arietta could feel the tears welling again. "Oh, Mum, I don't know, it's such a mess, and I don't know all the story."

"Arietta Rachael Clare," her mum said in a horrified voice. "Are you telling me you ran before you knew if there was a reason to?"

"Oh there was a reason," Arietta said bleakly. "Moss has a teenage daughter. One he forgot to mention."

"Oh dear."

That's mild, Mother-mine.

"How did you find out?" her dad asked in a soothing, uncritical voice, that went a long way towards calming Arietta down

"Evidently her mum didn't believe Moss had someone who he was going to her wedding with. Audie wanted to see who it was. I didn't even know I was going to the woman's wedding. He just told Audie I'd bought a hat to wear to a wedding he was coming to with me, so I could wear it to both."

"Ah," her dad said. "Hmm."

What a good way to sum it up.

"Whether he'd intended to bring her to see me, even if he'd managed to get hold of me, I have no idea. I don't mind him bringing her, well, not much," Arietta said, determined to be scrupulously honest. "Or the fact he had to take her home or whatever. What I do mind is we've been together now for a few months and he's never mentioned such a big part of his life. I feel…hurt, I guess. As if I can't be trusted. If he thinks that, then we shouldn't be together, end of." She took a deep breath. "Whew. Think that's it."

Her mum inclined her head. "Point taken, he should have told you, but no doubt he had a good reason not to. Anything else?"

What else could there be?

"He said he'd get back when he could and no more. After a bit I thought sod it and came here. I needed…your advice, stringent comments or anything else you thought necessary. And a hug of course."

"You've had the hugs and you've acted like a spoiled brat, coming here if, as I reckon, you didn't tell him you wouldn't be home and where you would be. Did you?"

"I waited for hours before coming here. I have messaged him now," Arietta said defensively. "Which is more than he did." Gah, how whiny did she sound?

"What did he say?" her dad asked.

Arietta wriggled uneasily in the chair. Why, when a few minutes earlier it had been the most comfortable place imaginable, did it now feel like it was full of nails? "I don't know, I haven't listened to his messages, or looked at his text."

This time it was her mum who exploded. "Are you really my daughter?" She pointed her finger at Arietta.

"Surely I brought you up better than that, scrub that, I *know* I did. Go and answer him, now, this minute."

Only her parents could make her feel like a toddler again.

Arietta smiled, shamefaced, and headed up to her room. The same king-sized bed she'd slept in since she chose it for her sixteenth birthday, albeit with new covers, was situated opposite the door. The room, now a cool, rich cream and apricot instead of the dark purple she'd favoured, was much more to her adult tastes, as was the deep pile carpet in matching apricot and cream tones. The en suite was as it had always been. White bathroom fittings and pale lemon walls, sconces for candles — evidently her parents had trusted her enough not to burn the house down — and deep shelves for towels and toiletries. She loved every inch of it. Those two rooms had been her sanctuary when her first boyfriend had broken it off — aged eight and three-quarters — saying she was too young for him. It had been a week after her eighth birthday and he had been three weeks and four days older. The rooms had continued in the same vein when she fell out with her best friend over bands — The Killers or The Zutons if she remembered rightly — when Thomas broke her arm and when she wasn't invited to the end of school prom by the then boy of her dreams.

Now it seemed they were about to be her sanctuary for grovelling to Moss.

Maybe.

The first thing, she reasoned, was to actually look at and listen to his messages and texts. Arietta took a deep breath and turned on her phone, half expecting it to beep that there were more messages.

There was only one. A voicemail left about ten minutes earlier.

Now where to start? Logic said at the beginning, intuition said with that last voicemail. She went with intuition.

It was as well she had. Moss' voice was loud and clear but oh-so very strained. "Sorry, can't get hold of you, sorry…for a lot more as well. Also sorry, I hurt you, I know I did. I had my reasons, which sound a bit spurious now, sorry. Ah hell, my turn to say sorry a lot, but I suspect you're not ready to hear me out. Let me know when you are. Oh and you might not believe me, and why should you, but I never wanted to hurt you. I'll leave it up to you whether you want to get in touch or not."

Arietta played it over again. He had it in a nutshell. He'd hurt her and if she were honest she'd not got rid of enough of that hurt to listen to him impartially and open-minded. A quick perusal of the other notifications were along the lines of 'not sure when I'll get back, will let you know', with a few variations of 'why aren't you answering' and one, just before her earlier terse text, 'are you OK? If you don't answer today, I'll notify the police'.

Thank goodness she'd answered.

She made her way back to her parents in a thoughtful mood and for the rest of the evening all talk of Moss, her and their situation was avoided.

The following morning, she headed for home. Not to be there in case Moss called by — she knew enough of him that she would have to make the next move — but in her own cottage she could do as she wanted when she wanted and how she wanted. And if that were mump, moan and munch chocolate, so be it.

Not if I want to get into those new jeans I bought the other day.

Chapter Eight

The last sentence of Moss' text went round and round her head over the next few days. He'd leave it up to her to call.

She lost count of how many times she scrolled down to his number, hesitated then shut her phone off. Why should it be her?

Because I've had enough time to sulk and it's time to pull my big girl pants up and get un-grudged?

Arietta went back to Regency Perth and Effie McSorley, her latest heroine, and took her frustration and sense of grievance out on the poor woman. By the time Arietta had put her through the mill — literally — she was in a better frame of mind and her manuscript was in a tighter, tenser place.

She shut her laptop down with a sigh of satisfaction and considered her situation. She was still a bit pissed off with life in general if she were honest, but just about ready to hear what Moss had to say. She'd text tomorrow, and ignored the niggle that said 'tomorrow never comes'.

Do it now. She bit her lip and thought about things. Was she ready to say all was forgiven?

No.

Was she ready to listen to him with an open mind?

Not quite.

Would she at least listen without going off on one? Act in a mature manner? Arietta couldn't honestly say yes.

That made her think a little longer and not be able to offer herself a definitive answer.

Would she be happy never to see or speak to Moss again?

Definitely not.

Therefore it was up to her.

Without letting herself do any more second-guessing, she sent a brief text.

Ready to listen no promises what my reaction will be.

She didn't think Moss would respond in a hurry, but to her surprise her phone pinged a few moments later.

Thank you, busy on set, speak soon.

Well it was better than silence. Arietta took a deep breath, put him out of her mind as best she could and got on with everyday life.

Which that week basically meant writing, deleting and rewriting until she was reasonably satisfied with the shape of her plot.

* * * *

By Friday afternoon, she decided she would be able to have a weekend of no writing and a lot of house cleaning and tidying up with a clear conscience. With regards to the writing anyway. The state of the house, not so much.

"Arietta, you are a slob," she said as she looked at the mess her bedroom was in. Her bed was unmade, the wardrobe doors open and several tops half-on and half-off their hangers where she'd rummaged as she'd decided what to wear. There were two empty water bottles on her bedside table, along with her Kindle, a chocolate bar — wrapped — and three odd earrings, none of which she remembered wearing. The bathroom wasn't a lot better. Toothpaste on the counter and what suspiciously looked like mascara on the mirror. Three pairs of pants and a skirt hung half-in and half-out of the washing basket, the reason for which was apparent. The basket was full to overflowing, and for the dirty clothes of only one person, that wasn't a good state of affairs.

Arietta made the bed, put the clothes back onto hangers, filled her wastebasket with the rubbish she'd found and wiped the toothpaste away. The dirty clothes she contemplated for a few seconds, then sorted them into colours and shoved all but one pile back into the basket, which at least she could now close. She stretched to get rid of the ache in her back — who on earth would start doing all that after sitting at a desk all day — picked up the load of clothes and dumped it in the washer. Then she contemplated the dusty windowsill.

The poor dust bunnies weren't half going to be upset.

"Needs must," she said out loud. "Long overdue to be a domestic goddess, sorry DB's, your time is up." She hunted out some dusters and a wet cloth and set to work.

* * * *

Two hours later Arietta was as grimy as the floor in the mudroom had been. She suspected she had cobwebs in her hair and a streak of muck on her cheek, but the downstairs of the cottage was as pristine as she'd ever seen it.

Time for coffee and a sit down. She'd only just achieved that when her phone rang.

Moss.

She contemplated for a few seconds and took the call.

"Hi, and sorry I haven't got back to you before now, but it's been chaotic," Moss said. "We do need to talk, well, I need to explain things to you, but I'm trying to do the correct thing here, and it's bloody difficult. If you say no, so be it. Audie went on and on about you, and that you said she could come back to see your dress. Her mum needs to be elsewhere for the day, and Audie begged not to be sent to her gran's. Would it be okay if we popped in sometime? I know we won't have a chance to talk, but Audie is convinced now you know about her it's over between us, and it's all her fault. If nothing else, could we come so you can reassure her? Lie if you have to."

That made her jump. "I have no need to lie. I'm going to be open-minded until we get a chance to talk," she said, not quite truthfully. "When did you think to come?"

"Tomorrow afternoon, if that's all right with you."

"That's fine. See you around two?"

* * * *

By one-thirty the following day, Arietta had made currant buns and cookies, spilled flour all over the floor and mopped it, and burnt her tongue on trying a bun just out of the oven. Plus she was in a tizzy and what her mum would call 'up to hi doh'. Of course she wanted to reassure Audie, but she wasn't sure how she would react to the young girl — or Moss. She'd just have to do her best to appear as normal as possible. Whatever that was.

The sound of a car made her take a deep breath, smooth her suddenly damp palms over her jeans and open the front door. Which, she ruminated, had had more use over the last few weeks than in years. Normally everyone went 'round the back'.

Moss smiled warily as they approached Arietta, and half-waved.

"Hi. Glad it was okay for us to come."

Arietta nodded. "Hi back."

Audie looked from one to the other, puzzled by their coolness. Arietta swore under her breath and lifted her face to Moss and kissed his cheek. "You look tired."

Gratitude flashed across his face. "Busy week, hon, glad it's over. Bet you feel the same." His breath feathered over her skin, and the scent of man assailed her. That peculiar smell of warm male skin and citrusy cologne she associated with him.

"You can say that again," Arietta replied, heartfelt. In terms of misery it rated in the top five, but that wasn't a tidbit she intended to share. "Just finished what I needed to do in the book, so I'm free to have lovely visitors."

Audie skipped up to Arietta and flung her arms around her. "I told Dad it would be okay," she said, then bit her lip. "Well, I hoped you'd let me come. You did say I could. You don't mind, do you?" In a split second she changed from a confident teen to an uncertain child.

"Of course it is," Arietta said warmly. None of this was the girl's fault. "I haven't had time to bake, though. I had a deadline to meet." Behind Audie's back Moss raised his eyebrows in disbelief. Arietta ignored him.

"For your book," Audie said sagely and nodded. "Dad explained you write grown-up historical thrillers. Do you think you could write a teenage one? And call the heroine after me?"

Arietta laughed. "Who knows."

"Audie, you wanted to see Arietta's dress," Moss reminded his daughter. "We can't take up all the rest of Arietta's day."

"No problem," Arietta said perversely, even though she'd thought the same thing not that long before. "I've done all I'm doing until Monday."

Moss' eyes narrowed. "That's good," he said. "Where's the crossword?"

I've done it. You've got the Sudoku."

He pulled a notebook out of his pocket. "I'll read my script for Monday. Then we can spend tomorrow together." He turned to Audie. "Behave or I'll call you by your full name."

Audie giggled. "Best behaviour, on parade."

* * * *

"What's the deep, dark secret of your name then? Why do you hate it?" Arietta asked casually as Audie oohed and aahed over the dress. "Is it not Audrey?"

Audie shuddered very dramatically. "I wish. Nah. My mum, in a fit of family loyalty, named me after her gran. Maude, would you believe. Maude-Therese Berkeley-Tonge. What a mouthful. Why not let me be Kirby like Dad? And when she marries Tarquin the wet, it could be even worse. She's talking of adding his name on to all the rest. Crazy."

Arietta experienced a lump in her stomach and swallowed bile as she fought back the urge to dash to the bathroom and be violently sick. Dots danced in front of her eyes and she grabbed onto the bedhead for stability.

Shit. I cannot faint. I will not be sick. But what the…

It appeared Audie didn't notice as she rattled on. "Mum is Kristin Therese Maude Berkeley-Tonge, and she's thinking of adding Smith to that mouthful. Can you imagine writing that on an immigration form somewhere? Plus, she calls herself Krystal for goodness' sake. I mean, I'm only thirteen but even I think that's daft. She and he are well-matched. Nice and insipid." Audie giggled. "Like cold rice pudding…they'll be very happy."

"And you?" Arietta asked once she was certain she could speak clearly and not stutter or croak. What she'd give for a glass of water. Or gin. "How do you feel?"

"Oh I'm happy," Audie said casually. "I split my time between Mum and Dad anyway and that won't change. It's not Dad's day today but Mum and T the G—that means Tarquin the groom, my shorthand—had to go and check out the hotel or something, so asked Dad to step in. Er, you wouldn't stop me seeing Dad?" Audie asked with an anxious note in her voice.

"Me?" Arietta said in astonishment. "Of course not. Why think that?"

Audie rolled her shoulders in an embarrassed manner. "Just wondered... One of my mates at school? Her dad remarried and his new wife wasn't overkeen on my mate being around so much. Got a bit fraught."

"I would never be like that," Arietta replied emphatically. "Plus, as far as I know I'm not in line to marry your dad. We're friends. Good friends, I grant you, but we're nowhere near thinking about that sort of stuff." Even if sometimes she had wished they were. "Anyway, I bet your dad would ask your opinion first."

"Maybe." Audie sounded doubtful. "Is your name really Arietta?"

"Yep, you couldn't use it as a nickname, could you? My dad is a great music buff, and decided I was his little Aria...so, Arietta."

"It's unusual. I like it," Audie commented. "Um, can I ask you something personal?" she added in a diffident way. "You can tell me to get lost if you want."

What on earth does she want to know?

"You can ask," Arietta said slowly. "As long as you accept I might not answer."

"Yeah, fair enough." Audie nibbled her fingernail. "Did you go to uni with my mum and the wet...I mean, Tarquin?"

"It seems like I might have done," Arietta replied cautiously. "Why?"

"Dad said you'd got an invite anyway because you knew them ages ago, but you'd not kept in touch. Mum was saying there's gonna be some people wondering how they got their invite. That's down to Gran. Poor

Mum. I wouldn't want to be in her shoes. Which are a size eight." She giggled. "Don't tell her I said that. You sort of jumped when I told you my full name so I sort of thought..."

"I was at St Andrews with them but not for long. I knew Tarquin briefly before he met your mum."

"Ah, okay." Audie sounded relieved. "I did wonder. You didn't know Dad, though?"

"Nope, and talking of your dad, we better go back downstairs before he thinks we've been abducted by aliens."

"I heard that." Moss appeared in the doorway. "I thought you'd both gone to sleep. Why do you both look guilty? What nasties have you been sharing about me? Spill."

"None, Dad," Audie said indignantly. "I don't know any and I bet if Arietta did she wouldn't tell me."

"Very true," Arietta agreed. "One person's nasty is another's okay." *Like your dad, mum and tacky Tarquin.* "We were saying what a coincidence that her mum and her mum's fiancé were at uni at the same time as me," Arietta said mildly. "And how surprised I was when I realised."

Moss reddened, coughed and nodded. He appeared uncomfortable.

Good, you bastard, so you should be. You were no help at all with all that. Arietta did nothing to help him. If she said any more, she might burst into tears or scream like a fishwife, neither of which would be appropriate with Audie around.

"Ah, right. Audie, love," Moss said when it was obvious Arietta didn't intend to say anything else. "If we don't go now, your mum will be imagining all sorts of horrors like I've crashed or lost you. You know how she worries."

"Witters, Granny says."

"Witters then," Moss said as Arietta chuckled.

"You do come up with some old-fashioned sayings, daughter mine. Right, we need to skedaddle. Has your granny told you that one?"

"Granny says it's her duty to tell me them."

"Good for Granny." Moss turned to Arietta, who had watched the exchange with interest. The fondness between him and his daughter was so obvious it was great to see. Arietta thought it was a pity he hadn't thought to mention her earlier.

"I'll be back as soon as I can."

Arietta managed a smile. "Don't rush, I'll be here," she replied in a stilted little voice. *Maybe.*

Audie stepped towards Arietta and gave her a hug, which after a second's hesitation Arietta returned. None of this farce was of Audie's making, and she liked her.

"I'm glad Dad has you and I'm glad you're real," Audie said earnestly. "If I don't see you before, I'll see you at the wedding. You in your cool hat and me in my yucky Alice band thingy."

Arietta laughed. "You'll be fine and look fab. Safe journey home." *Wherever home is.*

Moss stared at her intently. "See you later."

She nodded.

"I'll text or ring you to let you know what's happening when," he added.

He sighed when she didn't reply and didn't say anymore as they made their way downstairs. Arietta bit her lip to stop herself crying or shouting at him and opened the front door. After all it was reserved for strangers, wasn't it, and he seemed like one of them now.

It was obvious she knew very little about the important things in his life.

Back to square one. With a vengeance.

"You can kiss her, Dad. I don't mind." Audie grinned impudently. "After all, you're not sharing supper now."

"Gee, thanks," Moss said. "Arietta might object, though."

"Arietta doesn't." What else could she say? She stood on tiptoe and to all intents and purposes put her lips to his. Only they knew she deliberately missed. "Drive safely."

Moss groaned and rolled his eyes. "I always do."

She stood by the door and waved as the Ferrari drove off, shut it, leant back on the wood and exhaled slowly. Where was someone to cry over when you needed them?

* * * *

She'd decided it was time to discuss things with her parents again.

"Not only that," Arietta said an hour or so later as she brought her parents up to date with the happenings, "he also forgot to add that her mother is Krystal of the few weeks at uni fame."

"The one who decided to go to bed with your ex and gave him a better offer?" Jessie asked with incredulity in her voice. "That one?"

"The very one," Arietta confirmed with a wry smile. "There's more. The groom is the one who took her up on that better offer."

"Hmm... awkward," her mum said with unaccustomed restraint, as Arietta's dad choked on a mouthful of whisky. She patted his back. "Better, Tam?"

Tam nodded. "Went down the wrong way."

"So where does Moss and his—their—daughter come into all this?" Jessie Clare went on as if there had been no interruption. "You didn't know him then, did you?"

Arietta shook her head. "Nope, he wasn't about as far as I know so I have no idea. Audie, the daughter, is about thirteen, give or take, I guess, so after Kristin left uni, but not long after... How, why and where...anyone's guess, but as she's marrying Tacky Tarq, he must have got over it."

"How very unfortunate," her mum said, deadpan.

Her dad snorted. "That, Jessie love, is the understatement of the year. What do you want to do?" he asked his daughter. "Do you want my ten pennorth worth?"

Arietta smiled wearily. "Why not."

"What has he told you, how did you find out, and what did you or will you do about her, him and the pair of you?"

Trust her dad to condense it all into one sharp sentence. Arietta thought for a moment or two.

"He came over last weekend with her to tell me he'd be late as I hadn't heard my phone, and that is true. The connection is dodgy and sometimes when I think it's charging it isn't. It hadn't. He had his daughter with him, and said he'd be back so we could chat when I was ready."

That was said with brevity. She had no intention of going into all the nuts and bolts of the situation.

"Well I wasn't ready, and then when I was he had Audie with him because I'd promised to show her my dress for the wedding. Not that I knew that wedding was the wedding I'd also got an invite to. I discovered that a bit later on. I swallowed that, but what I still find hard to swallow is the rest of it. I *am* trying, though, and I made sure Audie didn't see how I felt. It's not her fault. But I still feel…betrayed. Which is daft."

"But understandable," her mum said. "Are you stopping?"

Arietta shook her head. "No, just wanted to chat face to face. Hopefully Moss will get over tomorrow and I want to be there. If he doesn't? Well, there's a lot of weeding needed in my veg patch. I can't see the peas for the weeds."

* * * *

He didn't come.

Arietta got a brief text.

Bloody film. Bloody arsy co-stars, bloody hell. Sorry, love, will need to take a rain check, and I mean rain. Filming storms for a week in the no phone signal wilds. Wish me luck.

* * * *

The idea she had for her next book and the research she needed to do for it were godsends. Arietta spent several days at her desk with some of her beloved ancient reference books open next to her, told Maggie what she was up to—with the only mention of Moss being that he was still working up north — and took an overnight trip to St Andrews. Once there she wandered along the cliffs and around the ruins of the castle for several hours and enjoyed the atmosphere. She hoped no one heard the notes she dictated to herself as she sauntered along, or she'd be met by the police as she headed back to the hotel she'd booked. Nevertheless, it was a very profitable day, and the excellent meal in the hotel, which overlooked the sea, added to the pleasure. A good night's sleep, full Scottish breakfast and a swift walk along The Scores, in brilliant sunshine, to the harbour the next morning and a glimpse of a dolphin was an added bonus and she almost wished she'd booked an extra night.

Well, why not? She was her own master and it *was* research.

She headed back to the hotel, who were pleased to accommodate her. Did she want dinner again?

"Why not? Yes, please," Arietta said and blithely handed over her credit card for an imprint to be taken. It had been a long while since she'd acted so impulsively. A quick text to Maggie to let her know got a 'go you' reply. Arietta went up to the same room she'd had before, left her case and headed to the shops. What a good excuse to buy clothes. Okay, she'd taken spare undies and a clean T-shirt, but who knew if the heavens were about to open and she would get soaked to the skin? How horrible not to have clean, dry clothes to change into.

With that spurious excuse in her mind, she began to look around her favourite shops in the town. With no students back at university yet, it was mainly tourists who crowded the pavements, and snippets of a lot of different languages could be heard as she walked along.

Arietta loved it. At one time she'd been very tempted to move to the area, but she'd seen her cottage and knew that was her place to be. However she'd happily have a second home in the town…if she could afford it. Which she couldn't, not if she wanted to enjoy the standard of living she had.

Instead she chose to visit when she could.

The shopping trip was successful and she headed back to the hotel with a gorgeous, smart casual dress she'd wear that night, two tops, a pair of trousers and some new undies. She's swithered over a pair of shoes, left the shop then thought sod it and gone back for them before, as an afterthought, she nipped into the supermarket for a bag of crisps and a lemon.

That was it, treat time over.

She asked for a bucket of ice, took it upstairs to her room and, after mixing a gin and tonic from the mini bar, added a slice of lemon cut with her tiny all-purpose Swiss army knife and went for a soak in the bath before dinner.

Dining alone never bothered Arietta. She would take a newspaper or a book—these days her Kindle—or simply people-watch. Sometimes, she remembered, amused, as she fastened on her watch and slid her feet into her new shoes, she would simply listen to those around her.

Eavesdrop.

Once, at a tiny bistro in York, she'd been fascinated by a woman explaining why she couldn't carry on with an affair due to her husband's demands for sex and the state of her greenhouse. Arietta never did hear the connection between those two things, but if she wrote contemporary fiction, it would have made a great plot. Her fertile mind had conjured up so many possible scenarios, it boggled. Did he get frisky among the tomatoes? Want to play strip peep, oh, between the runner beans and smash the pots? She could have had endless fun there. In fact, she had made notes — just in case.

Ever since then, she made sure her handbag was big enough for a notebook and pencil. Arietta picked up said handbag, checked its contents and headed for the dining room where, as the night before, she was given a table by the window, from which she could see outside to the sea and inside to most of the room.

Outside the streetlights were on and beginning to cast warm globes of gold in the gathering dusk. Inside, the tables were beginning to fill up. It was the sort of hotel where people tended to dine late and enjoy the pianist or band that played unobtrusively in the background.

It was her treat to herself.

The sommelier brought her wine. She'd decided against an aperitif due to the gin she'd savoured in her bath and chose a bottle of wine, which if she didn't finish — and unless she wanted to crawl upstairs she wouldn't — she'd been told she could take with her. He poured a taste. She agreed it was perfect and he added more to her glass with a flourish, just as people came into the restaurant and a ripple of interest circulated around the room. Even the sommelier turned to see what had caused it.

"Ah, yes…" He bowed to Arietta. "Enjoy your wine, madame." He turned on his heel and disappeared before she had a chance to thank him. She waited until he'd moved far enough away not to block her view of the doorway and did her best to try to see who had caused the stir.

At the far end of the long, curved window, partly shielded from the room by a couple of potted plants, was a table for two. Being escorted to it by the maître d'hôtel was a very glamorous lady in a red body-con dress and killer heels. Her very attentive dinner companion was either Moss or his doppelganger.

What the hell was he doing there? And even more what the hell, who was his companion?

Arietta couldn't help but stare. Whether it was her attention or his intuition she had no idea but he lifted his head, looked in her direction, paled and gave her a stiff nod. The sort you gave to a little-known acquaintance or someone you don't really want to acknowledge.

Then he turned back to his companion.

Well that showed me where I stand. Suck it up, serves me right? No it bloody doesn't, the bastard.

Pride kept her at her table through three courses of a meal that tasted like cardboard. Her stiff upper lip was challenged more than once as she heard his husky laugh, saw how he leant towards the woman and at one point gave her a brief — but loving — hug.

Bastard, sodding bastard.

"Ma'am? Is the food not to your liking?"

Arietta looked up into the waiter's concerned face and realised she was pushing the remains of her dessert around the plate. The same dessert she'd declared was delicious the night before had given her no pleasure this time.

"It's lovely," Arietta said with a bright, albeit forced smile. "I'm trying to persuade myself I've space for it when I know I really haven't. The food here is delicious and it's so easy to eat too much."

There, that sounded positive enough, didn't it?

It must have done because the waiter's anxious expression disappeared. "Good. Coffee and a liqueur in the lounge perhaps?"

About to refuse politely, she heard Moss' companion laugh and watched out of the corner of her eye as Moss kissed her cheek. *Bugger it, bugger him.* It was enough to make a saint swear, and she was no saint. The fact she had brought her solitary, no-Moss situation on herself didn't help any.

"That sounds perfect." Arietta took her time to collect her belongings before she headed to the cosy residents-only lounge with a brief incline of her head in Moss' direction. Whether he noticed or responded she had no idea. If he could be arsy, so could she.

Once in the lounge, where the waiter had somehow managed to secure her a comfy armchair and coffee table in the favoured bay window area of the room, Arietta let out the breath she hadn't been conscious of holding. She properly relaxed for the first time since Moss and his companion had appeared and chastised herself for caring so much. But as she'd long realised, she couldn't turn her feelings on and off like the kitchen tap.

The lounge was fairly empty, most diners either gone to the bar, their rooms or their homes, and she was able to sit and enjoy her coffee and the shortbread that accompanied it.

Until ten minutes later, Moss and his companion entered.

Oh shit, it's like one of those old-fashioned farces or weepies my mum loves. What next? She forced herself not to glance across the room—luckily they hadn't sat in her line of vision—and to sip her coffee as if she hadn't a care in the world. No way was she going to be rushed.

She opened her notebook and began to write. Meaningless, irrelevant drivel but who was to know. She grinned to herself as she wondered what a psychiatrist would make of asbestos, formaldehyde, panna cotta and sweet peas, who can make kailai…bright colours…BTW??

"Good evening, Arietta. I needn't ask how you are, you look stunning." Moss had approached unnoticed and stood by her side. She glanced up at him and managed a smile.

"Thank you." Did he appear thinner? Strained? "I'm well. And you?"

Moss shrugged. "So-so I guess. Alone?"

No, my fellow diner is under the table!

Arietta inclined her head. "As you see. A working trip. Nice to see you. *Not.* As you're not alone, perhaps you better rejoin your" — she paused — "companion."

"She's gone to the bathroom."

"So you popped over to say hi. Hi."

"Is that all?" Moss demanded. "No thoughts on us? Or the non-us?"

"Not here or now, no," Arietta said pseudo-sweetly. "I'm working, you're…whatever, enjoying the company of your companion, don't let me keep you."

"We need to talk," Moss said flatly. "I thought you were ready to listen. It seems not."

She shrugged. "I'll listen."

"Not here, soon."

"That," she said sweetly, "seems to be the story of our lives. Soon."

"Arietta, I…" He stopped and sighed. "Whatever I say will probably make things worse the mood you're in. Look, I've got to go back to my companion. I will ring, I promise."

Arietta studied his drawn face. "If you say so. I won't hold my breath." She stood up and stowed her notebook in her handbag. "Take care." That at least she did mean.

"And you. Let me know if you want to talk, really want to, and I'll decide if I want to," Moss said grumpily. "That might be arsy, but it's how I feel. I wish I didn't but I do."

"Shouldn't it be the other way around?" Arietta said with a snap she couldn't help. "When I'm ready to listen I'll decide if I want to."

He grinned, almost the old Moss. "That's not the other way round, just muddled."

Arietta's held-together-by-a-piece-of-string patience snapped. "Oh, go and boil your head."

His laugh annoyed her even more.

It was a relief to pick up her three-quarters full bottle of wine and head for the lift, conscious of his gaze on her as she left.

As she stood and waited — where the hell was it, she needed a good cry or to punch her pillow — Moss' dinner companion left the ladies loo, saw Arietta and headed in her direction.

Oh sod it. Come on, lift, come on, where the hell are you? The indicator showed it to be several floors above.

Damn and blast.

Arietta schooled her expression to be indifferent and gave the woman a polite, meaningless smile as she came up and stopped beside her.

"So," she said slowly. "You must be Arietta?"

"Must I?" Arietta didn't bother to confirm it or ask who spoke.

The woman smiled. "Oh yes, unless you have a double and no female twin was mentioned. Arietta, who has got Moss in such a mood he snarls at everyone and I'm supposed to sort him out. The joys of being an agent."

"Enjoy." *Ouch, catty.* Arietta shrugged. *Really his agent?* She'd think about that later. "I'm sorry he's being such a problem for you. I'm sure it's got nothing to do with me."

The woman patted her shoulder. "If you think that, why am I bothering?"

"I don't know, why are you?" Arietta said with blunt rudeness. "Look Ms whoever you are, I'm not his keeper. In fact, it rather looks like I'm not his anything." The lift arrived and she inclined her head. "Enjoy your evening."

Chapter Nine

Arietta drove home the following day in a sombre mood. It had taken an effort to go down to breakfast and not be a coward and order room service instead. She needn't have worried. Neither Moss nor his agent—if that was who she truly was—had been anywhere to be seen. She'd breakfasted, checked out and gone for a brisk walk around the golf course without a glimpse of the pair of them. She had noticed one D-list reality show host slice his ball, and introduce her to a new epithet, and a couple of tennis players having a go at a different sport to their own. However, in the main it was cheerful tourists who had strolled down the fairways and shouted the odd 'fore', or 'yeah, hey that's go-ood' and did or didn't take the long-suffering caddies' advice.

A couple of players had smiled at her. One had shaken his head and said in a very southern American drawl, *"Ah'll never get the hang of this, if I play till I'm eighty.*" He'd winked. "*Which, the way I feel after nigh on fifty-four holes in two days, is getting mighty close.*"

Arietta had recognised him as someone who had been big on the PGA circuit a decade or so before and laughed as she'd waggled her finger at him.

"*Is that you going for the sympathy vote or to be given a few free shots?*"

He'd grinned and winked. "*T'day, ahl take whatever I get. Shots, sympathy and the whisky in the nineteenth hole afterwards. Now where's that darned ball gone?*"

Arietta had thought it might be in the burn, but as he'd already walked on in that direction, she hadn't thought there was much point in saying so. After all, she might be wrong.

She'd headed back to her car and set off for home.

* * * *

It was strange to be there and not have a text, phone call or visit from Moss to look forward to. She knew it was up to her to set events in motion, but she still wasn't certain she was ready to do so. In her sensible moments, she accepted he had valid reasons for not being as open as she would have liked. After all, his explanations involved more than him.

However, the woman at the hotel had hit her hard and she'd felt betrayed all over again. Irrational when she'd said she wasn't ready to listen to him, but who said a woman betrayed should be rational?

Add to that her hurt side wasn't ready to accept he had any reason for anything that had happened with regards to the woman or the wedding. Especially as he hadn't mentioned he knew the bride or groom when he'd discovered to whose wedding he was to accompany her. That stung. He could have merely said 'I know them' or 'I went out with her for a couple of weeks but she preferred Tarquin'. Even 'I reckon I had a lucky escape, we really weren't suited' would have helped. He hadn't needed to say a word about Audie, she understood that—sort of—but not to mention anything at all was wrong. Then to intimate there were two weddings in the offing! Words failed her.

The crux of the matter was, Arietta acknowledged, she felt let down. That he had decided she was not worthy of that courtesy. Once she got over it, built the bridge and pulled herself together, maybe she'd contact him. Until then, she'd have to sulk and sort herself—and her new story—out.

With determination, a strong talking-to and her notes, she began to plot. As she'd hoped, once she got the outline of her story, sent it to her editor who came back faster than usual—which was actually pretty fast—with a "more please", and how did he get there in the first place, Arietta realised she needed a visit to Tentsmuir Forest. A gorgeous, wooded area that bordered a long sandy beach a few miles north of St Andrews. So sod it, she'd do the stay over and cosset herself again.

And if Moss was around, say hello and be polite. Maybe even say she hoped all was well and let her know when he had time free.

Or maybe not.

Arietta phoned the hotel—of course they had a room…well, actually it was a suite, a little more costly than last time, but with a large discount for a regular visitor. Arietta took that with a pinch of salt, added up her royalties, thought bugger it and said she'd love it for two nights and mentally thought of supermarket-basic meals for a month. It would be worth it.

This time, though, she'd go prepared. There really was no need to go and buy more clothes, even though she'd love to. It was a research trip, no more no less, and she should in theory be in the forest and on that beach not swanning around St Andrews all day. She'd even take some gin, lemon and tonic. Maybe not the done thing, but hey ho.

With good intentions, she set out early and headed for Tentsmuir before she checked in at her hotel. The right idea as it happened, because the weather looked threatening and she was darned sure it would rain later. Better to survey the paths and tracks now, see if she could reconcile them with Regency Britain and add the town bits in later.

Arietta hummed to herself as she hefted her rucksack over her shoulder and headed from the car park to the grassy dunes then on to the windy beach. It was the perfect pace for her heroine to discover what was going on and have to hide. And an even better place for the hero to have to find her. She was glad she'd made herself some reminders on what to check, and how she hoped her story would pan out.

Hands-on research, when possible, was a great thing to do, and in the sunshine, on a deserted beach, with waves rippling nearby was probably as perfect as it could get. Arietta sat down in the lee of a sand dune, where the marram grass sheltered her from most of the ever-increasing breeze, took out the flask of coffee she'd prepared and sipped the still-hot liquid as she checked what she'd discovered. It was a relief to note that she'd covered everything she had on her list, and for now there was nothing else needed there. Next, a swift visit to East Sands and the harbour in St Andrews, and hopefully she would have everything she would need. Then she could enjoy her not-really-necessary, but oh-so appreciated night of luxury.

Tomorrow it would be, as her mum used to say, *"bread and scrape and get on and budget once more"*. Not that Arietta lived outside her means, anything but. Her money was too hard-earned. She budgeted well and could afford such things as decent holidays, a good mid-range car and the odd night away. However not all the time to the level of this night – and the couple she'd almost enjoyed earlier.

The almost annoyed her, especially as she was conscious it was her own fault. After all, how much would it have cost her to be civil?

Nothing.

Arietta moved uneasily at that thought and shivered as one particularly strong gust of wind got through the grass that topped her particular sand dune and hit her head and the back of her neck. *Time to get a move on.* She repacked her rucksack and returned to the car to do the short journey to her hotel. It was easier to park there now the students were back, rather than fight for space in the centre of town.

She checked in, left her luggage in her room – not the same as one last time but with, she judged, a slightly different view, a very ornate bathroom and a big squishy sofa she'd love to sink into. However, work first and chill later. Arietta changed her somewhat scruffy trainers for a pair of smarter but comfy shoes and headed out again. She wanted to have time to enjoy her evening.

The walk along the harbour wall was invigorating as the wind was now gusting enough to make it interesting. If it had been much stronger, she'd not have thought it safe.

Nevertheless she was glad to get back to the safety of the beach, and at least the weather had sorted some more facts out for her. Her smuggler would have had trouble getting his goods to the shore. The caves beneath the cliffs worked well for that part of her plot.

Satisfied she had achieved all she could, Arietta wandered back through the town, dodging students just out of lectures, tourists exclaiming at the students, some of whom wore the university red gown in the proper way for the year they were in, and school kids and their parents shopping or walking home.

Rush hour.

She grinned as one red-haired youngster stood outside a shop selling toys and pleaded for a horse, with the words 'I'll be good and go to bed when you tell me'. How many times had she and Thomas said that? She smiled in sympathy as the child's mother rolled her eyes and mouthed 'Oh I wish'. She bet their parents had thought that as well.

In a much better mood than she had been for a while, Arietta headed back to the hotel, showered and changed and, after enjoying the comforts of the squishy chair, headed down to the bar for a gin and tonic before her dinner. She couldn't only drink her own.

It was as good as it had been before.

This time, though, there was no one staring — or not staring — at her from across the room. Not sure whether that was a good thing, Arietta ate her meal with relish, went to the lounge for coffee and headed back upstairs replete. She slept for seven hours straight and enjoyed an early morning cuppa before she went for breakfast.

She spent the next day checking she'd done everything, enjoyed another excellent meal and woke up the following morning refreshed and raring to write.

All in all, it had been a very successful trip and she wished she had an excuse to stay longer. She was darned sure her bank account gave a groan of relief when it realised she had no intention of doing so. Arietta chuckled to herself when she noticed she had given it a brain and a conscience. Perhaps it was well it didn't have those things.

She headed for home via the supermarket and the fresh fish shop and took the scenic route that avoided motorways. It might take longer, but she was in no hurry, and happy to let the traffic dictate her speed.

That traffic included a tractor and trailer, five horses—luckily not all together—a guy on a trike and three sets of temporary traffic lights.

All of which meant it was almost five before she turned down the lane to her cottage, avoided the potholes and drew up in her drive.

Behind a well-known, slightly dirty car, one wing dinged as a result of a meeting with a rock on a narrow road *'up north'*.

Damn and blast. A frisson of worry skittered over her skin. Trouble? Surely not?

It wasn't Moss, just Thomas…or was it? If Moss had accompanied him, did he have his woman with him? If he did, she'd give him a mouthful, and in her mood it would be a mighty long, and strong, one.

There was only one way to find out. Arietta took a deep breath and mentally counted to twenty. Time to discover the reason for the unexpected and, she suspected, what might be an unwelcome visit.

Not that she didn't love her twin—she did—and enjoyed spending time with him, but she could have done without him being about right then. She had enough to think about without watching what she said. He was sharp to pick up on her moods and intonations. He'd be equally as alert to what she said—or didn't say—about anything or anyone.

Which brought her back to her original thought. What the hell was Thomas doing there mid-week, and as she understood it, halfway through a film? It spelt trouble and she wasn't sure for whom.

She switched the car's engine off, engaged the handbrake and opened the driver's door just as Thomas came round the side of the house.

He scowled.

It didn't look good.

"Thought it was you, thought you'd be back earlier, or so Ma said when I phoned her to ask where you were," he said loudly enough for the cows in the next field to lift their heads. "You never mentioned going away. Ma said you'd gone to St Andrews for research. *Again.*"

Tell the world why don't you? He made it sound as if she'd done something illegal and definitely not acceptable to any sane and sensible person.

"Yup, I did. Why?" If he could be arsy so could she. "There's no law against it."

"You were due back this arvo, so I was worried."

Arietta sighed. "If I'd have known you were coming I would have been back. Not to sound rude, but *why* are you here and not where you're supposed to be?"

Are you alone?

"To see you," Thomas said impatiently. "What the hell is wrong with you and Moss?" he said as soon as he got within speaking, not shouting, distance. "What's going on?"

"Hello, Thomas, nice to see you too," Arietta said dryly as she hauled her shopping out and dumped the bags in his arms. "What shall I attempt to answer first? Or refuse to answer at all?"

Her brother reddened and did a mock stagger under the weight of the bags. Or she hoped it was mock. She didn't think they were *that* heavy.

"What the hell is in here? Gold ingots?"

"I wish. The weight of your nosiness maybe. What else do you want to know? What I ate for dinner? How many pairs of shoes I bought? Anything more?"

"No need to be snarky," he said. "Just all of it, in any order."

"Oh good," she retorted. "That makes a change."

"Give over. Well, not yet." Thomas followed her round the side of the house. Two bottles clinked together ominously, but neither mentioned it.

Arietta was conscious if she said anything he could easily drop the bag or tell her to carry it herself. She assumed her twin chose not to bring her notice to it, just in case a calamity was in the offing.

"Any grub going?" Thomas put the bags down on a work surface and rubbed his stomach. "Not eaten all day. Too worried about my little sis."

"Ham actor," Arietta said, unmoved. "Do you mean going or available to eat?" she asked as she followed him into the kitchen. Obviously Thomas hadn't been there long. There was only one dirty mug in the sink, and one solitary teaspoon. No plates, knives or forks and no telltale crumbs on the work surface or draining board. "When did you arrive?"

"About half an hour ago," Thomas said as he picked an apple out of the bowl and took a crisp crunchy bite out of it. "Why?"

"No reason," Arietta said. "But it figures. So give me a clue. What are you hoping I'll feed you?"

He tilted his head to one side. "We...ll, as you've been to St Andrews and I know you, I'm guessing fresh fish and sticky toffee pud? Maybe that and chips? I brought a bag of oven ones with me and put them in the freezer." He smiled as if he'd given her the Holy Grail. "And I come bearing gin. I didn't put that in the freezer." He waved towards the cupboard where she kept her few bottles of alcohol.

"Now you're talking. What make?"

Thomas reached into the cupboard, took a bottle out and showed her the label.

Arietta whistled. "Very nice. What have I done to deserve that?"

Thomas grimaced. "Not a bloody thing, but I want answers. Who drinks rum and what the hell is going on between you and Moss?"

"Why not go straight to the point, brother mine, instead of going round the houses?" Arietta said, more to play for time than to be provocative as she began to unpack her bags. "Rum is for mojitos." It was also for Maggie's Doug, who enjoyed rum and Coke and who sometimes popped in with Maggie for a chat and a drink. Or, rather, she and Maggie chatted and Doug hunted out any odd jobs Arietta needed doing and did them. His way, he said, of relaxing.

"You know? Those lovely long drinks with lots of mint in. And limes. That's what the limes are for. The mint of course is also for potatoes and lamb," Arietta said mischievously, playing for time as Thomas scowled at her. "Which reminds me, I must get some more wine vinegar next time I do a big shop."

"Ari…etta," Thomas said in a flat, vaguely annoyed tone. "Cut it out. I was chatting to Moss, asked when he'd next be down because I'd try to make it as well, and got told how the hell did he know. That you were a bit hurt about something and next time I saw you, tell you it's okay to tell me whatever it is that's got your knickers in a twist. That's my interpretation of what he actually said," Thomas added hastily as she pointed at him in indignation. "He said he'd upset you big-time and you didn't seem inclined to forgive him everything any time soon. But that you could share whatever it was with me if you wanted to. He even wrote it down so you knew he said it and I didn't make it up." Thomas fished in his pocket and drew out an envelope with her name scrawled on it in Moss' handwriting.

Arietta took it from him silently. She slipped her finger under the flap and opened it.

The message was short and succinct.

You can tell Thomas what you feel necessary. I trust him. Love, (and I mean that) Moss xx

There was a p.s.

Audie sends her love and is looking forward to seeing you again soon. She's got the dreaded Alice band and, yeah, hates it.

Bugger it. What had seemed so clear-cut suddenly appeared so much more complicated.

"Well?" Thomas demanded as Arietta bit her lip and stared at him. "Anything to tell me?"

Arietta sighed. "Yes, no, maybe." More to have something to do with her hands than the need for coffee, she began to fill the coffee pot.

Thomas took it from her firmly, steered her to a chair and pushed her into it. "I don't think playing with the coffee pot is the answer. Is it a gin and confession time?"

"Probably."

"Then you work up the courage or the way you need to say whatever it is that has you both looking like you've lost a million and found a fiver and I'll make the drink. What if it isn't sun over the yardarm time. Let's live dangerously." He rummaged in the fridge to find what he needed. "Where's the lemon?"

"Second drawer where it always is. Next to the limes."

"Ha, ha, and the oranges. Pimms next time." That drink was a favourite hot-weather tipple.

"You buy the Pimms then. Talking of living dangerously, shouldn't you be filming somewhere?"

Thomas glanced up and grinned. "My part finished yesterday. I have a month of lotus eating. I, er, might be going to Hong Kong."

"To see Jan?" Arietta wondered what the outcome to that meeting would be. If ever two people managed to rub each other the wrong way, without really doing anything, every time they saw each other, it was her brother and her friend. "She never said when she sent me a text saying she hadn't been invited to the bun feast and make sure I took plenty of pics."

"She doesn't know. It's to see about a TV series."

Arietta raised her eyebrows. "I can always tell when you're lying."

"Half-lying," he corrected her. "I've got the part already, filming starts in a month. I thought I might go out early. And stop changing the subject."

"Wow, congratulations. What is it?" Arietta took her drink from him. "Should this be fizz?"

"Mystery with a touch of intrigue, with a bit of luck it will fly. Fizz later, once you've spilled the beans. Come on, love." Thomas became serious. "I hate to see my twin and my best mate at odds. I get *your* vibes and they're rotten and *his* temper, which is just as bad. We had one evening out together recently and he growled at everything, drank half a pint and left the rest, ate three mouthfuls of curry, pushed it away and said he wasn't hungry, and made small talk until it was time to go. With a doggy bag he gave to me. So not like him. Tell big brother all about it. Let me sort things out for my little sis."

If only he could.

"Even with your big brother magic wand, I don't think you can work your magic this time," Arietta said morosely. She paused for a moment, impressed when Thomas didn't ask any questions but sat quietly sipping his drink. If Moss said she could share, then share she would. After all, Thomas might, just might, say something helpful. "What do you know about Moss' past?"

Thomas put his drink down and stared at Arietta. "How do you mean? Girlfriends? The usual, but I've never known him to be serious about anyone, and he tends to stay on a friendly basis with them once their romance is over. Friends with benefits? Haven't we all, but I don't know of any he's had for a while, though. Nasty infections? I'd be very surprised. He's too careful, scrupulous and sensible." Thomas answered the questions as he posed them. "Vomiting over flowerbeds, dancing naked in fountains? Mega debts? He hasn't to my knowledge. What have I missed out?"

Arietta frowned. "It's a bit difficult, and I guess isn't general knowledge and it would be bad for someone if it got out."

Thomas nodded. "Then it's about his child then," he replied in a very matter-of-fact way.

Arietta put her drink down. "You know?" Just what did he know?

"Not a lot. Don't get all het up."

"I wasn't," Arietta said, stung by the accusation. "Not much anyway. I just didn't know what you knew."

"Very little. Just that when he was a lot younger, he got involved with an older woman who was, from the sounds of it, slumming it for a few weeks while her rolling-in-it boyfriend was away. He—Moss, not the rolling-in-it bloke—used a condom, but as many people discover later to their cost and all that they're not infallible and she got pregnant. Told Moss it was his but she wasn't going to be with him. However, he was welcome to see the child, etcetera, etcetera. Not that he wanted her then. The woman, not the child. I mean, talk about a convenient itch scratcher, but who knows? The boyfriend was fine with it, and that was that. Moss doesn't publicise it all, wants the child to have a normal childhood, not be seen as Moss'…God knows what it's being called these days. Is that it?"

In a nutshell. "Did he say anything else?"

Thomas shook his head. "No, and I didn't ask. That's the sort of info he'd share if he wanted to and if not, not my business. No idea what sex it is, how old it is or whether he still sees…him or her. I hate saying it."

Arietta took a deep breath. "You needn't say it anymore. She's a she, and she's thirteen or fourteen years old."

Thomas whistled. "Ah...and? I'm guessing you didn't know?"

"Correct. None of it, until they appeared the other weekend, out of the blue. Actually not strictly true, but I didn't know it was him and her," Arietta added, determined to be as precise as she could. "I'd been to the market by the loch, saw someone I thought looked like Moss, but when he was addressed as 'Dad', thought I must be mistaken. Came home, got ready for a nice, lazy weekend in with my fella. We had all sorts of doing nothing planned. Then a few hours later, the said fella turns up with the girl I'd seen at the market. One and the same." The old sense of hurt and rejection reared up and she ruthlessly quashed it. Now was not the time to do a wilting violet act.

"Bugger," Thomas said succinctly and whistled.

"Well put. Both the situation and him. It transpires he couldn't come that evening as he had his daughter and I hadn't heard my phone."

"Bit of a shock," Thomas commented. "But surely he explained? I mean, about not telling you about her. What's she called by the way?"

"Audie and she is lovely. However that's not all."

"No?" Thomas leant forward, his eyes bright. "This is better than a soap any day. Give me more and yeah, it's confidential, I know."

"If it was in a soap or a book, we'd say it was too far-fetched to be true," Arietta said with a laugh. She could see how farcical it sounded even though in actuality that was the farthest from the truth. "First off, I saw Moss with a glamour puss when I was in St Andrews and they were oh-so cosy together." She tensed as she remembered that. "The woman had the cheek to try and talk to me about him as well." She scowled at the thought. "Said she was his agent. Hah. Bloody cheek."

"What did you do?"

"Ignored her."

Thomas let his breath out in a long hiss. "Okay, go on."

"It seems that Audie's mother is now getting married to the rich boyfriend who, according to Audie is okay, she likes him but he's a bit wet and she thinks he's a numpty. Nice, but a wet numpty, who sadly doesn't even like watching golf, let alone playing it."

"Damned with faint praise. Oh, how I remember us being like that. Over Uncle Harold and his why on earth would anyone want to sit on a horse, let alone jump over things. Poor Audie and the wet numpty. Must be a teen thing, I reckon."

"So it seems. Mind you, I don't remember him like that," Arietta said mischievously. "Not Uncle Harold, he was exactly what we thought. The bloke. Although I do remember the horror at my tendency to wear odd socks. Poor sod must have lost his whatever it was he almost had."

Thomas blinked. "You mean you know him?"

Arietta nodded.

"Shit." He whistled again. "To add to which, Moss wants you to go to the wedding with him?"

Arietta nodded again. "Yes and yes."

"Okay, what's the punch line?"

She grinned. "Hold on to your hat. I know the bride as well."

"You do? Ohhh, more and more intriguing."

"Yup. Oh, and I was going to the wedding anyway. With Moss."

"With…" Thomas stood up, walked across the room, came back and flopped on his chair. "You mean that the woman Moss had a fling with, the mother of his child, is the bride-to-be of the bloke you blew off? Tarq the Tosser and Krystal of the pouting lips?"

"Yes and yes again." Arietta sat back and watched a flabbergasted expression appear on Thomas' face. "What do you say to that?"

"Bloody Nora. Could be interesting."

That was an understatement again.

"You'll have to talk to Moss," Thomas said earnestly. "You've got double the reasons to go to the wedding now. Get your grovelling hat on, love. I think you're going to need it."

So did she.

"Oh and by the way?" Thomas said in a casual not that it really matters voice, as he filched a carrot and crunched into it. "The woman in St Andrews?"

Arietta nodded. "Yes?"

"I could have told you she's his agent."

Chapter Ten

"I'll pop into the parents' and spend the night with them before I head off to see *my* agent," Thomas said the following afternoon. "After which, I think I'm going for a week or two's breather before I start filming. No idea where yet, but somewhere will grab me" He heaved his bag into the boot of his car, and straightened. "Life will be full-on when I get back from wherever I end up."

Arietta didn't press him, although she had a good idea where he *hoped* to end up. If he chose not to share, it was up to him.

"What are you going to do about Moss?" he asked as he stood with one foot in his car, the other on the drive. "You can't keep on like this, can you? You really aren't the bitch you're showing yourself to be."

"Thanks, bro." Arietta rubbed the toe of her trainer into the gravel under her feet. "You mean I overreacted." He'd said as much the night before when slightly tipsy—they had the champagne—they'd meandered upstairs to their respective bedrooms.

"Well, love, didn't you?" Thomas looked at her quizzically. "Or is it me now doing the overreacting bit?"

"Maybe. Possibly. I don't know."

He gave her a long-suffering 'Oy, this is me, your twin, you don't fool me' look.

"Okay," she said, goaded by his tolerant expression. "I guess, but I was hurt."

"And now you're sulking. Not pretty. Sort it out for both your sakes. And mine. Even if you still say goodbye, make it a less antagonistic one. Yes? He's my mate, I'd like that status quo to stay."

"Yes, maybe, do my best. Now shoo, you rang Mum a good half an hour ago to say you were about to set off. She'll start thinking you've crashed or been abducted by aliens before too long."

"That's maybe on the cards for next year." He got into the car, tooted the horn and drove off as Arietta laughed.

She went back indoors, deep in thought. Thomas was correct of course, she had been indulging in a mega sulk. And she was a bitch, first class, no doubt about it. She actually didn't like herself very much at that moment.

A sulk was acceptable up to a point but, she allowed, this one had gone on too long. Deciding to stop mumping was easy. Actually doing it, not so much. However, she was allegedly grown up and above such pettiness as to still hold a grudge. She had two options. Either forget about Moss or forget about the hurt and move on. It was her choice.

When it all boiled down, there was nothing to think about. Only one possible recourse. Arietta took a deep breath, found the correct phone number and pressed the connect button.

And waited…

The answerphone clicked in, with an impersonal voice asking the caller to leave a message and they would be contacted as soon as possible.

As what she wanted to say couldn't in all honesty be left on a voicemail, she clicked the phone off. She'd try again later.

Balked at being able to give the apology she'd screwed herself up to make, Arietta wasn't able to settle. If Maggie had been around, she would have invited her and Doug to pop in or suggest they go to the pub and take part in the fiercely fought dominoes tournament that took place every week. However, as it was the beginning of the school's half-term holidays, Doug, a head teacher, had the week off and at that moment they were en route to the airport and seven days of, as Maggie put it, sun, sand, sea, sangria and the other 's' if and when possible.

She envied them, especially the other 's' if and when possible.

As any one of those s's was unlikely at that moment, she'd have to do some r—research—and w—writing—instead.

Her mental meandering was enough to make her grin and head for her laptop. She could get a good hour's writing in before she needed to think about dinner. Happy now that she had decided not to carry on cutting off her nose to spite her face, she typed faster. By the time she surfaced, two hours had passed and her tummy was making rumbling noises. She checked she'd saved and backed up her work then headed for the kitchen. Her mobile phone stared at her in reproach.

"You are not my conscience," she informed it, and sniggered. She'd really lost the plot if she gave a phone a persona with a mind of its own, as well as her bank account. Nevertheless it reminded her to try Moss again.

She got the bloody answerphone again.

It would have been oh-so temping to put the phone down and say well, that's it then. However now she had made her mind up to contact him and move on, and in whatever direction she was shown. She decided she had to at least let him know. Otherwise she could be trying for weeks. Arietta took a deep breath and left her brief message.

"Hi, it's me, er, Arietta…" What next? She panicked then knew exactly what to say. "Just to say I've got over my snit. I'm sorry I reacted so vehemently and was a complete bitch. Hope to speak to you soon." She pressed Send and thought over what she'd said. Was 'vehemently' the right word? She mentally shrugged. Hopefully he would get the gist. She put her phone on charge and headed to the kitchen. Now she'd made the call, she was ready to eat, and she wanted something quick and easy.

Halfway through her paella ready meal, her phone rang. Her heart missed a beat as she dropped her cutlery and picked up the phone.

It wasn't Moss. It was her mum asking if she fancied going over the following afternoon.

They made plans and she went back to her food.

* * * *

Typically, she was in the loo at her mum's when her phone next rang, and by the time she'd washed her hands there was only a voicemail and, she noticed, a text. They were both from Moss, who in his text had only managed a brief, 'Hectic, will call asap so we can talk, damn I'm wanted. thank you'.

The voicemail was a bit more informative.

"Sorry it's taken me so long to get back to you. Kristin has been rushed to hospital, suspected appendicitis, and, typical, might have broken her ankle…not related, so I have Audie with me for now and no idea how long for. Heaven help me when I have to go back to work on Monday, but I'll cross that bridge when I come to it, if need be. I agree we must talk. I'll let you know when I can get over. Um, not a bitch, just a bit catty… Justified as well. What's a male bitch? I guess that was me. I could have been more open." He laughed. "That sounds dodgy, doesn't it? Anyway, you know this number. Take care."

The call ended.

Ten fraught minutes later, she was satisfied with her text.

Just got this.

A bit of creative typing there but she felt it best added.

Sorry to hear about Kristin, hope all works out well. If there is anything I can do, let me know. I'll be at mum's until Sunday afternoon, but can come home early with a couple of hours or so's notice if need be. p.s. all cows, cats and other assorted animals now banished.

Knowing Moss, he'd get that cryptic p.s. and appreciate it. She headed back to the lounge.

Her mum looked up as she re-entered the lounge. "Dad's making fresh coffee and I've some homemade shortbread. Sorted?"

Arietta shrugged self-consciously. "Don't know, to be honest. Just got a message saying he still has his daughter with him as Kristin's been rushed to hospital with suspected appendicitis and a maybe broken ankle, no idea how. I've sent my hope all goes well and said I'll be home on Sunday if he needs my help."

"Do you think that's likely?"

"No idea, Mum, but I thought I should say it."

"Ah, but do you mean it?" her mum asked with shrewdness. "Or are you paying lip service to appearing helpful?"

"That's something I'm not yet sure about. I guess I'll find out if he asks for help, won't I?"

* * * *

After a satisfyingly energetic session of gardening with her mum on Saturday, and an equally enjoyable trawl around the local flea market on Sunday morning, Arietta headed home in a much better frame of mind. She had a coolbag full of goodies, including one of her mum's excellent lemon drizzle cakes, a half leg of lamb, a couple of rump steaks and some chunky, drool-making pork chops from the freezer — well-insulated — and veg from her dad's allotment. She wouldn't need to shop for basics for at least a fortnight.

She drove home happier than she'd been for a while. A text saying that Kristin was being kept in for the time being for 'monitoring', and he'd remember her offer for help with thanks had been her only communication from Moss. A short text from Thomas — "Oh shit, WTF is going on?" — she had no idea how to reply to. In the end, as she had no idea what Moss had told Thomas, she just said Moss had a lot on.

Thomas' answer was short and sweet. "So it seems. Crap, isn't it? Hope you can do something to help."

Once she'd parked her car, unloaded and put her still-frozen meat in the freezer, she changed into shorts and a tank top, made the inevitable cup of coffee, grabbed a bottle of sparkling water and a slice of cake, and took them and a notebook into the garden. Even with all that had been going on over the past few days, a germ of an idea for a story had grown, and she wanted to make notes before she forgot the gist of it. Normally she'd use her laptop but she wanted to enjoy the sun while she could. The weather forecast was to use a favourite phrase of Maggie's...'minging'. As in rain, wind and a good eight degrees lower than that day's balmy twenty.

She could — would — be inside the next day. This afternoon was a sit and think in the garden session. Within half an hour, she was immersed in making notes, reminders of what to research, and thoroughly engrossed in her slowly forming ideas. Once she'd chosen suitably Regency names for her working-class hero and aristocratic heroine, she'd be happy and ready to write. She put down her pad and pencil, stretched out on the ancient lounger and shut her eyes.

* * * *

Something tickled her nose, and she tried to brush it off.

"Wake up, sleeping beauty. I've not got long."

She opened her eyes and glanced at her watch to discover she'd only been dozing for around ten minutes.

"Long for what?" she asked Moss warily as she squinted up at him, his silhouette dark, outlined by the sun. "Hold on, let me sit up." She adjusted the back of the lounger and felt a lot more in control of the situation once she no longer was conscious of being at a disadvantage. She waved at a nearby garden chair. "Have you got time to sit down?"

"Do you want me to?" he asked, putting, Arietta decided with an annoying use of the idiom, the ball firmly back in her court.

"Up to you." She had no intention of making his mind up for him — or making it easy. He might be here, but what for? "Oh, sit down, you're making the place appear untidy."

Moss gave her a cautious smile as he did as he was bidden. "Thanks." He didn't seem in a hurry to say more.

Arietta was conscious she needed to go to the loo before long and didn't fancy saying so. "You said you hadn't got long?" she prompted. "For?"

He exhaled deeply. "Your explanation, my explanation. Grovelling, more explaining. Begging for help, coffee... Sod it, can't add alcohol. Take your pick."

"I'll make coffee." All of a sudden the grovelling didn't sound so satisfying. She'd hate to have to do it, so why put Moss through it? "You can explain as I do."

"I can try and explain," he said as he followed her indoors. "Whether I do it well enough for you to listen to why I need your help is another matter entirely.

Apropos of which, I've been a grumpy, miserable sod all weekend."

"Really? Why?" She filled the coffee pot and put it on the stove. "Guilty conscience maybe?"

"Tell it how you see it, why don't you?" Moss said as she got out mugs and he retrieved the milk jug from the fridge. "Don't give me any breaks."

Arietta glanced at him and gave him a quizzical look. "Should I?" she enquired sweetly.

He grimaced. "Probably not. I do have my reasons for what I did or didn't do, but whether you agree with them or not remains to be seen."

"I couldn't have put it better myself. Do you want to talk in here? You know, in case hedges have ears?" She poured the coffee out, somewhat annoyed with herself as she'd remembered how Moss took his coffee and added the correct amount of milk without thought. "Here you go. Well?"

"Indoors, in case those ears are that Josephine woman's. I think I saw her towing a black ball of fluff behind her as I turned into the lane. I'm in Tarquin's Land Rover, by the way. He's got my car, as he took Audie to see her mum and their other car decided it was poorly. His words, not mine. Audie said it had probably broken down in sympathy with her mum and did cars have the equivalent of an appendix? I choked on my non-alcoholic beer, Tarq looked blank and she winked and went out whistling *Sucker* by the Jonas Brothers." He grinned as Arietta chuckled. "Not that the words are suitable for that occasion, and maybe I shouldn't have taught her how to whistle so well, but I did and that's my daughter for you." He stopped suddenly. "About whom I need to explain, don't I?"

Arietta looked at him, considering how best to reply. "That's up to you."

He firmed his lips. "Actually, no, it's up to you. If you're not interested or don't care, then I'll not share confidences. All I'll ask is you don't go telling the world and his wife about Audie. It's not fair on her."

Arietta tamped down her rising temper. "Sorry if I was sounding like that animal we said we weren't going to mention, but if you have so little belief in my ideals and honesty, then just go. Anyway, I can't share what I don't know, and to be honest, would anyone be interested?"

"Oh yes, they sure would. Love child, born before I was nineteen, never with the mother. People wondering how and why. Can't you just see the headlines?" he demanded. "I will not allow Audie to be put through that *or* hounded by the press. Yes I was naive, yes we were stupid, no I didn't realise I was a convenience, yada yada ya." He stood up, and put his mug into the sink, contents untouched. "Oh forget it, sorry I disturbed you, sorry I lied, sorry for whatever I need to be sorry for. Let me know if you still need a partner for the bloody wedding. I've been told it's still on." He headed towards the door and had it open before Arietta found her voice.

"I'm sorry as well," she said quietly. "You hurt me, Moss, really hurt me. I thought we'd been open and honest with each other, then wham. I saw you and Audie at the craft market and thought I was mistaken and it was just someone who looked like you."

Moss turned around and slowly walked back to her side and sat down again. "You did?"

She nodded. "Then you turned up with a daughter, whose mother is the woman who went off with the ex I ditched. Who she's marrying. Whose wedding I got an out-of-the-blue invitation to, and to where you said you'd escort me. But where I guess you'd have been going anyway?"

"All of that. And the rest. Will you listen now?"

Will I? Arietta nodded again. "Tell me.""

"I met Kristin on an advert set," Moss began. "In those days it was take what parts you can get. I played a baked bean."

Arietta choked. "A what?"

"A baked bean. Do not snigger," he said mournfully. "Someone had to do it, and it paid my rent for a month. Allegedly I was excellent and conveyed what was needed. I declaimed such powerful sentences as…there's no better baked bean than a Brontesauralies Baked Bean or some such name, lost in the mists of time," Moss said in a modest tone, which he spoiled by crossing his eyes. Another trick Arietta envied. "Put me off beans for years, though I love 'em now. They went bust soon after, mind you."

"No wonder, with a name like that," Arietta observed. "What a mouthful."

"I might have got the odd letter wrong here or there. It wasn't very memorable," Moss said. "But it *was* where I met Kristin."

"How can you convey a baked bean's attitude?" she asked, intrigued.

"Heaven knows but it seems I did. Now where was I? I've lost the thread."

"Being a baked bean and meeting Kristin."

"Ah, yeah. Kristin was, I think, something like the third assistant to the producer's assistant, if there is such a thing. As in the gofer's gofer. She came on to me, I was flattered, we went out and well, you can guess the rest. Two weeks later she told me it had been fun while it lasted, but her boyfriend was back now, so it was over between her and me. She was sure I was enough of a gentleman not to talk about what had happened and say if questioned, we were just friends. That all changed when she discovered she was pregnant and it couldn't possibly be Tarquin's."

"She was sure?" It sounded a bit fishy to Arietta.

"Mumps," Moss said briefly. "Him, not her. But she was adamant she didn't want anything from me, was happy for me to be acknowledged as the father. Her mum and dad backed her, and it didn't appear to bother Tarquin, still doesn't, and Kristin is agreeable to what we decide."

I bet money had to be involved somehow, somewhere and sometime.

"Anyhow, to go back a bit, Kristin had Audie, she and Tarquin stayed together, albeit often apart, and here we are. I share Audie's time and love with them as best I can. When I'm away, I don't see much of her, and it's not generally known I have a daughter. When I'm around, Audie spends as much time as possible with me, and so far no one has twigged who she is. We try to have a good give and take between all of us. It seems to have worked."

"That I can see, but it doesn't explain why you didn't mention a daughter to me when we were…happy as a couple. Like recently." She understood why he hadn't at first, but later? That question kept going round and round in her head.

"Because I was scared it might change how you felt towards me," Moss said bluntly. "Especially when I discovered all the ins and out of why you didn't want to go to the wedding. I know Kristin could be a bitch, and I didn't want you to go to the wedding alone. Or cry off. Then when I accepted I had to tell you—whatever the outcome—I couldn't get away. So, this weekend was going to be the first chance I had and look how that ended up. Shit creek and no paddle. I did try to get in touch and say maybe we'd be best to put the weekend off, but…well I'd hoped there would be no need, so when I couldn't catch you I thought oh well, maybe it's a good omen." He stared at Arietta and she caught the nervous tic of his eye. "I accept it wasn't, and I've been an insensitive jerk."

He could say that again.

"What now?"

Moss shrugged. "Up to you."

Arietta thought of something. "What's the favour?"

"Pardon?" Moss said in a puzzled voice.

"What favour did you want to ask of me?"

"Ah…a big one."

"Well spit it out so I can say yay or nay." She got up and poured out two glasses of wine, more to do something with her hands and for something to hold than because she wanted one. If anything, she could have done with a large brandy

"Do you forgive me?" Moss asked in a very serious voice. "*Freely* forgive me?"

Arietta didn't answer straight away. She did, but she wanted to make sure she showed him how his lack of trust had affected her. "I suppose so, as long as there's nothing else you've forgotten about that I might find out later."

He smiled. "No gov, honest gov. Well, I can't think of anything."

She grinned at the put-on accent. "Then ask away. I reserve the right to say no."

"Fair enough, and it is a big favour. Audie's school is closed next week for midterm break. Kristin won't be able to look after her — even if her appendicitis is only an upset tummy, the dodgy ankle is exactly what it's purported to be. Her parents are in the South of France and can't get back for a week due to, wait for it, her dad breaking *his* ankle and her mum refusing to drive on motorways or for more than a few hours at a time. Which knowing both French motorways and Kristin's mum, I can well understand. Tarquin has to go to the States in the morning on a make-or-break deal for his firm and I have to be back at work or else all hell breaks loose. We're at our wit's ends to know who we could ask to take care of Audie for us, and it's not helping Kristin's recovery. It would have to be someone Audie likes of course, and someone we feel happy about leaving our daughter with."

Arietta began to see where he was heading. Unless he was about to ask her advice on a live-in housekeeper or child minder, it appeared he might have that role in mind for her. Would she agree? She waited to hear what he said next.

"I can arrange to be with her most evenings, but I would need to leave at some ungodly hour in the morning to get to the location on time. Which leaves a problem."

"During the day," Arietta said matter-of-factly. "It's hard when you have commitments, isn't it? I know I feel the same when people assume because I'm at home all day without what is generally called a proper job. They take that to mean I have spare time on my hands and can run errands or whatever. Bloody annoying."

Moss went red, just as she realised how those words sounded. "I didn't mean—" she began, at the same time he uttered.

"Oh hell, I didn't think—"

Arietta put her hand in the air. "Let me go first. I didn't mean you, you knew I hadn't started my next book." A slight white lie, she thought as she crossed her fingers behind her back and thought of all the notes she had. Sometimes you couldn't have it all your own way. "Plus, this is an emergency. If you're going to ask me to look after Audie, I will of course." She thought rapidly about the next week's diary. "Well, until Friday, then I have meetings and so on. Any help?"

Moss nodded. "You don't know how much. Tarquin should be back on Thursday. You're sure?"

"Certain. I can get her to help me research the gory bits for my next book." She could always recheck places she'd been to and get Audie's input.

"She'd love that," Moss said. "All bones and baddies?"

"Something like that. What next?"

"I go and get her, explain to her and head here, then head up north to sort out getting back as often as I can, thank you over and over, and ask what sort of gin you want?" He inhaled long and deep, sniffed his wine and handed it over to Arietta. "Save it for me, please. So next. Get my breath back and wonder what I might have missed."

Arietta laughed. "What Audie likes to eat, do you have a list of dos and don'ts, and do I make both spare bedrooms up? If so is the bigger one for her or you now? What do we tell anyone who asks who she is? Can my mum come over if she feels like it? We had a tentative mooch around town booked for Tuesday. Oh, and what's the rest of our story?"

"Hmm." Moss pondered for a few seconds. "Her likes are longer than her dislikes, so I'd check with her. I think they might change as often as the wind changes direction. No problems with your mum as long as she knows what you and Audie cook up between you."

"We'll think of something. By the way, my parents are sworn to secrecy. They'll abide by it."

Moss nodded and didn't ask any more questions. "I'd like to be honest and open if you're okay with it. Say it's early days, but we know we want to spend more time together." He winked. "And in more interesting scenarios. Once Audie is back at her mum's."

It was Arietta's turn to nod. "I'm okay with that." *More than.* "And our story?"

"Tell your parents whatever you and Audie decide to make up and let them know they're fabrications. To anyone else, how about saying she's a daughter of a friend who is spending a few days with you because you get on well? Make up something you can both remember for the rest?"

"Will you remember it?"

He rolled his eyes and struck a pose. "Darling, I'm an act…or. You tell me, I won't forget."

It sounded fair enough. She agreed, Moss kissed her cheek. She let him, and watched as he drove away after promising he'd be back before eight.

"*Just in time for supper,*" he'd said cheerfully. "*Via a well-known burger drive-through I reckon.*"

Arietta had grinned. "*You'll enjoy it.*"

"*Sure will, but there'll still be space for your supper.*"

She laughed and waved him off. How the hell could she go from being in a blazing bad mood with him to offering to look after his daughter all in an hour or so?

Because deep down she accepted she'd overreacted and not even given him a chance to explain. Happier than she had been for a couple of days — was it so short a time? It felt like weeks — Arietta went upstairs to make up the spare bed.

* * * *

Before Moss and Audie arrived, Arietta had one other important thing to do — type up the other notes she'd made for her new book and decide what she could pretend she needed to check out with Audie. Although she thought for once her bullet points were reasonably legible, she was under no illusions that she'd still know what she'd meant by such things as check flu, best kill, how, and Potomac, liquorice when, without the scribbles she'd added as she'd thought of them and which weren't so clear.

Over the years, as her typing had improved, she was certain her handwriting had deteriorated. Was it because she wrote in longhand less and less, or was always in such a hurry when using a pen or pencil she didn't take enough care? Probably a bit of both.

She typed up the notes, including the deciphered scribbles — why did she want a cat, cot, cut, or was it oat, oath or oaf biscuit? — and made a mental vow to try to write more legibly in the future. Maybe she needed to set aside half an hour or so each day to write in longhand and be able to read it back the next day. She knew exactly the best way to do it as well.

Arietta saved her notes, closed her laptop, got up from the chair and headed to the old and well-loved antique bureau she'd treated herself to with her first decent royalty cheque. Inside the top drawer was a diary she'd got in the family Secret Santa present exchange the previous Christmas. She'd guessed it was from her brother, due to the slightly risqué 'writers do it with scribes' on the front cover. Arietta had intended to write in it, she really had, but she'd received edits for her book, spent a fortnight in the Canary Islands ostensibly researching pirates for a book—but in reality enjoying some winter sun—and forgotten all about the diary until she came home. At which point she'd put it into a drawer, thinking she really would use it at some point.

That point had arrived.

Arietta took it into the lounge and opened it at that day's date. What to write without giving secrets away? She bit her lip and thought for a few moments before she wrote.

Started notes and typed some up etcetera for next book.

What else?

Mum gave me enough food to feed a family of four for a fortnight.

Innocuous...boring...factual... Better than nothing. She put the diary into the leather-lidded footstool by her favourite chair. If she could read that next week, she'd count it as a success.

She had a thought, went back to the bureau and rummaged through a drawer until she found what she was looking for. A new notebook with 'Be careful what you say or it might be in my next book' written across the front, a new ballpoint and matching propelling pencil with an eraser on the end. Hopefully Audie would be happy to help using her own 'tools'. She added a folding clipboard, tiny notepad, Post-It notes and some marker pens — the sort of stuff she always had on hand when she went out and about on a research trip, and often when she didn't — and put it all in a new shoulder bag she'd earmarked as a present for someone someday. If Audie didn't want it, so be it. It would all get used at some point.

Arietta mulled over what she'd agreed to. She could only hope that A, Audie was happy with the situation and B, they got on well after such a short time of knowing each other. At least, she temporised, it wasn't for too long and surely they could manage a few harmonious days in close proximity.

Please, God.

Chapter Eleven

Moss was true to his word and arrived back just before eight after a text he'd sent an hour or so before.

Burger turned down in favour of whatever you might have for supper (sorry, I did try). Pantechnicon van more use than my car. Hope the garage is empty.

It was accompanied by a winking emoji. As half of Moss' stuff was in her garage and her car in the other half, she hoped he was joking. Meanwhile she'd see what she could get ready to have for supper. Not easy when you had no idea what one-third of the party — she assumed Moss was staying with her and Audie that night — would eat.

Quiches — no cheese for her, three types for Moss — a couple of pizzas, one laden, one not, an assortments of salads, cold meats and jacket potatoes, along with the inevitable baked beans Moss now loved and ratatouille that she could eat with almost everything, and frequently did. With a bit of luck there would be something amongst that selection for Audie. If not, there was always toast, or tough luck. Hopefully Audie would be happy with what they had. Arietta made a note to ask the teenager what they might need food wise and take a trip to the supermarket the following day.

For now, though, it was potluck.

A toot of a car horn ended her introspection. Whether she'd made the right or wrong decision it was too late to alter it now. It was about to happen and they would all have to make the best of it.

She headed round the house — she really must find the front door key she'd put somewhere after Moss left the last time and had no idea where — just as the noise of the car engine stopped.

Audie almost tumbled out of the car, headed towards Arietta with a rush, then stopped hesitantly, obviously unsure how to greet her hostess.

Start as I mean to go on.

Arietta moved to the young girl's side and hugged her. "Hi and welcome."

Audie smiled tremulously. "Am I really?"

"Really," Arietta assured her. "As long as you don't ask me to cook cheese and accept I'm a grumpy bu...er, blighter before I've had a cup of coffee in the mornings."

Audie laughed. "Same as Dad then. Do you fight over who gets up to make it?"

"Often," Moss assured her as he rounded the car and unselfconsciously kissed Arietta. "Hi, love. We all thank you massively for offering to put up with Audie. Do you know what you've let yourself in for?"

Arietta laughed as Audie did the long-suffering teen act and pulled a face as she said, "Da…ad." She seemed to think it was a done thing that her dad and Arietta were a couple. "Honestly, I'll be good."

"I guess we'll find out," Arietta replied cheerfully. "Where's your stuff? I've put you in the bigger of the spare rooms."

"Mainly because the other is full of my stuff," Moss said as he hauled a suitcase and a sports bag out of the boot. "Poor Arietta didn't just get landed with me, she got my favourite books and so on."

"So on covers a lot," Arietta said as she took hold of a large cardboard box Moss handed her. "I dread to think what we might find in there."

"Ghosts and ghouls and things that go bump in the night?" Audie said with a giggle. "Bones and bats and bits of bodies?"

"Repellent child," Moss said. "Where do you get such ideas?"

"Probably from you and your films," Audie said very straight-faced as they walked towards the back door. "Or Arietta's books."

"Eh? You don't read them, do you?" Moss asked. "Scary stuff." He dropped the suitcase and headed for the door once more.

Audie gave him a butter-wouldn't-melt-in-her-mouth look, which she spoiled by sniggering. "Nah, I just looked at the 'read me bits' online and decided too much too soon."

"Thank heaven for that," Moss said in a heartfelt way as he held on to the doorjamb. "Stick to Horrible Histories."

"Just as gory in their own way," Arietta observed as she put the box on the table. The contents clinked, but she wouldn't be so rude as to ask what the contents were.

She didn't have to. "A necessity after too much Audie," Moss said with a grin as he reappeared carrying a box and a carrier from a well-known food store. He dodged a pretend thump from his daughter. "A wee minder, as Thom says."

It didn't sound that wee—small. "Then many thanks. I'll savour whatever it is. And while I remember to mention it, Audie, yeah, don't read my books, yet, please."

"Too much love and icky stuff amongst the blood and gore?" Audie asked with a cheeky smirk. "Would it gross me out?"

"Definitely," Moss said. "Right, let's get this stuff upstairs. Anyone would think you were here for four months, not four days." He hefted the suitcase and staggered. Arietta picked up a box of what appeared to be shoes and followed him.

"You always say prepare for every eventuality," Audie said as she carried her sports bag upstairs. "And I didn't. No skis or snorkelling stuff, and I didn't even put my golf clubs in."

Arietta laughed. "Just as well, not my thing. Though I can play lawn bowls and skittles, and skim stones. I got eleven once and Thomas has never forgiven me. Mind you, the record is about eight times that, so I'm no Wonder Woman."

"Ohh, that sounds fun, can we do it? I've got my wellies."

"Homework?" Moss asked as he nudged the door open with his foot.

"Dad." Audie sounded disgusted. "Spoil things, why don't you. Actually," she added in a lofty tone,

"I've done most of it, except for a book review of a book I hated. We have to find at least three positive and three negative things about it. The only positive thing I can say is thank goodness I'll never have to read it again. It's daft."

Arietta laughed. "There you are. That's one, and if you can explain why you think it's daft, that's two. We'll have a look at it one day."

Audie punched the air. "Yeehaa, and you can tell me what to write?"

Arietta shook her head. "No," she corrected and Audie's face fell. "I can help you craft your answers. There's a difference. You'll know what I mean when we sit down with it. You better tell me the book."

"Bummer." Audie wrinkled her nose as Moss looked skyward.

She named a famous children's book. "So not my thing."

Arietta understood that. It hadn't been hers either. "Fair enough, now while we do other stuff, think why not and remember it for when we start to do your review."

Audie pouted. "That's so not fair."

Moss looked at her sternly and she went pale. He then spoiled it by winking. "It's so not raining either. Get over it, sweet. It's more than a lot of your mates will have."

Audie nodded. "That's true. Boy, I am so looking forward to the next few days. Oh not just because of my homework, though if I tell you what I think—politely Dad, politely—and write it as I think you can sort me out so I'm not in detention all year."

Arietta nodded. "To say it sucks might not be the best review ever. Unless you say it sucks because it's two dimensional or unrealistic or no one would say that or some such thing. We'll sort it out. In your view and words."

Moss sent her a grateful look. "Sounds good. Ladies, I'm going to have to love you and leave you in a sec. I need to get to my basic not very homely accommodation before people start screaming for me. I need to be up, wide awake and willing by four a.m." He yawned. "Not an attractive thought."

"Aw…I hoped you'd stop here for tonight," Audie said in a disappointed voice. "And I would…okay, might have, waved you off tomorrow. Depending on the time."

So did I. And so would I, and it wouldn't be time dependent either.

"I hoped so as well," Moss answered. "I'd intended to until my call was brought forward. But let's look on the bright side. The sooner we get going, hopefully the sooner we get finished. Which means the sooner I get back. Now, my lovely ladies, be good while I'm away."

Arietta smiled. "If we can't be good, we'll be careful."

Moss blinked. "Oh glory, I hope so." He kissed them both. "Right. I'm off. If you need me, phone or text. I will get it."

"We will, but we won't," Audie said before Arietta could reply. "I'll be good and Arietta will be stern. Sorted."

Moss didn't look too sure. "Yeah, yeah, I can wish. Right. I'm outta here and see you both soon."

He sketched a wave and headed off.

As the noise of the engine faded, Arietta looked at Audie, who she decided didn't seem nearly as confident now. "Food?" she suggested.

"Good idea," Audie confirmed. "Sorry and all that, but I'm starving."

"No need to be sorry. I'll cook, you see if you can find the crockery and cutlery and set the table."

* * * *

The meal went down well, and Audie was complimentary about the quiches. She liked cheese, she admitted, but thought the cauliflower and smoked salmon cheeseless one was much better.

"Different, not boring." She blushed. "That didn't come out quite how I meant it to, sorry. Dad always says I open my mouth and shove both my feet in it."

Arietta laughed. "Snap. I know what you mean. Glad you like it."

"Oh do I ever," Audie said earnestly then gasped. "Oh, oohh, roulade, my favourite." She proclaimed it as ace and ate three portions, until she finally decided enough was enough. Arietta was mighty glad, because to see Audie tuck into so much food with relish made her feel slightly sick.

"Wow, now I know what Dad meant when he said you were a brilliant cook. Will you show me?" Audie asked. "Mum is great at pretty food, but it's just that. Pretty, not tasty or filling. Yours is all three." She began to stack the dirty plates. "Tarq makes a good curry, but mum says it stinks the place out so we don't have it that often. Which is weird cos I reckon fish smells just as bad and we have that a lot. Just as well I like fish."

"It's healthier," Arietta said as she loaded the dishwasher. "Especially oily fish. What's your favourite?"

"Whatever I've caught?" Audie said with a twinkle that belied the statement.

"Oh, great stuff. Shall we go out one day?" Arietta said mischievously. "I've a mate who has a rowing boat we can use on the loch."

Audie blanched. "Actually, er, no, ta. I can't do the take off the hook and thwack over the head thingy. Makes me feel icky. My favourite is probably sea bream. Or fish shop battered with mushy peas."

"Good, because the fish and chip van comes to the village on Wednesdays so we can have that for tea if you want?" That meant one less meal to plan. She had to get into the two-not-one to cook for mindset again.

"Sounds good," Audie said. "With pickled onions and mushy peas?"

"Of course."

"Brilliant. Um, Arietta?"

Arietta glanced at the young girl. "What's up?"

Audie bit her lip and looked thoughtful. "Can I ask you something and will you answer me honestly?"

Good lord, what does she want to know? A myriad of possible questions ran through Arietta's mind, some palatable, some not. "If I can," she said slowly. "As long as I'm not answering on behalf of someone else or saying something that might hurt another person."

"No, just on behalf of you." Audie wrinkled her nose. "Is it honestly okay for me to be here? I mean, I know you write and work from home, because Dad told me. Won't I be in the way? I promise I'll be quiet and try not to disturb you while you're writing, but...well..." Her voice trailed off. "Are you sure you don't mind?"

The poor girl. Had she been worrying about that all this time? Arietta made haste to reassure her. "You are not in the way of my writing, your dad, your mum, Tarquin's work or any other little or big thing. If I had a lot to do or something planned I would have said so. Which I did. I'm off to meet my agent on Friday, and I said as much to your dad. Hopefully Tarquin will be back by then, but if not, you'll have to sit in a corner with a book and pretend not to listen when I say how poor I am and how I can only afford cheap wine and budget-range cheese for when she visits. Betty is a dear, but she's a fine wine aficionado and all her cheeses come from the posh cabinet. No such thing as basic cheddar. I always get a good lunch, and she does do well for me, but I do like to tease her. She can't believe I hate cheese."

"It is hard to understand that. I can't imagine not liking cheddar," Audie observed. "Or Port Salut. I hope Tarquin doesn't get back. Your agent sounds an interesting lady. I'd love to meet her."

"We'll see," Arietta said vaguely. "Now, tomorrow I could do with a visit to the harbour at St Andrews." The car would know its way there before long, but as much as she wanted to visit Dollar Glen and Castle Campbell, she would need to concentrate there so would wait until she was alone. "Do you fancy it? I've an idea one of my protagonists might try to lure the heroine to a gruesome death there."

Audie's eyes were wide open and round. "Ohh, does he manage it?"

"I hope not, or it would be an awfully short book. Anyhow it might not work, so we can go and check it out, and either have our fish and chips there or wait until Wednesday."

"Or have them twice?" Audie said hopefully. "They are my favourite."

"Boy, you are your father's daughter."

Those few words evidently pleased Audie enormously, as she relayed them to Moss when he rang later. When she handed the phone over to Arietta, Moss sounded amused. "You're high up in the favourite list now, you know. Fish and chips."

Arietta checked Audie was out of earshot and heard her going upstairs to sort her books out. "Don't forget the mushy peas, and pickled onions."

Moss laughed. "Every day if she was allowed. Tell me honestly. Are you okay with the situation? You were rather inveigled into it."

"No one inveigles me unless I want them to," Arietta replied firmly. "She's lovely and helpful and tomorrow we're off to St Andrews."

"Again? I thought you'd been there, done it and got the T-shirt as well as the info you needed."

"I forgot to check something," Arietta said lightly.

"Hmm." He didn't sound convinced. "If you say so."

"I do say so. We'll be back by teatime and both have phones."

"Enjoy then. Think of me knee-deep in mud and gore."

"Oh I will, sounds delightful."

"Not as delightful as if you were in it with me. Mind you, I'd rather be in bed with you and no mud or gore in sight. Love you, sleep tight." He laughed and rang off before she could formulate her reply.

Arietta went to bed a couple of hours later in a thoughtful mood.

* * * *

She was woken by the sounds of her visitor creeping down the stairs. After she squinted at the clock, Arietta groaned. Five-forty-seven. *What on earth?* Thoughts of Audie having smuggled a hamster or a kitten in with her luggage got her out of bed and down the stairs at a rate of knots before she thought to remember what she might or might not be wearing. Thank goodness she'd put a pair of PJs on the night before.

She entered the kitchen silently to see Audie open the back door and peer out.

"What's there?"

Audie turned round with a gasp. "Oh shoot, you startled me. I could hear a strange noise. Like someone sawing a door or a window. I was worried."

"So worried you didn't think to get me?" Arietta asked with a raised inflexion at the end of her sentence. "Wow. Would you say that was brave or stupid?"

Audie blushed. "I was gonna check and then get you."

"Stupid," Arietta confirmed as Audie looked bashful. "What if it had been a burglar?" Arietta asked. "A big one. With a gun or an axe. What then?"

"Then I'd scream."

"Maybe not the right answer. Maybe come and tell me before you did your super sleuth act?"

Audie grimaced. "Yeah, well, I thought of that after. Anyway, there's nothing here. Nothing out of place, nothing on the doorstep. Not a thing."

"Of course not." Arietta gave her a sympathetic look. "It's Mrs Cranshaw's cockerel. It's lost its voice."

Audie started then giggled. "Pardon?"

"Lost its voice," Arietta said again obligingly.

"A cockerel who's lost his voice? Honestly?"

"Honestly," Arietta confirmed. "No one knows why, including the vet, but we all know what the noise is. So do you now."

"You sure?" Audie still didn't sound certain.

"Oh yes... many early mornings sure. Peregrine the cockerel is voiceless."

"Peregrine? For a cockerel? Why on earth?" Audie asked, clearly puzzled. "I mean, it's not really apt is it?"

"Nope, but evidently they wanted him to be brave and bold."

"Good grief." Audie must have picked Arietta's favourite expression from her.

It was the understatement of the year. Even on their journey to St Andrews Audie kept referring to it. By the time they parked the car on The Scores—free parking even if it meant a few more minutes' walk to town, it was very close to the castle—Arietta was sick of the cockerel and its name.

"Enough," she said and held her hand up. "I'm cockerelled out. Have you got your notebook ready?"

Audie giggled, nodded and held a bulging backpack up. "All present and correct. Oh, and tissues, two pens, three pencils, a wee bottle of water, sweeties..."

"Casserole set? Cuddly toy?" Arietta said, referring to the prizes on an old game show her parents used to watch. It had been a standard joke of her dad's to say it when as children she and Thomas loaded themselves up with an assortment of items before they went anywhere.

No wonder Audie looked blank. "Pardon?"

"Oh, nothing," Arietta said hastily. *Sheesh, I'm turning into my parents.* "Great, let's get started."

Audie almost danced out of the car.

"I am so looking forward to this." She nigh-on carolled the words as she settled her backpack across her shoulders. "Much more interesting than going round the shops with Mum or helping her decide on what sort of place name thingies she wants."

"Oh, we'll be doing that as well," Arietta said as she locked the car and glanced up at the thickening clouds. They looked ready to shed their wet contents any moment. At least, she thought as she sniffed the air, it didn't smell like snow. It was considered to be too early for snow in that part of the country, but if there was one thing she'd discovered at an early age that the Scottish weather had a mind of its own and you couldn't rely on what *should* happen.

"Well, we will check out some of the shops but, I don't need place name thingies," she added as Audie giggled. "There's only space for half a dozen people round my table, and it's usually sit where you want."

"They're for the rehearsal dinner, and then she wants different ones for the reception. Dad is sending her demented, as he won't tell her your name. He's even got me to call you 'Dad's lady' and not mention your name. When Mum asks, I say I've forgotten and I just call you Clarabelle and that I'm sure that's not your name, just Dad's nickname for you. It isn't, is it?"

Arietta shook her head. "No, thank goodness. Where on earth did you get it from?"

"Dad. He said to use it if Mum pressed me. I think he's teasing her, and she really doesn't have a sense of humour where the wedding is concerned. Evidently there are a few people who have replied they're bringing a partner, but not given a name and it's infuriating her. Tarquin just says put 'partner of whoever' on the name place thingies, but she says it's not…" She wrinkled her nose, something she did to great effect. "Symmetrical," Audie finished with a triumphant inflexion. "Where are we going first?"

"For a drink and something to eat," Arietta said and steered her into a small independent coffee shop she liked. "My one slice of toast seems like a long time ago now. They do great bacon sarnies here and, so I've been told, thick creamy hot chocolate."

Audie swallowed. "I hate it. Could I possibly have tea and a bacon sandwich? I've got money," she added hastily. "I can treat you."

"Next time," Arietta said firmly. "I'll pay now, you can get the ice cream." There was a splatter of hail on the window of the café. "Or soup."

"You're on. Oh wow, are *they* the bacon sarnies? They look amazing." Audie had noticed a plate being delivered to a nearby table. "They should keep me going until lunchtime." She looked towards Arietta and grinned. "Dad says I've got hollow legs."

"Your dad was right about your hollow legs," Arietta said a few hours later as they walked back along the harbour wall and she let Audie take photos. The hail had stopped but it was grey and gloomy and the very atmosphere Arietta needed for the happy ending of her book. The dangerous will they, won't they succeed in their plan would take part in bright sunshine. Exactly the opposite to what she hoped the readers would expect.

"I'm a growing girl." Audie pointed the camera at Arietta. "Upwards and, Mum says, if I'm not careful, outwards. But I am careful. Pose and smile."

Arietta laughed as she struck a pose. An unexpected gust of wind caught her hair and whipped it around her face.

"Perfect, Dad will love it. Can we please pop into the old-fashioned sweetie shop and get some puff candy? It'll keep me going on the way home. I'm almost out of carrot sticks."

What Audie said was true. The young girl ate a lot of food, but not a lot of junk. The junk food she devoured with relish, but as she pointed out, except on the odd occasion, as with the roulade, she was careful how much she consumed. Her backpack might have sweets in it, but it also had the carrot sticks, which she crunched with gusto.

Arietta blew her hair out of her eyes. "In deference to your growing, then, shall we hunt out some lunch? I think I've got all I need here. You can pick where we go to eat. There's the chippie, a salad, Chinese, Indian, pizza… Up to you." They reached the end of the harbour wall and began to walk back towards the town. "We'll go via the shops. I saw a rather lovely jumper the last time I was here, but the shop was closed." A bit of stretching the truth, but Arietta loved her wee wander through the streets. Not too many shops, some nice independents and a pleasant way to spend half an hour.

"Hmmm…" Audie put her finger to her mouth in a parody of someone deep in thought. "Decisions, decisions. I think I'd like a curry, and save fish and chips for Wednesday night. I like the idea of a chip van, especially if we eat it out of the box thingy. Although, do we have to use one of those awful wooden forks? They make me shiver."

Arietta agreed about that. "Nope, plastic, or we take our own with us. Fair warning, if it is blowing a hooley, we drive up to get them. You can still eat out of the box, though."

"You're on. Er, where's the Indian restaurant?" Audie looked around them. "I'm ready for lunch."

"Follow me. It's after the shop I saw the jumper in."

Audie sighed. "You're just like Mum."

Arietta judged that to be high praise from Audie. Knowing who Mum was, she wasn't sure she agreed.

Chapter Twelve

Either Audie had become used to Peregrine's croak, or she was so tired she slept through it because the following morning Arietta had been up well over two hours before the young girl surfaced. She rushed into the kitchen yawning and apologised.

"Oh gosh, I'm so sorry. I hardly ever sleep in."

"No apology necessary," Arietta assured her. "You must have needed your sleep and it's awful weather. Nothing much to get up for." Arietta pointed to the window. It was almost impossible to see to the end of the garden due to the rain and mist. "A day for staying inside and doing your homework?"

Audie groaned. "Must I? It's only that blooming book review."

"You must." Arietta sympathised but forced herself to be firm. "Get it over and done with, then if the weather is better, tomorrow we'll go to the safari park or on the steamer on the loch. This is the last week before they shut down for winter. Deal?"

"Deal. As long as you help me explain this book is boring and sucks."

"The boring bit, maybe, the sucks bit, maybe not. Unless you can expand on that?"

Audie groaned. "It just…"

"Sucked?"

"Exactly."

"Then think of other words that are more acceptably descriptive and why. What do you want for breakfast?"

* * * *

Fed, watered, washed and dressed, Audie sat down at right angles to Arietta in the study, and nibbled the end of her pencil. "Where do I start?" She gave Arietta a beseeching look. "I'm stuck."

"You haven't started," Arietta pointed out. "Therefore how do you know you're stuck?"

Audie pouted. "You and Dad always manage to do stuff like that."

"Like what?" It intrigued Arietta to see how a young teenager operated. If she thought about it, the last teen she had had a lot to do with, apart from herself, had been her twin. Not a lot of help in the circumstances.

"Make me realise how stupid I sound."

"Ah well, it happens to all of us. Right, I'll start you off. Reread what it says you have to do."

The resigned sigh, hastily suppressed, made Arietta hide a grin. She well remembered the annoyance of homework over the holidays. She didn't say anything, just waited.

Audie read over the printed pages slowly, and if Arietta understood correctly, long-sufferingly. She kept her patience—just. At the end, she tapped Audie on the shoulder.

"Look, love, I don't care whether you want to do this and get it done properly, mess around with it or just not bother and get into trouble. It's up to you. I did say I'll help and I will, but you've got to meet me halfway. If you don't want to, just say so, and I'll get on with my work. Your choice."

Audie went red and for a second Arietta regretted her words. Only for a second. They had to be said or she could be sitting there twiddling her thumbs for who knew how long.

"I'm sorry," Audie said slowly, as if she hated to have to say the words. "I know it's got to be done, I *am* happy you've offered to help. It's just that even the blooming question is boring. I mean, give a reasoned explanation why you did or did not enjoy this book. Give at least three positive and three negative comments and your reasoning for thinking so."

"That's straightforward enough, isn't it?"

"Not when you can't think of three positive things. I mean, what did you think of it when you read it?" Audie asked in an expectant tone. "You did say you'd read it."

"I did, but you're not getting out of it that easily. You first," Arietta said. "Do the negatives first."

Slowly Audie began to explain why she thought the book was boring. Once Arietta started questioning her reasoning, demanding that she expand and at one point arguing—not because she disagreed, she didn't—Audie became enthusiastic. She stated firmly all her grounds on why the book wasn't for her, and was even able to grudgingly find those three needed positives, albeit they were very minor.

At last Arietta nodded. "Well done, you. That in my mind is a very fair, well thought out and constructive critique. Now all you need to do is write or type it up, and voila. Homework done. Unless there's something more you've conveniently forgotten about?"

Audie put her head to one side. "We...ll," she began and burst out laughing. "Oh you should have seen your face. Honestly, there's no more. I did the rest over the weekend, it was only this that had me stuck. But the way you helped me sort out my mind was brilliant."

"Rotter," Arietta said good-naturedly. "You had me worried. Celebration time? How about you choose how we spend the rest of the day?"

"It's stopped raining. Can we walk into the village and I could get some of those mini sticky toffee puddings Dad likes?" Audie asked. "We could have it for afters when Dad comes to get me."

Moss had texted to say he'd get Audie on Thursday night and drop her at her mother's house. Kristin, who was now at home, had insisted they'd be fine for the few hours until Tarquin returned from his work trip. It was, Moss had said, a good all-round answer to everything.

"And if we're celebrating, can we have pizza tonight please?" Audie said in a beseeching tone. "Homemade. Well, homemade as in we buy the bases and make them up ourselves. If you're happy with that?"

"Fine by me, I have mine without cheese anyway," Arietta reminded the young girl.

"Not a pizza then..." Audie squealed and dodged out of the way as Arietta went to tickle her. She'd admitted how ticklish she was, just like Moss. "Okay, okay, a pizza...ish."

"That'll do. Right, let's go before the weather changes its mind again."

* * * *

There was a watery sun as they made their way up the lane, circling round the biggest puddles and at one point jumping over one. Even though it was almost after the midge season, there were still enough of them around in the warm dampness for Arietta to be glad she'd put repellent on and insisted Audie do the same.

After she fished the third beastie out of her mouth, Audie blanched. "How on earth do you cope in the middle of the summer?"

"Go away. Or wear a net and stay indoors when need be."

"I'd do the go away bit," Audie said frankly. "What's the point of living here if you can't go out and enjoy it?" She skirted another puddle and pointed towards the field they were passing. "It's all so gorgeous, I'd want to be able to go and see things. You know what I mean? Not think, oh it's too midgefied today, better stay in and do the ironing."

Arietta laughed at Audie's disgusted expression. "I've wondered that, but then I remember the other seven or eight months of the year and think, yeah, even with snow and ice it's beautiful. Anyway, it's not every summer day we get hit with the little darlings. Or everywhere, especially during the daytime. If you climb a hill, for instance, or it's windy, there should be very few around. It's just the perfect weather for them today. And of course my godmother left me this house, which is everything I want in a home. I love it, so guess it's a no contest. Though on days like this I'll admit, Devon, the Cotswolds or Lanzarote do have a pull."

"Harder for Dad to get to you in the Canaries, though," Audie observed. "It's not exactly nip-able to for a pizza and a pint."

"Very true, and as you see I'm still here. Even when I moan that summer in Scotland is three days in May. It's all part of what makes Scotland the wonderful place it is. Gah, now I sound like a travelogue, or the tourist minister, but honestly days like this are few and far between and the further east you go, the less midges you find. Here endeth my preaching."

Audie giggled. "Preach on, it'll help in my next geography block. We're doing Scotland, and I can now say some very important things about midges." She glanced at Arietta with a very mature and thoughtful expression for someone of her age. "I sort of get what you mean. You find somewhere that's special and know that's where you want to be?"

"Exactly that."

"And sometimes you find someone who you want to be with wherever they are?"

What was she hinting at?

"So people say," Arietta replied in a cheerful insouciant way — she hoped. "Sometimes you *both* give and take and come up with a suitable compromise."

"I get that. We can't be selfish all the time, can we? Do you think you and Dad will get married?" Audie asked as they approached the first house of the village proper. "It's fine by me. As long as I don't have to wear an Alice band thingy."

Ah... "No idea, we're just really getting to know each other. Early days. I like him, I think he likes me, and we'll see how things go."

"Mmm." Audie didn't sound as if she was sure whether to believe Arietta or not. "Arietta, who is that woman waving at you like a ship's sail in a high wind?"

Arietta half turned, saw whom Audie meant and groaned. "Ah shit, oh, sorry, ignore the language."

"Why are you apologising? Mum, Dad and Tarq all cuss, even though Dad tries to tell me it's a sign of a limited vocabulary. At school we make up words so we don't actually swear but we know what we mean if we say custard or tuck it in."

Audie definitely didn't have a limited vocabulary.

"Josephine, the vicar's wife. Do *not* tell her anything," Arietta said fiercely. "She's the biggest gossip this side of the Irish Sea. I think you better be the daughter of an old friend come for a few days while...oh, I don't know, we'll think on our feet if need be." She swung around as the newcomer shouted "cooeee" over and over.

"Oh, Arietta, who is this?" Her eyes lit up. Probably with the thought of gossip.

"Hello, Josephine," she said, resigned to an interrogation. "How are you? How's the family? Is Dorothea still in Glasgow? Can Maynard make proper coffee yet?" That was naughty. However, Arietta decided, unrepentant, it would show her inquisitiveness could work both ways. She waited.

"Doing as well as could be expected," Josephine said in a stiff voice. She stared at Audie. "You remind me of someone, dear. Do I know you?"

Before Arietta had a chance to say anything Audie grinned. "Ohh really? I hope it's someone rich or famous. A pop star? Or a film star? Then I can say well, my mum or dad are rich singers or actors and away for work. So I'm here annoying Arietta." She spoke in the sort of voice that made anyone listening sure she was having them on. "Though, if that's too far-fetched, how about I say my dad was a dustman and mum a stay-at-homer? Or Mum is a perpetual student and Dad a government assassin?"

Arietta bent her head, got a tissue out of her pocket to ostensibly blow her nose but in reality to hide behind.

Josephine tutted. "Telling stories is not the thing to do, dear. People might get the wrong idea."

"Really?" Audie opened her eyes wide. She let out a big sigh. "What should I choose then?"

"The truth, every time."

"But it's not really…" Arietta kicked Audie.

"Very interesting," Arietta finished for her, even though she was fairly certain that hadn't been what Audie was about to say. "The daughter of a friend and we're off to get something nice for dinner. Must dash." She grabbed Audie's arm and walked briskly away, leaving Josephine staring after them.

"Oh shooterooney, I'm sorry," Audie said as soon as they were out of hearing distance. "But honestly, what is she like?"

"Bored, lonely, upset, frustrated…" Maybe she shouldn't have added that. She'd got the frustrated bit from Maggie, who had overheard Josephine telling someone the vicar had better things to concentrate on than carnality. "We all have worries. Josephine seems to have more than most at the moment. Her husband is a busy bloke and she has time on her hands. She should get a job and not just float around." *Sticking her nose in where it's not wanted.* "Josephine thinks she's showing good parish interest and that she's around to be helpful, but in most cases it's exactly the opposite. She's too…"

"Intense?" Audie said. "We discussed that at school just before half term and I think it fits her perfectly. She must be awfully disappointed at times."

"You got it. I feel sorry for her. She doesn't even work in the charity shop anymore because she says she might be needed elsewhere." Arietta was about to add she'd heard it was more that her attitude put people off shopping there but thought better of it. Audie was only a teenager and didn't need to hear things like that. After all, it was also gossip, and incredibly catty gossip at that.

"That's sad, but I guess she's the only one who can sort it," Audie said as they arrived at the tiny village bakery. "A bit like my godmother used to be. Aunty Gail. She lived in a flat in London cos she said she loved the, hold on, let me quote, 'vibe and buzz and immediacy of it all'. That doesn't make sense to me, but what do I know? Mum insisted Auntie Gail was lonely and to justify her lifestyle she, and I'm quoting again, 'did things, often not relevant to herself'. That doesn't make sense either."

Arietta could subscribe to that.

"Then she met Marcello," Audie said. "Ended up as a merchant seaman captain's wife and goes around the world with him. I get postcards from some amazing places. She said she had to take a leap and she did and landed safely. I'm going to do that."

"Good for you." Arietta was impressed at the common sense Audie showed. "Sticky toffee pud?" She opened the door and they went inside.

Ten minutes later, they exited with three of the puddings, a very sickly-looking coffee, chocolate and cherry cake that Audie almost drooled over, and some more mundane but in Arietta's opinion equally as delicious, if not more so, coconut macaroons. Those had been Audie's gift to her and she was bowled over by the way Audie had asked if she could buy them for her hostess as a present, and insisted it was her own money, not her dad's.

After that Arietta had no intention of refusing. It was thoughtful and a lovely gesture. A bag of bread flour, yeast and some of Nettie's homemade jam had also gone into the bag.

"Ohh, it looks lovely," Audie said and Arietta laughed.

"Audie, my love, you've got hollow legs."

Nettie had stared at Audie then Arietta intently, but hadn't made any comment as she totalled up their purchases, except to wish them a lovely day. The only other person in the shop, a stranger, was busy on her phone as she glanced at them then turned away.

Arietta wondered about that look — had Josephine been gossiping? More than likely, but unlike Josephine, Nettie was the sort of person to keep her own council. She hoped.

"It's just as well we've got two backpacks, isn't it?" Audie said as after a quick foray into the paper shop and a bag of jelly babies later they began to walk back down the lane. "Cos seriously, there's a lot of weight here." She did a pretend stagger. "Argh... I'll be half a foot smaller and —"

"Better not eat any of that cake then or you'll also be half a stone heavier," Arietta said. "I'll have to eat it all myself." She didn't say she probably wouldn't eat any of it. She might have a sweet tooth, but not that sweet.

"I'll need some to keep my strength up," Audie said. "And I've run out of carrot sticks till I cut some more. Oh fish, here's that Josephine woman again."

"This time don't get carried away," Arietta warned her. "She might be daft but she's not stupid."

"Sorry." Audie sounded contrite. "I'll be good."

Josephine evidently hadn't sought them out. She crossed their path and, apart from one deep searching glance in Audie's direction, did no more than nod and speak briefly. "I've got to dash, the vicar will be waiting for his cup of tea and currant bun. It's his evening for parishioners to come and talk to him."

Arietta almost said enjoy, before she realised how inappropriate that was as an answer. She murmured something that could have been 'mustn't keep you', and smiled. "Busy man, the village is lucky to have him."

Josephine preened and nodded. "We all are." She bustled off.

Arietta watched her go. "I must stop getting so annoyed with her. She means well."

"She made me feel like an insect under a microscope," Audie said and shuddered. "It wasn't nice."

"No, I bet not. Sorry. Let's hope we don't bump into her again. I'll give her what for if she does it next time. Nudge me if you get that feeling again." Arietta hoped there wouldn't be a next time.

"Will do. Hey." Audie grabbed Arietta's arm. "I'm getting paranoid. There's that woman from the shop stopping Josephine and asking her something. She's got her phone out again. Do you think she's a super sleuth? Jewel thief doing a stakeout in the pub or renting a hideaway?"

"Probably thinks our lane is the way to town and got lost."

"Could be. Oh, she's going away now and Josephine's gone as well. Not with her. At least she's not come in our direction."

"Thank goodness, now let's get ourselves back and argue over what film to watch and decide how early we want to head off in the morning." Audie only had one more full day with her and Arietta intended to take her to the safari park as promised. With luck Josephine wouldn't be around.

* * * *

She wasn't, and Arietta and Audie spent several happy hours touring the safari park then walking around the pedestrian areas, watching the various animals as they enjoyed their large living quarters.

"Though I'd still love to see them in their proper place," Audie said as with an ice cream each they made their tired way back to the car. "This is the next best thing and it is making sure they don't die out, isn't it? Dad says he'll take me on a safari when I'm a bit older. Mum says she'll take me on a cruise and I can learn to snorkel. I like the sound of the snorkelling but not so much the cruise. I mean, what do you really see but the sea?"

"The places you stop off in?"

"Maybe, but I bet they'll all see the harbour, go to one busy beach, be expected to talk to people you don't really want to, and it'll probably be a ship full of oldies." She giggled. "That's what Dad would tell me is a first-world problem, and I should be grateful I get the chance to do everything I do. I am, but I'm more grateful for some of them than I am for others. Yeah, I know I'm spoiled."

It sounded as if Audie had it all thought out.

"I'm sure cruises aren't like that," Arietta said diplomatically. "You'll probably enjoy it."

"Hmm." Audie didn't sound convinced. "Have you been on one?

"Well, no," Arietta confessed. It sounded like her own personal version of hell. She was no fan of crowds and forced conversation. "But then, I'm generally a loner."

"till you met Dad?"

"You've got me there. Okay, until I met your dad. So head home, have a wash and go into the village in time for the chip van?"

"Oh yeah. High five." Audie held her hand up and they slapped palms in the ritual. "Looking forward to it. Can we eat it as we walk?"

"As long as you're not too tired."

"Walk for fish and chips? I'd never be too tired. Well, unless it was miles, then I'd walk there maybe, and ask for an Uber home."

"No Ubers around here."

"Probably as well the chippie isn't far then."

Arietta shook her head in amusement. "Just like your dad, got an answer for everything."

Audie skipped to the car. "I try."

* * * *

"These are delicious," Audie mumbled through a mouthful of hot but not greasy chips. "You know it was weird, up at the van in the queue? I'm sure everyone was staring at me as if I was a performing seal."

"A what?" Arietta said, amused at how Audie really did have some interesting thoughts.

"Well, you know what I mean. I thought I ought to do a magic trick and take a bow or pass my hat round and ask for 'change, missus, any old change'. Then Josephine was strange. She went red and rushed away without picking up *her* change when she saw us. Don't you wonder why?"

Arietta did. She'd noticed that as well. "Probably just a bit ashamed of herself. She's like all of us and hates to be in the wrong for any reason. I bet she realised how she sounded the other day. Don't worry about her."

That was easier said than done. Audie had nodded and began to talk about going back to school and the end of term play. Which she was adamant she wouldn't appear in. "I want to direct, not be told what to do."

Arietta laughed and told her why not and the subject was forgotten. However, as she got ready for bed, she found herself worrying about Josephine's attitude once more. Moss hadn't been able to ring, which was something he'd warned them about earlier. They were filming late and as he was getting, as he put it, time off for good behaviour to pick Audie up, he wasn't going to complain. A short and to the point text to Audie just said, "All on schedule behave yourselves".

To Arietta it was even briefer.

Love you x

She'd sent 'sleep tight when you get a chance', thought about it and added, 'PS love you too'.

She hoped she could do as she'd asked of him and get some sleep.

* * * *

The noise of someone hammering on her front door, her mobile doing the muted buzz it did when the sound was switched off and she had a call, plus her land line ringing, combined with Audie shaking her, woke Arietta up with a start. From a dream about doing a double ride on a zip wire with Josephine, who was threatening to get off halfway because she wanted a kebab and a man on a pedal boat beneath them was waving one in the air.

"Waaa?" she said groggily, half her brain still full of the zip wire dream. She could swear she could taste the kebab. "Where's the fire?" She sniffed. No scent of smoke hit her nostrils, which was one good thing. Arietta relaxed a couple of muscles she hadn't realised she'd tensed. "What the hell's going on? End of the world?" She had a terrible thought, and no idea why it was the first thing that properly hit her. "Your dad? Is he okay?"

"Hopping mad but unharmed," Audie said gloomily. "Can't say that for us, though."

Arietta did her best to unscramble her brain. "Say it slowly and in words of one syllable. I'm not all with it yet. Why is your dad okay but we aren't?"

"Someone knows who I am, or rather they've guessed it part wrongly and it's all over the papers that you're my mum and Dad is my dad and he didn't know he had a love child and where on earth they think I've been hiding is beyond me." She gulped and took a breath. "It's got everyone's knickers in a twist according to my mum, who says there's no need for them to be and some people need to keep their noses out of what after all has nothing to do with them."

Arietta held her hand in the air. "Slow down, I'm still having trouble following you. I'm supposed to be your mum? And you've just appeared like a genie out of a bottle?" Was she still asleep and this was the follow-on dream? *Please don't let Josephine pop out from behind the loo door.* "How did we manage that?"

"No idea, and it seems so, though not the genie bit."

Thank goodness Audie had no problem following her befuddled thoughts. Arietta sat upright. "Ah, okay." Which was another stupid thing to say as it obviously wasn't okay, anything but. "Stolen by the kelpies? Scrub that. It's daft. I'm not with it yet."

Audie smiled. "Thank goodness! I mean not that you're shattered, but that you understand your words are crazy. Kelpies is a bit too far-fetched, even for this. Mind you, now I wonder if I've been living on a farm in Australia or with foster wolves in a cave somewhere?"

In spite of the seriousness of the situation, Arietta's lips twitched. "And just teleported here on a whim?"

"Who knows? Someone is quoted as saying 'we all reckoned she', I guess they mean you, 'had secrets but not that one was like this!' Barstewards. Dad is fuming, on your and mum's behalf, and worried for me. Mum thinks it's funny that no one has cottoned on who I really am before or, well, not really now either, and Tarq is threatening to sue anyone he can think of who's got anything to do with this, except Mum and me. Weirdly he says the jury is out on Dad, because Dad says it's got to be some wally and does Tarquin have any idea who, so now Dad is ready to punch Tarq. Who wouldn't have a clue how to defend himself. Sadly then, Mum admitted Grandma and Gramps said you did it and now Dad wants to give *them* what for, but hey ho…" She shrugged and made a funny face. "Goodness knows who is who, on where, or what they want. Here's a cup of coffee. I made it, so no guarantee what it'll taste like, but at least it's hot."

Arietta did her best to be fully awake, concentrate and understand what Audie was saying. "Stitched up?"

"Seems so. What shall we do about it? Who do we kill? I mean metaphorically," Audie added hastily. "I'm anti-violence in real life."

I thought I was. I'm not so sure now.

"Me, honey, not you. You need to keep out of it." Arietta took a sip of coffee, pulled the landline out of the socket and sighed in relief as one of the persistent noises was silenced. "Hot and good, thank you."

"Stay out of it? Not in a million years," Audie said indignantly. "It's me as well they're talking about and it's not fair on you or Mum or Dad or Tarq for that matter. I'm gonna wave the flags and man the barricades." She started to sing *Do You Hear the People Sing* from the musical *Les Miserable* in a very tuneful voice. "Dad says he'll be here around ten and he'll come in the back way. There's people out the front, probably reporters, and did you know your mobile is still going crazy?" She sounded as if she didn't know whether to be alarmed or excited at all the commotion. "Totally crazy."

Arietta nodded. "Let it, that's why I've not put the ringtones back on. It can vibrate away and we can ignore it." Unless it was Moss. She'd check the names before she did anything.

"I've had three of my mates from school text and ask if it's me cos there's a reward for my name and so on from one of the pap rags," Audie said. "I said I wish, so hope they'll leave it for now. Mum and Tarquin are staying out of it at the moment, but as Mum says, once people get hold of a clear pic of me, it'll all be out and the poo will pile on the fan. Do you mind? I mean, you've been dropped into something that's not your fault. Will it really be all right for you?"

Audie sounded about ready to break into tears. Arietta hurried to reassure her. She got out of bed and pulled Audie into a bear hug. "I'm flattered, to be honest. If I ever have a child, I hope it's a girl as nice as you. Even if you do eat all the carrots." It had become a standing joke that every carrot in the veg box became carrot sticks within minutes. Audie ate them like other teens might eat chocolate.

"They make your hair curly and help you see in the dark." Audie tugged on her straight-as-a-die hair and crossed her eyes. "I think someone had that wrong or I'm the whoosit to challenge the saying."

Arietta grinned in spite of the seriousness of the situation. "Definitely got it wrong. It's my least favourite veg after fennel, and I straighten my hair. If I left it to do its own thing, it would be a mass of unmanageable curls. I'd swap with you, even if it means eating carrots. But I daren't risk it." She looked at her bedside clock and groaned. "What time did you say your dad would be here?"

Audie glanced at her watch and yelped. "Ten minutes. I'll go and unlock the back door, shall I? And not open the curtains. Or answer to some persistent twit trying to call through the letterbox and not knowing he's actually shouting into a real wooden box. Er, if I unlock the door, what if one of them gets in? Maybe I'll stand behind it ready to do a quick open and shut around Dad?"

"Good idea, I'll get up." *And get ready to do battle. How dare any of them think this is my doing?*

By the time she'd had the shortest wash on record — no time for a shower — pulled on clean jeans, a newish and smartish blouse, and brushed her hair, seven of those ten minutes had gone. She spent another one and a half putting on mascara and eyeliner and a speedy colour on her lips before she did a quick check over in the mirror. It was as well she did because when she studied herself, she realised she'd only got one earring in, and remembered she'd taken the other one out in the middle of the night as the wire had been digging in. It returned to her ear in record time and she decided she was as ready as she could be. If she was heading into battle she was going in wearing full war paint and with all guns blazing. Whatever that meant.

She headed downstairs and ignored the rattle of the letterbox and the thumping on the door. As it was Scotland, where there was no law of trespass, she couldn't call the police on that account, but maybe she could say she was being harassed? And that there was a young, frightened child in the house? One glance at Audie's face scotched that idea. She'd obviously decided to come down on the side of excitement.

Or maybe I'll be arsy and see what Moss is going to do about it — or not. Why the hell didn't I unlock the back gate? Hold on, he's got a key.

"Dad's just texted. He's on his bike and going to be a courier if anyone asks who he is. He'll come up the lane at the back and through the garage. I suggested he drive straight down the front lane, rev up and pretending to run them over, but he said he'd get fired if he did that and got found out. Pity really cos one of them has a voice like a foghorn. Or he's got a foghorn, I dunno which. I bet it means he's a tiny wimp with a tiny — "

"Audie B-T or whatever name you use, how old are you really?" Arietta broke in before Audie said exactly what she meant.

Audie sniggered. "I was going to say tiny mind… I'm thirteen and a bit and I use B-T cos it's easier to have the same name as Mum. Or I did do. When she marries Tarquin I'm not going to swap to Smith. If I changed to anything it would be to Dad's, but that would upset Gran and Grandpa and as Dad says, why do it? I know he's my dad and so does he."

So does half the world now.

"I think that's Dad now." Audie was peering through the tiniest gap in the curtains. "No one's realised there's a back way in yet, have they?"

"Hopefully not. It's rarely used by anyone, except Thomas when he wants to dodge people." More than once he'd been glad of that getaway. Some of the locals could be persistent in asking for autographs or photos. If it were bad for her twin, what on earth would it be like for Moss?

"And now Dad."

"And now your dad."

Arietta joined Audie at her peephole as a helmet-clad figure wheeled a well-known motorbike inside the garage and a few minutes later headed to the house. Audie flung the door open, and Moss — if it was Moss, it wasn't easy to tell with most of him covered — moved swiftly inside the cottage and shut and locked the door behind him.

Chapter Thirteen

He took his helmet off, put it on the nearest work surface, dropped a tatty rucksack on the floor by his feet and hugged his daughter, all without looking at Arietta.

Doghouse again? I must get new carpets. The ones here play havoc with your knees. And a fridge… It needs a fridge.

"Earth to Arietta… You with us?" Audie gave her a peculiar look. Sympathetic and pleading at the same time.

"Sorry," Arietta apologised. "I was miles away. What did you say?"

"*I* said why the hell did I not threaten them with God knows what?" Moss said in a flat, angry voice. "How dare they? I am so, so, sorry, love, but seriously, they need to grow up and be sensible. Are you holding up? Can we sue them?"

"If you explain what they say I'm supposed to have done," Arietta said in a soothing voice, "perhaps I can help you."

"You know what the hell I'm talking about. The bloody B-T's. Sorry, Audie, but I'm off your grandparents big-time at the moment. They automatically think it has to have been Arietta because you're here and being taken advantage of. I told them in that case they could come and get you, Audie, and sod their bridge and trip to Bruges. And I added for good measure, Arietta would never do such an unfair and unfriendly thing to a young and vulnerable child."

"Dad, I told you," Audie said angrily, "I'm not vulnerable. That means in need of special care due to disability or age or that I'm at risk of neglect. Come *on*, do you honestly look at me and think that? No, I thought not," Audie answered her own question. "You're right on one thing, though—Arietta would never do anything like that But a nosy co…woman in the village said I reminded her of someone, and she'd seen you around before. Put two and two together and made whatever it is you make when you get half the answer correct. And well, I did sort of give her a stupid answer when she was going on at me. I told her if she wanted I could pretend I had a dad who was someone famous, or a dustman or anyone really. I hinted at my vivid imagination. I know it was daft but seriously she wasn't at all nice to Arietta and it annoyed me. The woman wasn't best pleased."

Moss dropped into the nearest chair and put his head in his hands. "Shit. Who?"

"In theory there could be more than one person," Arietta said. "In practice I'm not so sure. But—"

"Hold on," Audie said excitedly. "According to my phone news app, which I've just remembered and gone onto, whoever was their source was 'a good friend of Arietta's'." She looked from one adult to the other. "As you both know and therefore so do I, Arietta wouldn't have that sort of friends. Now do we play sleuthing?"

"No need. I have a good idea who it is. I tell you she never was and never will be a good friend," Arietta said explosively. "Because I bet it's sodding Josephine. I'll have her guts for garters."

"Stand in line," Moss said. "I want first dibs. I'll blue alien her all right. Long story," he said to Audie, who looked expectant. "Another time. Any coffee going?"

Audie nodded. "I made it today. It's more than likely cold, but Arietta said it tastes okay."

"More than okay," Arietta said. "Lifesaver."

"Shove it in the microwave, love," Moss said. "Forty seconds will do. Just what's needed. Hold on, I forgot, I've a stash of newspapers with me. Had to go incognito to several different places to buy them, so as not to appear screwy. Some rags, some not." He unzipped the top of the rucksack he'd left untouched on the floor and took out a wad of newspapers. "Shall we do some sleuthing and then have a phone conference on what to do next? I've a feeling I saw a quote somewhere that might help us. Kristin and Tarquin say it's up to me and the unknown you." He put the papers onto the kitchen table. "I can't believe they haven't twigged that Arietta here, who they now know is the Arietta I'm taking to their wedding, is the Arietta they were at uni with and all the rest."

Arietta went hot, cold and hot again as he winked to show he had no intention of divulging more of the past acquaintance. *Thank goodness. After all, they may have improved.* Or more than likely didn't show the side of them she knew to Audie.

"That's because they were convinced I was a Harriet and I never bothered to correct them. I wore glasses instead of contacts then and my hair was my natural corkscrew curls, not straightened. About as different as I look now as you can get. Plus, let's face it, it's a long while ago and you don't half change over that many years." She chose not to add that she'd been a stone heavier as well, never mentioned her brother and was a lot more of an introvert. If that were possible.

"I didn't tell them, like you said not to, Dad. I think it'll be great for them to discover they know Arietta when they see her. I bet they'll laugh."

Arietta wasn't so certain, but she was human enough to look forward to relishing the expressions on their faces when they did find out. If, of course, they recognised her these days. Which brought her up with a start.

Recognition.

"You know," she said slowly. "I've been thinking about it. If it *was* Josephine, she won't have done it maliciously. More likely just wanting to feel important. It would be typical of her to do the bull in a china shop approach and not ask me first. She'll have a friend of a friend who knows someone who would jump at something like this. Sure to."

"She wouldn't check because she knows you'd tell her to take a hike," Moss said. "To mind her own business."

That was true.

"I've thought of something else as well," Audie said suddenly. "Remember that woman in the cake shop who gave us a funny look? Not the owner, but the customer."

Arietta nodded. "Yeah, she did, didn't she? No idea who she was, I'd never seen her before."

"It was as if she was weighing us up." Audie went and stood next to Arietta. "Do we really look similar in any way, Dad?"

He grinned. "You're both female."

"Daaad," Audie said indignantly. "You know what I mean." She looked at Audie and rolled her eyes as she gave a long-suffering sigh. "Men. Honestly. What are they like? Now, Dad, give it serious thought."

Arietta laughed as Moss winked.

"Yeah, sorry, love," he said. "Let me think. Sort of but not a lot. I guess it's the shape of your faces—both very similar and you both have a dimple when you grin. Grey eyes, but that's like me and your mum and three percent of the population. Rare-ish, but I wouldn't see that as a positive connection between the two of you. After that... Nope. But people can put any slant on any little thing if that's what they feel like doing. I could say, oh you're both left-handed or you both like fish and chips but that means blooming nothing. I think whoever it is decided for some reason there was a connection and liked the idea this was it, did a bit of digging, and added two and two together and only got half the answer."

"Recognised you, saw me with you. Saw Audie with me and drew the lines?" Arietta said. "Sounds feasible, but who? We know it's not Maggie, her and Doug wouldn't do that, they'd be more likely to say Audie was a relation of theirs and her parents were abroad and I'd come to the rescue cos Doug has flu or something."

"Has he?" Moss asked. "Poor bloke."

"I have no idea, but you get my gist?"

Moss nodded. "So... I reckon it's like you said. Which doesn't help us much."

He was silent for several minutes.

Someone else hammered on the front door, then there was a soft knock on the back.

"Open sezme. Gimmeabreak." That came from outside the back door, not the front.

"Thomas," Arietta said. "Our childhood password." She went to the door and opened it slightly. Thomas almost fell through the narrow gap. He stumbled, righted himself and rocked on his heels.

"Sheesh, you two—three—what have you done now? Mum and Dad were on the phone to me at silly o'clock saying they would do whatever you want or need and asking if I was on my way. Which half an hour later I was. Audie, my lovely, you look as if you've grown a foot from the photo Dad showed me the other week. In height, not in body extremities. I came to get love and hugs and I end up almost being mowed down by a bloke on a moped and a four-by-four with what looked like three goons in it. Josephine Whoosit saw me and almost ran in the wrong direction and Maggie waved me down to warn me to come in the back way. She says you ring her if you need them for anything, and Doug has his spade ready if Moss wants him to help bury the body." He shoved three cups and a plate to one side, perched on the work surface and winked at Audie, who had gone pale. "Joke, love. It means they're hopping mad and want to help when and if they can. So, spill the beans. Talking of which, got anything to eat?"

Arietta hugged him. "I was about to start on breakfast. Moss will fill you in."

"Not literally, I hope," Thomas said. "I need sustenance, not duffing up. Unless it's plum duff and not up the—"

Arietta coughed and glanced at Audie, who was listening to the exchange with avid interest.

"Yeah, well, eggs and bacon would be good. With mushrooms and tomatoes and black pudding. Or haggis? That would be ace."

Arietta opened the fridge door. "If you and Moss clear the table and the work surface, maybe. But I need space."

"Front room?" Thomas took the coffee cup Audie gave him with a smile of thanks. "Out of your way."

"Don't you dare. Audie and I want to know what you're plotting, and if we're cooking we're listening as well, or no food," Arietta warned. "Set the table and start thinking about what we need to do."

* * * *

A couple of hours—and a phone call with Kristin and Tarquin—later, they'd fleshed out a story to put out if need be. It had gone quiet outside and Thomas, who had slid out of the back door, walked via the fields to the village and back down the lane, reported no one still hanging around at the cottage but a few nosy bods in the village, mainly in the pub.

"I went into the bakery and Nettie was all a-goggle. She asked if you'd sent for me. I asked why and she said well, now the news about your daughter was out. I did the 'you what' thing and said what daughter. She tried to say it was obvious and I was, ohhh, you mean our mate's child? I wish, she's gorgeous, but sadly not ours. Then she said a weird thing. That a woman had been in the shop and said she was certain she knew you but hadn't realised your daughter was so tall. What was her name because she'd forgotten. Nettie said she'd heard you call her Audie."

"Shit, sorry. Shoot," Arietta amended hastily. "When we were in there I told Audie she had hollow legs."

"And that woman customer heard and she was busy with her phone," Audie said. "And she spoke to Josephine as well."

"Camera maybe?" Thomas said.

Moss nodded. "More than likely."

Arietta dished up the food and slid onto the bench next to Moss. He took one look at her and pulled her close for a hug. "All right, love? We'll sort it, I promise. We can always ask Thom to do something outrageous and he can be the next news. This is probably because it was a quiet news day."

She sighed. "I know, but it is so not fair."

"Not raining," Moss said with a grin. "It's not bothered Audie. Kristin and Tarquin know it's not you and Kristin's mum and dad can go take a hike. I've set my agent's brother onto tracking down who said what, why and when — he's good at things like that — and Kristin and I are going to do a joint statement." That had been decided a few minutes earlier. "All will be well. Life will go back to normal. Talking of which, have you looked at your phone yet?"

Arietta shook her head. "Nope."

"Want me to do it for you?"

"Please. It's in the bedroom."

"Once we've eaten then."

* * * *

He was as good as his word and once he'd scrolled through all the texts and messages, Moss leant back in his chair and accepted his fourth cup of coffee. This one made by Arietta while Thomas and Audie washed up and argued amicably over who could bake a better Victoria sponge. Arietta waved them towards the pantry. "Go and find out." She was grateful to Thomas, who seemed to have accepted his job was to entertain Audie for a short while.

"Well?" she asked as Moss put her phone down. "What's there?"

"Not a lot really, and only a few interesting ones. Josephine saying she didn't mean to and what should she do? Maggie reiterating they're here if need be and one from someone called Maisie Day who is a reporter for a Sunday supplement asking if you'd like to tell her about your love child."

"I bet that's who we saw then."

Moss nodded and handed his phone over. "I Googled her."

Arietta stared at the recently seen face. "That's her, the bastard. How dare she?"

"Very easily it seems, but you got the last laugh. We've given the so-called story to a rival paper. One of Kristin's mates works on it. Poetic justice."

* * * *

If only it could be that easy, Arietta thought as she drove towards the station to catch her train to the meeting with her agent. Moss and Audie had waited until it got dark, used the back lane and driven off in Thomas' car, Moss admitting he'd set off on the bike without thinking about the logistics of him and Audie leaving. Thomas had spent the night in the spare bed and bagged a lift to the station from where, he'd said, he'd head to Perth, which was where Moss and he had arranged to meet. He to get his car back and Moss to head back to work, using, as Thomas said enviously, a car and driver provided for him.

Arietta didn't mention that Moss had slipped into her bed in the wee small hours. He had started the night on an airbed which, he assured Arietta, had gone flat. Therefore it was imperative he had a cuddle and a kiss. He'd left a couple of hours later after a bit more than a cuddle and a kiss. Not how she'd expected her love life to resume, but oh boy it had been worth it. Even the shushes, muffled giggles and muted shouts due to the close proximity of the other overnight visitors. She was exhausted, which could account for her frequent yawns.

The big reveal was due to be on Sunday and already the paper was full of hints and innuendos. Audie didn't seem fazed by it all, just saying she had great parents and didn't care who knew it. The interest in Arietta and their whereabouts appeared to have died down and the lane was back to normal with the only other occupants a few cats, one fox and several kamikaze pheasants bent on self-destruction.

"It's not," Moss said, "as if we'd deliberately kept this big dark secret. There never seemed a reason to shout about it. We all did what we thought was right."

Which was fair enough, but somehow Arietta had to sort out certain inquisitive people and remind them what damage they could have done. She wasn't sure if she was happy about that or not.

She forgot about it while she found somewhere to park, and forgot about it all over again later as Betty, her agent, greeted her with "Good news or even better news first?"

"Hit me with it all."

"Good news, the last manuscript is great and will be out next year. Even better news, I've been approached by Antigone Productions. They want *The Dogs of the River* as a film and they want Moss Kirby to play Baraquin. How about that?"

Arietta sat down with a thump. "Say again. Moss Kirby as Baraquin?" She hadn't really fleshed the story out yet, but she had used a certain someone's image as her protagonist.

Betty nodded. "Why? Don't you think he'll fit?"

"Oh I'm sure he will. Does he know?"

"He should now. They said they'd tell him and we could all meet up for a late lunch. He had a prior morning engagement."

Yeah, swapping cars and so on.

Arietta schooled her face into appreciation. "Sounds good. I wish I'd dressed up now."

"You'd look good in a sack, but that blue colour suits you. So are you happy?"

"Very," Arietta assured her. "Thank you." She thought for a second. "You do know I know Moss, don't you? You must have seen all the crap in the papers?"

"That *is* you?"

Arietta nodded. "Me, but not my daughter. Though she is Moss'." She and Moss had decided she'd better tell the truth wherever possible, but not offer any information otherwise.

"Then I saw a lot of half-truths, untruths and maybe smidgeons of truth," Betty said. "Along with what I assume was a good dollop of fairy tales and wishful thinking. Yes?"

"Very much so, yes."

Betty inclined her head and began to discuss what she thought Arietta needed to do over the next few months. As she could be as passionate about research as Arietta, they were mainly in accord. Arietta made copious notes in her own peculiar version of shorthand, ready to type up as soon as she could. Several times people had suggested she type them on her phone or iPad, but she had a terrible habit of pressing the wrong letters and finding it even harder to decipher the type than with her pencil notes. If she was alone, she could dictate herself a message, but after one embarrassing incident when the village policeman had caught her appearing to talk to herself about where a body could be, she was very careful as and when she did that. Or pretended she was on a phone call. But no mentioning bodies or graves.

"That's enough." Betty closed down her laptop. "Time for lunch. I'll just add some slap." Betty, an energetic fifty-something, was, as she cheerfully confessed, addicted to flame-red lipstick and Louboutin shoes. Along with her oversized handbags and raucous laugh, she enjoyed life and was never afraid to admit it. Arietta loved her and often said she was as near a mum as anyone who wasn't your relative could be.

"You and your lipstick. What would you do if they discontinued it?"

"They almost did, once." Betty carefully outlined her lips before she continued. "I was about to get a petition up or chain myself to their head office door when some celeb did a thing in the paper about it and it was saved. Anyway, I have a stash in my bedside table. Just in case." She clicked the lid on. "You ready?"

Arietta put her own lipstick back in her somewhat smaller handbag. "Just need to pop to the loo and then yep."

"Then on you go after which, we can go. To lunch, not to the loo."

* * * *

"What else do you know about Moss Kirby?" Betty asked as they walked the few hundred yards to Betty's favourite lunchtime venue. "I meant to check him out but didn't have time. This was all arranged in a hurry."

Which could have been why Moss hadn't mentioned the meeting when he'd left her earlier. Mind you, if she were honest, he'd dashed, she'd not been fully awake and their parting had been very short and extremely sweet. Her body tingled as she thought about it.

"I thought he was filming up north at the moment. There was a bit in the papers that a lot of the plot was high-tech, very physical and under wraps, all of which he told me as well."

"And that he appears to have a love child and no one knows who with except the woman looks like you, and you've told me it isn't but not whose child she is."

"I wondered when you'd mention that," Arietta said, resigned to the fact she'd need to be a bit more open. "It was going to be my info once we'd done with work. I do know him, we're more than friends—I think—and she really *isn't* my daughter. It's a long story, and one I'm not telling in a restaurant or anywhere we can be overheard. Audie spent a few days with me while her mum was in hospital and we were seen together by some nosy reporter. She was in the village, by chance I think, but I'm not certain, saw us and came to an incorrect conclusion. That's it in a nutshell. The truth will be out on Sunday in a rival paper so that should be interesting." *Thank goodness not all the truth. I'd rather my early acquaintance with them both be lost in the mists of time, and I bet they would as well* and *how Moss and Kristin were together.* That as much for Audie's sake as anyone else's.

"You can fill me in with the missing links later then," Betty said as they reached the restaurant. "Did you know he'd be here?"

"He never mentioned it."

"Probably not had a chance. Like I said, it's a rushed meeting fitted in, I was told, between an early morning call and a night shoot or something. I'm a bit hazy how it all works."

"So am I," Arietta confessed as Betty pushed open the door and was greeted with a beaming smile and a vigorous handshake by the maître d'. He was more restrained with Arietta before he escorted them to a round table at one side of the room.

"Your guests have not yet arrived," he informed them in such a manner that Arietta fought to keep her face expressionless. "I will bring them over immediately when they do."

"Well if they were here, would they be hiding under the table?" Betty muttered once the man was out of earshot. "Harold is lovely, I've known him for years, but boy does he have a habit of stating the obvious." She put her handbag under the table and wriggled in the well-upholstered chair. "A wee fizz?"

"I drove to the station but if need be I guess I could leave my car there. Yes, please."

"By the time you get back, one glass of fizz should have worn off," Betty said. "This is definitely time to celebrate."

"In that case, why not?"

"One for me as well, please." Moss stood next to the table and, seemingly oblivious to anyone around, bent down and kissed Arietta long and thoroughly.

She savoured it and blushed as Moss straightened and Betty fanned herself.

"It's as well you two *do* know each other," Betty said. "I never get a welcome like that from a tall, dark handsome man."

Arietta composed herself with difficulty. "That's because Davey is tall, blond and handsome."

"Was," Betty corrected her. "My lovely husband is now tall, *bald* and handsome."

Moss hooted as another man, neither tall, dark, bald or handsome, but with a homely face and mousey brown hair joined them.

"Sorry," the man apologised. "Phone call. You've got three hours, Moss, so let's get cracking." He kissed Betty on the cheek and turned to Arietta. "Dan Colby. And this is—"

"She knows me," Moss said with a grin. "The alleged mother of my child. Which she isn't. She's a good friend who was helping us and got hauled into the rubbish that's been going on. Arietta, meet Dan, who is my conscience, damn him."

Dan chuckled. "Someone has to keep you on the straight and narrow, though if Arietta wants to do it, she's welcome."

"No, thanks," Arietta said hastily. "I'm busy. Anyway, I lo…like him as he is."

Moss kissed her again before he sat down in the empty chair to her right. "Just as well. Okay so, food and chat, then I'll need to hie back to the set." He squeezed Arietta's knee under the table. "I begged and managed to carve these few hours out but we're busy-busy. Getting close to the end and tempers are short."

"Worth it, though?" Dan said.

"Hope so," Moss replied. "Except it keeps me away from my lady. I'm savouring the thought of some us time."

Arietta mentally nodded. She loved the sound of that. Now all they needed to do was to try to arrange their schedules so they actually were both free at the same time.

Not much to ask…was it?

She tried to kid herself that she believed it, but if she were honest she wasn't that hopeful. She'd seen Moss' diary, and apart from the wedding weekend, it seemed almost every day had something happening.

Oh the joys.

Betty coughed and Arietta came out of her somewhat depressing reverie and concentrated on the matters in hand.

* * * *

Moss had dashed off with an apology, Dan had left soon after, and Arietta spent another hour with Betty then headed for a swift foray around the shops before she headed to the railway station. After her one glass of fizz, she'd stuck to sparkling water, and was satisfied she would be well below the limit and able to drive home. It had been no hardship, as she'd wanted to concentrate on what was said and what was intimated.

Betty had promised to let her know once a satisfactory deal was concluded, and when she'd have to sign on the dotted line.

She perused a rail of dresses, found one that shouted, 'buy me', and realised it was twenty percent off. That went into a basket along with a scarf she thought would appeal to Audie. The thought of Audie reminded her she still hadn't purchased a wedding present for Kristin and Tarquin and that she still had no idea what to get. The note in with the invitation had been a coy, 'please, we don't expect gifts but if you want to celebrate this special day, then any gift will be lovely'. There had been a p.s. with a list of their favourite charities as alternatives, and she rather thought that might be the answer. However, she resolved to ask Moss for his thoughts. Would they do two presents? A joint one? She had no idea.

It really would have been much easier to send her apologies. As that was no longer an option, unless she came down with a dreaded lurgy or broke a limb — neither of which appealed — she purchased a wedding card then headed for the train. At least she'd done one more positive thing with regards to what she still privately called the Day From Hell.

Which, she mused as she settled in her seat on the rapidly filling train, was daft. The happy couple might not realise who she was, but no doubt they would find out, either the coming weekend when the big reveal was in the paper, or when she was introduced to them on the wedding weekend.

The train set off, and the last few remaining passengers began to occupy the few empty seats left.

"Excuse me, but..."

Arietta looked up at Josephine's shocked face. "Do I need to?" she said, deliberately misunderstanding. "Did you do something wrong?"

Josephine flushed and waved at the seat. "Is anyone sitting there?"

Which Arietta thought was a stupid question. "As you can see. Help yourself." She opened her Kindle and pretended to read. Nasty no doubt, but she was in no mood to help Josephine out, or give her an opening to say whatever was on her mind. It was up to her to do that.

For several minutes Arietta flicked the pages in her Kindle, not seeing one word. Which was a pity, as she had been enjoying the book, and she'd have to flick back so she didn't miss any of the drama as it unfolded.

The conductor checked their tickets and, once she'd gone, Josephine cleared her throat. "Can I talk to you for a moment please, Arietta?" she said diffidently. "If you don't mind."

Arietta closed her Kindle and half turned in her seat. "Of course. What do you want to say?"

Josephine narrowed her lips and swallowed. "I owe you an apology for something I unwittingly did and may, no, not may, I'm *sure* I did, cause a lot of upset and problems for you and others and I really had no idea and my goddaughter was so underhanded, I could —" She broke off and took a deep breath. "Sorry."

"I think I followed most of that. Start again slowly. Remember to breathe." It reminded Arietta of Audie when she was imparting big news. Josephine's news may or may not be big, but evidently it was important. "When you're able."

"I'm able, just not very coherent," Josephine said. "I called at your cottage this morning but no one was in. I wanted to apologise then. My goddaughter was visiting, saw you in the village and said she recognised the man you were with. Then on another visit saw you with the child and said didn't the child look like you both. Well I was shocked but agreed with her, and off she went. I'd said you'd lived in the village for a while, but I'd not seen the young girl before. Evidently it was enough for her, and the result?" She sighed and shook her head. "She used to be such a nice girl, but this reporting lark has gone to her head. I told her I didn't know anything else and she said, well, other people might and we all would once she got her facts sorted. How she sleeps at night I have no idea." She sounded flustered and disgusted at the same time. "I know I'm inquisitive and like to know what's going on. A result of where we used to live and how I was expected to be aware of everything. And of course I know all about your brother and his propensity for coming and going without any fuss, and so understand that. I liked the idea I realised when he was around — double milk orders and so on — and others didn't. So when your new visitor was around, and you weren't forthcoming about him, I think I felt left out. That I should be in the know and I wasn't. I'm sorry. Not very Christianlike, and my husband would be oh-so disappointed in me if he knew."

She sounded so despondent Arietta decided to help her out. "Don't worry about it, I'm just glad we know how everything happened. I'll tell Moss." There was no point in denying who he was now. "He'll be glad to know it wasn't properly your fault." She wasn't going to let Josephine off scot-free.

"Just improperly?" Josephine said with a humour Arietta had no idea she possessed. "I was out of order more than once, wasn't I?"

"Oh yes, but at least you realise it," Arietta said cheerfully, just as the train slowed at their local railway station. "Do you need a lift?"

"Oh, no, thank you, my dear." Josephine sounded so much better than she had a few moments before. "The vicar will pick me up. He's been to the supermarket while I went into town. I wanted a new dress," she confessed. "I'm the Women's Institute president this year and want to look good at meetings."

"Congratulations, and before you ask, no, I can't guarantee to get to meetings so I won't join or go on the tea rota."

Josephine's face fell then she smiled. "Ah well, we'll see you when you can make it, and you did say you'd be a reserve speaker if need be and if you were free. It's a lady talking about basket weaving next month. So exciting."

Arietta nodded. Exciting wasn't the word she would use, but interesting certainly was. *Each to their own.*

She'd make a note of the date once she got home.

Chapter Fourteen

Moss appeared the following morning, cloudy-eyed and hollow-cheeked. "Lack of sleep," he said when Arietta exclaimed at his appearance. "I wanted to spend time with you, so arranged to be driven here and not to my hotel room. If I can have a few hours' sleep I'll be fine." He yawned. "Grief, I'm knackered. Sorry, love."

"Go up then, I'll wake you when?"

He glanced at the kitchen clock. "Around noon. Thanks, hon. I'm so tired I won't even ask for a coffee, and it takes a lot for me to say that."

"Well, it's supposed to keep you awake," Arietta pointed out. "Not that it does me."

"Nor me." He yawned again and Arietta turned him around to face the hall.

"Go now before you fall asleep on the stairs."

"I could sleep standing up the way I feel," Moss said frankly. "I'm off and —" He yawned once more and sketched a wave. "Love you."

"And me you." Arietta watched, alarmed, as he swayed a little and headed stairwards. Two thumps told her he had kicked his shoes off, followed by the loo flushing, running water then silence. She turned off the ringers on the house phone — not that it was used often, but it would be Murphy's law someone would ring while he was sleeping.

She collected her laptop, went back into the kitchen and closed the door to the hall behind her and made herself a coffee before she remembered what she had said.

Oh lord, I told him I loved him. Do I? She thought about it. *It appears I do… Hell's bells. That came out of the blue.*

Her mobile did its muted hello it's a phone call noise. She checked the caller and answered it. "Hi, Maggie, how's it going?"

"I was going to ask you that," Maggie replied. "Seeing as it's all been talked about very briefly in our one quick meet-up and cryptic conversations on the phone."

"I'd say let's meet today, but I've had an unexpected visitor," Arietta said. They'd covered everything that had happened and Maggie had been loud in her condemnation of people who couldn't keep their mouths shut and their noses out of other people's business. "And I've lots to tell you."

"Ohh, visitor wise or otherwise?"

Arietta laughed. "Both, I guess. The visitor is you-know-who, I've no idea how long he'll be here, and he's in bed at the moment after working all night. Which is why I'm in the kitchen with the doors shut, and not in my study." The kitchen was at the far end of the house to their bedroom, her study underneath it. "The rest of the news is hush-hush so I'll tell you when I see you, oh, except I've seen the other you-know-who and found out what happened."

"Best not say on here then, walls have ears and phones have hackers," Maggie said in a knowledgeable tone, which she spoiled by laughing. "Says she as if she knows what she's talking about. I wish. Give me a shout when you're free. I'll bring the wine gums."

"Will do." Arietta shut her phone off and grinned to herself. Wine gums in Maggie-speak meant a bottle of wine and some crisps—their go-to goodies when they wanted a good chat.

She opened the fridge and rummaged through the contents. She had no idea whether Moss would be around for dinner or not but she'd need something. The weather was inclement, and an overnight hard frost was forecast. To her mind that meant winter warming, comfort food in the form of a hearty stew. The best part of that sort of meal was she could freeze what she didn't eat. Arietta set to and collected the ingredients she needed. Thank goodness she'd popped into the supermarket on her way back from the station. She had swithered about whether she could be bothered or not, but the thought she'd have to turf out the following day—i.e., that day—had made her mind up for her. Get it over and done with.

Now she was very glad she had. Not only because she had been at home when Moss arrived, but she could feed him if necessary.

Win-win.

She prepared the stew and with one eye on the time decided she'd better cook it in the microwave. She could give it an hour in the bottom oven of the Aga—the equivalent of a slow cooker if there was time. If not, well it might not be as rich as she'd liked but it would, as her dad would say, *"fill a hole"*.

In a cooking mood, she put the stew in to cook and started beating all the ingredients together for an apple sponge pudding, another 'could be cooked in the microwave' recipe. She was so intent on what she was doing that when something touched her neck she yelped, spun around and flung a greasy spoon heavy with the sponge mixture in the air. It headed towards Moss.

"Shoot, sorry, you startled me. Duck."

"Good shot, you almost got me." He jumped back, caught the spoon before it hit him in the face and licked it clean. "Nice. Sponge cake?"

"Apple sponge pudding, if there's enough left after I almost splattered you with a lot of it."

Moss peered into the bowl. "Loads left. Even enough for me to have another spoonful if you don't scrape the bowl out too cleanly."

"Maybe."

He nuzzled her neck. "Pretty please. With bells on. I love raw cake mix. Go on…"

"Urgh, not if you do that. Your hair is all wet and cold and dripping on me."

"Cold-ish shower," Moss said. "I woke up, knew if I went back to sleep I'd feel the worse for it later and decided to really wake myself up. Mind you, I reckon that it was more a lick and a promise than a proper shower. I smelled coffee."

"Don't know how, there's none on." She grinned. "Aww."

"No? Then I dreamt I smelled coffee and hoped it would come true." Moss did a long languishing sigh. "Prayed."

She laughed. "Over to you, you know where everything is. I want to get this finished."

"Cheers, want one?"

"Why not?" She finished off her sponge as he made the coffee.

"I hate sounding whiny or needy, Moss, but how long can you stop? I...I miss not having you around now," Arietta admitted as she took out the stew and replaced it with the apple sponge. She set the timer, picked up her coffee and sat down in one of the comfy chairs near the warmth of the Aga. She grinned mischievously. "My feet get cold in bed."

"I'll buy you a hot water bottle," Moss said. "With a picture of me on a furry cover."

"Then I'll have you at my feet whenever I want?" Arietta sniggered. "Like it."

"Ha, ha, I'd rather be in your arms. Or have you in mine."

"I'll cuddle it as well," Arietta assured him. "When I can't have the real thing."

"Real thing here for now." Moss drank some coffee. "I've got a request, but feel free to say no."

For some reason the way he spoke didn't instil any confidence in her that she would like what he was about to say, *or* willingly agree. "That sounds ominous. Go on, ask away, put me out of my wondering misery."

Moss twisted his cup around in his hands. Arietta took it from him and put it on the work surface. "Just tell me."

He took hold of her hands and kissed them. Such a daft thing to do, but it made her go stupidly gooey.

Get a grip. If something like that made her go weak at the knees, what if he did something even more romantic? Would that mean she'd do the fainting female thing? Heaven help them both if she did *that*.

"Quick, before I worry."

"Right then, here goes." Moss squeezed her hands but didn't let go of them. "Your hands are freezing," he said. "Why?"

"Waiting for you to tell me what you want to do? No, not really, it's because I've had them in cold water." She hadn't, but to say worry made her shivery sounded ridiculous, although it was true. "Go on."

"I made a swift detour on the way to the set yesterday, at the request of Kristin and Tarq," Moss said. "We've been invited to go and stay with them, and Audie of course, for tonight, so we can present a united front if need be tomorrow. It means they will know who you are sooner rather than later, but I honestly think it will be better to get all the news, shocks and denouements over in one fell swoop. And it should make you happier about going to the wedding. Audie wants you to as well. Oh, and the B-T seniors won't be there. They're not happy with any of it, so have headed to a very exclusive, no doubt excruciatingly expensive hotel near, but not quite, on the Costa Brava for a couple of weeks until the brouhaha dies down. I'm fairly sure I heard Tarquin say he hoped they'd forget to come back in time for the wedding, and in that case I could give Kristin away."

"Oh blimey."

"Oh yes. So what do you say?"

"What did Kristin say?"

"Well, as I wasn't supposed to be eavesdropping, I think she said it would suit her and was there any chance they could bring the date forward, or even elope." He smiled in a reminiscent way. "Then Tarquin said, oh how he wished. Audie came back downstairs and I had to pretend I'd come down with her. I'd been on the way to the loo, but I missed my chance and had to get my driver to stop halfway and let me disappear behind a convenient but not-very-bushy bush. Just in time on more than one account. I'd just zipped up and was back at the car when a coach full of old ladies drove by. I went hot and cold at the thought of them catching me mid-pee or unzipped. I whipped my phone out, pretended to take a call and got inside the car PDQ before they clocked me, stopped the coach and wanted pictures. Not that I'd mind in the normal scheme of things, but we were cutting it fine to get me back by the time I was needed. We did it with fifteen minutes to spare. A close-run thing with the damned coach holding us up. What it was doing on a one-track road to hardly anywhere I have no idea."

"More than likely a mystery trip," Arietta suggested. "With fish and chips before they headed home."

"Yeah could be, so…? Shall I ring and say we'll be there after dinner or make our excuses?"

"You'd do that for me?"

"Of course I would. And make it sound plausible as to why we couldn't go." Moss hugged her. "You matter to me, more than K and T."

"What about them not realising I'm me, if you know what I mean? What if they take a hissy fit?" Arietta said in a worried voice. "I don't want to cause trouble."

"Then we take ourselves somewhere incognito and let them sort it out by themselves. Simple. However, seriously, I doubt they will."

"But there's Audie to think of as well." That fact had been niggling at Arietta. "What about her? How is it going to affect her?"

"I'd explain to her, she's sensible and would accept it," Moss reassured her patiently. "And as she says, what a story to tell her mates now she can. Which reminds me, we must make sure she only gets general details and that she doesn't choose to embellish them."

Was it fair for a young girl to have to do, or not do, that? Arietta made her mind up. "Tell them we'll be there at whatever time you want."

"After stew time," Moss said as he kissed her. "Which isn't yet, and once I text and say we'll go this evening, I can think of a really interesting way to pass the time."

She twisted around to look at him. "You can?" she said, wide-eyed and guileless. "How?"

"Give me five and I'll show you."

* * * *

The time passing did exactly as Moss had said it would. Very satisfactorily. Sadly, though, much too quickly.

Arietta stood under the shower and leant against Moss as he soaped her back. "This is so nice," she said dreamily. "I wonder how long the hot water will last for?"

"Too long for us to find out." Moss tapped her bum. "Right. Dry, eat, go." He turned the taps off, opened the door and handed Arietta a big, fluffy bath sheet. "If I had my way we'd go from here to bed, back here, and back to bed again. But duty, or whatever it's called, calls. We can't turn up at midnight."

"Where are we going anyway?" Arietta asked as she towelled herself down and dressed in newish jeans and an oversized shirt. She was going comfortably dressed or not at all. "You never did say."

"The other side of Perth, take about an hour. They're expecting us for supper and before Audie is shooed to bed. I reckon we should leave around seven, seven-thirty?" He said it as a question. "Only need clothes and toiletries for one night. I'm back on set at four-thirty a.m. sharp on Monday anyway so can't spare any longer, and I said you'd have writing things to do. Gives you a good getaway." He zipped his jeans up and pulled a T-shirt and sweater on. "I think this is the time to tell you again how bloody sorry I am I got you into all this."

"You couldn't have got me into it if I hadn't wanted to be got." Arietta packed an overnight bag with ruthless efficiency and wondered what she'd forgotten. "Damn, I better shove in some PJs."

"Why?" Moss asked. "There's no need. We'll have an en suite and an electric blanket if need be. I'll lend you a T-shirt if you think I'm not enough to keep you warm." He twirled an imaginary moustache in the silly over-the-top way he could. "Let me show you…damn, no time now."

Arietta laughed. He could keep her more than warm just by looking at her. Not that she intended to admit that. "What if there's a fire or Audie comes in or…well, or anything. I'll shove my PJs in. I don't have to wear them."

"Fair enough. I've got a basic wardrobe there. Weird as it may sound, we all get on well, and I've stopped there many times before. It's helped Audie and it's good to have somewhere around there as a base if need be."

It all sounded very pally-pally. Would she fit in? Arietta blocked that scary thought. She would or she wouldn't and at that moment there was nothing she could do to change it. "That's everything, I think. I'll go and dish the stew up."

"And make custard for the sponge." Moss rubbed his stomach. "Can't have apple sponge without custard."

"You'll want it? Is there time?"

Moss nodded. "Yes to both. I factored it in." He laughed at her disgusted expression. "I'm not missing out on your home cooking. No way. I've been looking forward to it. Kristin will have nibbles ready for supper but, as posh as they more than likely will be, they won't be made by you and they'll still taste shop-bought. If you know what I mean."

Arietta nodded. "Yeah, okay. Flatterer. I'll go and make custard. With powder. I'm all out of vanilla pods." They weren't high on her list of shopping priorities—powder from a packet made up as sweet as she wanted it was good enough for her, and tough bananas if it wasn't good enough for anyone else.

"Powder is good. Vanilla pods don't feature in my kitchen. And tins aren't high up on my must-have list." Moss snagged an apple from the fruit bowl, stared at it for a minute, put it back then picked it up again.

"Nor mine, though they do come in handy at times." Arietta took the plates out of the warming oven. I don't like tinned custard or rice or tapioca stuff." She didn't bother to ask Moss how hungry he was—he always said 'not starving but well ready to eat'. "Were you going to eat that apple or juggle with it?"

"Eat and then remembered the sponge." Moss waved towards the pantry. "I just wondered, if you don't like tins of rice pud, why do you have seven of various sorts stashed away?"

"Those tins? Seriously, I do sometimes think I need my head examined. You may well ask. Blame my dear brother. Thomas loves it. He brings some with him every visit so there's always one here if he fancies some. He's been known to eat two tins, cold, at one sitting. He's another one with hollow legs, and I suspect arms as well at times."

Moss winced. "I feel sick. Not sick enough not to eat dinner, though."

* * * *

By the time they were halfway to Perth, Arietta was in worry mode once more. "Are you sure this is the right thing to do?" she asked as they joined the dual carriageway and Moss set the speed of the car to the permitted limit. "What happens next?"

"No idea. As to are we doing the right thing?" He shrugged. "I—we—and you, it appears—aren't sure, but it seems to be a sensible precaution. We get there, we have a drink, alcoholic or not, our choice, we sleep." He flashed a quick grin in her direction. "Maybe. We wait and see if anything happens or we need to do anything. Then we leave sometime tomorrow."

That was another thing that worried her. "You put other stuff in the car, I know you did." While she was tidying up, checking switches were off and any food that needed to go in the freezer had been put in there, he'd disappeared upstairs to, as he'd put it, *"make sure they hadn't forgotten anything"*. She'd been in the loo when he'd clattered downstairs and gone out to the car so had no idea what had been stowed in the boot, just that something must have been. "What, why, and after tomorrow, what then?"

"Sure did." Moss ignored her last question as he pulled out and overtook a lorry and a car struggling to tow a trailer twice its size. "Accident waiting to happen," he commented as they pulled ahead and he went back to the inside lane. "I have an idea for after tomorrow, if you're agreeable."

Arietta watched a train on a nearby line go by. She hoped the passengers weren't worrying as much as she was. "That we leave ASAP? Get a flight to Bora Bora or somewhere till it's all died down? Dye our hair green and say we're aliens? I'm all for that."

Moss howled with laughter. "Well, we could, though I fancy sky-blue-pink with spots myself. Problem is, if we went to Bora Bora, I bet someone would recognise us and there would be no easy getaway. My suggestion is not so drastic."

"Go on then, I'm all ears."

"I have a house not a million miles away, but it's in a place you have to be signed into. So unless someone has legit business and you, as in we, say it's okay, then they don't get past the guy on the gate. Even deliveries are held at the gate and if necessary brought up to the delivery address later. Overkill maybe, but really useful at times. Like now."

"The one that was flooded?" If she were honest she'd love to see it. *And* see if it really had been flooded.

He nodded. "It's all dried out, re-plastered, re-painted and re-whatevered. We could go there, and you could stay while I work. I can get back easily when I'm not needed. Think of it as a mini break. Or a trial run."

A trial run? For what?

"Um...what are we practising?" There that didn't sound too over-the-top surely?

"Well, now, I've lived with you and we didn't fall out."

Arietta snorted. "We didn't?"

Moss reddened and cleared his throat. "Well, apart from that. I miss you when I'm not with you. I'm hoping you feel the same?"

"That I miss me when you're not there?" she said deadpan.

Moss groaned. "Clever clogs."

"Okay, okay, sorry, I couldn't resist," she said with amusement in her voice. "It's weird because when you're away for work it feels okay, because you're working and that's how lots of couples live their lives, but when you're just not there it doesn't. If you get me?" It sounded muddled but she wasn't sure how to explain what she meant without sounding needy – or pathetic.

"I get you," Moss said. "Which is why I thought you might try and live with me, at least until the wedding. It's only a couple of weeks after all. Then we could negotiate where, when and how we carried on."

"But where? And what about the cottage?" She couldn't just walk away from it like that. There were flowers that would need water, food in the fridge that needed eating, freezing or throwing out. As she'd thought she was only away for a night she hadn't thought any farther ahead.

"Could you ask Maggie to keep an eye on the cottage? You said she's got a key. Maybe she could sort out what's needed for now? And tell Thom as well so he can do his, 'ooh, I was in the area and just popped by' act. If you don't want to see him, we can tell the gateman he's persona non grata at the moment."

"Maybe." Was it fair to Maggie? Thomas she wasn't worried over. As far as he was concerned Moss could do no wrong. However it did mean she was nigh on certain if she stopped at Moss' house they would have a regular visitor — work permitting. Perhaps she could suggest *Thomas* get a job in Bora Bora? His appetite was as voracious as Moss'. For food anyway — she had no inclination to ask about any other appetites he might have. Arietta enjoyed cooking, but not all the time.

However she was interested in seeing Moss' house, and if it meant they could spend more time together…

She made her mind up, but before she could reply to Moss he spoke again.

"If you don't want to, no worries, I'll just drop you at home tomorrow and I'll head north."

That didn't sound very good at all.

"I'll ask Maggie to house watch."

His smile was all she could have asked for.

That was one hurdle over. Now all she had to do was successfully navigate the rest.

* * * *

The car drew up outside a long, low and rambling farmhouse. Not at all like a place Arietta had envisaged Kristin and Tarquin would live in. Moss noticed her amazed expression and laughed.

"Not like you thought it would be?"

"Nope," Arietta said honestly. "I expected something more elaborate, more in-your-face." She paused for a moment. "Like I remember them."

"I've a feeling you might be in for a nice surprise," Moss said as he unclipped his seatbelt. "A bit more mature since then."

Arietta forbade to say they would need to be a lot more mature—she was determined to have an open mind. "Well, we'll see," she said non-committedly. "I'd hope we are all a bit more mature than we were at the heady age when we went to uni."

"Well judge for yourself, here they all come now."

The front door of the house had opened and Audie, followed by two adults—the female on crutches—approached the car. Arietta looked at them covertly. Both recognisable, when you knew what to expect.

Older of course. Tarquin had a lot less hair and Kristin's was a browny blonde, not the brassy blonde Arietta remembered.

Remember, open mind.

Moss helped her out of the car just as the trio reached them.

"You're here!" Audie jumped up onto her dad and wound her legs around his waist as he held on to her. "I've been waiting ages."

"We're *early*," Moss said mildly as he hugged Audie and gave her a kiss. "Arietta wouldn't let us be late."

Arietta would have been happy never to arrive.

"I knew you'd keep him in line," Audie said to Arietta. She gave her a wicked grin. "Come and meet Mum and Tarquin." She slid down from her dad and held her hand out to Arietta. Moss took Arietta's other hand. They must look as if they presented a united front, which Arietta considered, may or may not be a good thing.

She took a deep breath. "Actually," she said slowly, "I know your mum and Tarquin, though they might not realise it."

The two adults mentioned both started. "You do?" Kristin said. "How?"

"It's a long while ago now."

Tarquin squinted at her. "You sort of look familiar now you've said something but sorry, no idea how and why."

Next to her, Moss tensed. Arietta squeezed his hand in reassurance. She hadn't forgotten Audie was there, and neither did she want to make it seem like Tarquin's and Kristin's behaviour had had much effect on her.

"We were at uni together," she said lightly. "I looked somewhat different, apart from all those years younger of course." She paused for effect. Naughty but, she thought, unrepentant, it would be worth it. She had enough residual snarkiness in her to know she would enjoy saying it.

"You spent the time we all knew each other calling me Harriet."

A crutch clattered to the ground.

Moss picked it up. "Shall we go in?"

Chapter Fifteen

Audie had gone — protesting — to bed before the four adults sat down on two comfortable couches and metaphorically faced one another. The couches were at right angles.

Tarquin handed glasses of wine out before he took his place next to Kristin.

"Right, I'll start. I was a bloody arrogant sod who thought he should get what he wanted. When you didn't oblige, I spat the dummy out. For what it's worth, I'll apologise now, only, what, fourteen or so years too late."

"I wasn't any better, was I?" Kristin said. "I was older than the rest of you, you all meshed and I just couldn't get onto your wavelengths. Plus, I freely admit, I was as jealous as hell that Tarq chose you and didn't seem interested in anyone else. Okay, scrub the anyone, in me. So when I saw my chance I jumped at it. Bitch, cow, whatever, yeah that was me. I'm a bit more mature now. Though as you can tell by the well-loved and never regretted result upstairs, it took me a while to get there." She smiled wryly. "When I look back at the then-me, I can't say I much like what I see."

"We were all younger and sillier," Arietta said. "And all made mistakes."

"I guess we all learnt from them," Moss said. "And the us we were then has brought us to the us we are now."

"That's damned profound for this time of night on your second glass of wine," Tarquin said. "But I'll echo it. So" — he turned to Arietta — "when did you realise we were *us*, if you get my meaning?"

Arietta laughed. "It's a long story, goes back to when I got my wedding invite and — "

"And I didn't mention that the wedding Arietta had been invited to was to this one. I sort of let her think there were two weddings," Moss broke in. "Plus of course Arietta's invitation was addressed to Harriet."

"For which we apologise," Kristin said. "I wouldn't have been so crass. Mum and Dad, though, are sending me demented, trying to make the bloody day OTT. We'd prefer low-key. I told them to invite close friends and I'd starred those. They ignored us and invited the world and his wife. I mean, you wouldn't have expected an invite, would you?"

Arietta shook her head. "I was gobsmacked and showed it to Moss. It was a bit naughty not to refuse and explain, but okay, I wanted my two minutes of revenge."

"Only two? I'd have gone for a hundred at least," Kristin said and yawned. "Oh lord, I'm so sorry. I'm not sleeping very well at the moment. Let's go over tomorrow's maybes, then, sorry again, I'll have to go to bed."

"No sorry needed," Moss said smoothly. "We're not a lot better what with my early mornings and late nights. I say let's see what happens, if anything, and just present a united front. As in all friends, all happy, and just had to put the record straight, no big deal?"

"That sounds good to me." Kristin struggled to her feet. "I'll love you all and leave you."

"I'll come up," Arietta said and got to her feet. "I'm shattered. No, you stop and finish your drink," she said to Moss. "I'll bag the shower first."

He winked and she narrowed her eyes and smiled sweetly. "And make sure you don't hog all the bedclothes."

Kristin laughed. "It's a man thing. Tarquin is as bad. Right then, you promise not to laugh as I go up the stairs on my bum?"

"Not to your face anyway."

"That's good enough," Kristin said cheerfully, as different to the girl Arietta had known as possible. "If nothing else I hope it'll tone said area up."

"I better do the same then," Arietta said. "But I won't break a bone so I have to."

"Don't blame you, much too uncomfortable. All I hope is I don't have to go down the aisle on them."

"Is it likely?" Arietta asked as they got to the bottom of the stairs and Kristin handed her the crutches to carry up the stairs for her. "I'm hazy about it all."

"It's a fracture, not too bad, and the crutches are a precaution now more than anything. Easier to say a break and keep my parents out of the way. They love Audie but say she's a handful, which in their lifestyle she no doubt is. Plus my dear mother is not any good in a crisis or near a sick bed. I reckoned I'd get better faster without her hovering." Kristin began to bump up the stairs one by one.

Arietta followed her slowly. It looked most uncomfortable.

"Also, between us, Tarquin will be sharing the news with Moss about now, I'm pregnant, luckily not throwing up yet, but I couldn't stand Mum either doing the cotton-wool wrapping or the telling me my timing is bad, what about the wedding. We are amazed and delighted, as Tarquin was certain after he had mumps he was infertile. Turns out he's not. Audie was over the moon when we told her this morning and was sworn to secrecy until we say otherwise." She retrieved her crutches and limped as far as the door of the room. "For two pins, you know, I'd say sod it and elope."

"Well, why don't you? You could always have your wedding day as a big celebration."

Is this really me offering advice? "Not that I'm an expert on any of it, you know," Arietta added in a hurry.

"Is that what you would do?" Kristin asked her. "Elope?"

Arietta thought about that. "Not quite elope, but have just a few very close friends and relatives, then celebrate with others later." She couldn't say the last thing she fancied was the sort of wedding Maggie described as a bun fight, and the idea of a big wedding brought her out in hives.

"Hmm..." Kristin was silent for a moment. "I wonder. Ah well, time for bed." She didn't elaborate, and after wishing Arietta a good night and with a reminder that no one stood on ceremony and she knew where the kitchen was, took herself off to her own room.

She had no idea how much later it was when Moss got into bed, except she half woke up and registered him there as he snuggled up to her, kissed her cheeks and said something she didn't hear. "S'night," she muttered and went back to sleep again.

* * * *

It was still dark when she surfaced again and wondered what had woken her. The bedroom door was half-open — Moss had either forgotten to lock it or knew there would be no need, as Arietta had told him they would be circumspect while they were there.

Audie peered around the door. Arietta slid out of bed and put her finger over her mouth before she held five fingers up. Audie nodded and pointed to the stairs before miming drinking coffee. Arietta did a thumbs-up and, as soon as Audie withdrew, headed for the bathroom.

Moss rolled over and did the male hog-the-bedclothes-and-most-of-the-bed thing. He grabbed a pillow and cuddled it.

Arietta grinned and wished she had her camera handy. *On second thought, maybe not.* She could imagine the furore if someone got hold of that.

She washed the necessary parts of her body for her to feel clean, brushed her teeth and put on her clothes. A clean T-shirt and her comfy jeans. The make-up and whatever else might be warranted could come later. Coffee came first.

Moss opened one eye as she picked up her shoes and tiptoed past the bed. "Running away?"

"Nope, going for coffee."

He grunted. "What time is it?"

Arietta glanced at the bedside clock. "Just after six, go back to sleep."

"Thanks." He was snoring softly before she left the room.

She smiled and shook her head. Some things never changed. When he had to be up, he would be—bright, awake and cheerful. If he didn't, he could sleep on for hours. How when the day could go either way she had no idea. Only time, and the papers, would tell them that.

With that not-overly-pleasant thought in her mind, Arietta headed for the kitchen. Kristin looked up from the newspaper spread all over the table and grinned. "Coffee on the Aga, Audie's making egg and bacon sarnies and it's girl time. I had hoped we'd get half an hour to ourselves so I could do some more grovelling and ask you a favour. Could you take the grovelling as read, please? Audie will be back in a few seconds. She's gone to collect the eggs. Yes, we have chickens," she added, laughing. "You look gobsmacked."

"I am," Arietta said honestly. "I really didn't know you before."

"You did, but this is the new me, and so far I haven't regressed. Even when provoked," Kristin said. "Like when my mum decides it's her way or no way. Which is what I want to talk about."

"Okay, grovelling seen to be done, what's the favour?" Arietta was intrigued.

"Keep the Wednesday before the wedding free, please. We might, no, probably will, need you both. Tarquin is going to ask Moss, and we don't want to say anything to Audie or say any more yet. Will you?"

Arietta's curiosity was well and truly aroused. "Okay as long as it's nothing nefarious. I am not kidnapping your parents so you can enjoy your wedding day."

Kristin giggled. "Nope, not that, they aren't coming up till Wednesday night anyway. And we might not need you both, we'll see."

"Fair enough," Arietta said just as Audie came into the room, clutching a basket.

"What's fair enough?" she asked

"I am a fairy, my name is nuff…" Arietta said. "Fair enough. Which means I'll not moan if you break my egg as you're cooking it."

"I'd just say I'd changed my mind and was making omelettes instead." Audie nodded towards the paper. "Well? Am I famous as 'legendary film star's love child in a triangle'?

"No you are not, you objectionable child," Kristin said with a laugh. "I hope not anyway, I've not got that far yet. We're not front-page, thank goodness. I was reading about an obnoxious bloke I worked with who's just won the lottery and been told he's got to share it with a syndicate. Serves him right, he was a bully. If the deal was you only added more money when asked and he forgot to ask, that's his fault."

"Yeah, guess so." Audie had obviously lost interest. "Where's Dad and Tarq?"

"Still asleep."

"Are not." Moss came in and kissed Arietta on the cheek, hugged Kristin and winked at his daughter before rubbing his unshaven cheek across hers.

"Urgh, Dad, puleeease. That's scratchy." She rubbed her cheek. "Honestly, men."

"Got to be, need it like this or they'll glue fake ones on." Moss scratched his chin. "They're a bu…devil to get off."

Kristin gave him what Arietta's mum would have called 'the glance' — as in, watch your language.

"Sorry, yes, anything in the papers?"

"She's not looked yet," Audie complained. "Too busy gloating over some bully-bloke she used to work with getting his comeuppance. Two rashers or three?"

"Er, three please, and two eggs."

"Glutton. Arietta?"

"Two and one thanks."

"And Mum's the same. Tarquin will be like Dad."

"Am I last? Someone taking my name in vain? Ah well, less time to wait for breakfast." Tarquin strolled in, kissed everyone except Moss and nodded infinitesimally at Kristin.

Evidently whatever might or might not be needed, it appeared that Moss had agreed as well.

Arietta waited for an answer. None was forthcoming. She ate her breakfast, complimented a blushing Audie on her cookery skills, then turned to Kristin. "Right, put me out of my misery. As Audie once asked me, who do we metaphorically have to kill?"

Kristin laughed. "No one look." She passed the paper over. "All aww and soppy hearts and flowers. Sort of how nice to see how well people get on. And no one's cottoned on to our past meetings, thank goodness."

"Why thank goodness?" Audie said with avid interest. "What did you do, Mum?"

"Mum didn't do anything," Arietta said. "We didn't know each other well, or for long."

"I was not a very nice person," Kristin said and bit her lip. "Thank goodness I've changed."

"We both fancied Tarquin," Arietta added in a hurry. "He was immediately attracted to your mum."

"But," Moss added, "he was slow on the doing something about it and your mum and I got together. I must add I didn't know Arietta then, not even as Thom's sister. Come to think of it," he said reflectively, "I didn't know Thom either."

"Dad, you're rambling," Audie said with a giggle. "Get on with it."

"Where was I?" Moss sent Arietta a quick wink. "I've lost the thread."

"You and Mum together."

"Oh yeah, well, we liked each other but decided we were better as friends than lovers. Then she and Tarquin got together."

"Which was a bit weird when very soon after your dad and I did the friends-only bit, I discovered I was pregnant. I told Dad and Tarquin and how things were going to be. And they are," Kristin finished. "I love you to bits, and luckily so do they."

"Wow." Audie looked impressed. "Go, you lot." She picked up the paper and began to read it.

We really ought to write fiction. Talk about creative accounting, history-style.

"They don't half go on, do they?" Audie said after reading for a minute or so. "Hold on, this bit is all about the wedding," Audie said. "Ohh gosh. You two never told me *that*," she accused Arietta and Moss. "Why didn't you?"

"Told you what?" Arietta asked as Moss blinked. "What have I missed sharing?

"That Dad is best man."

You what? Best man? Maybe because it's the first I've heard of it?

"Audie, put both feet into it, why don't you?" Moss said. "None of us had a chance to tell you and Arietta didn't know. There was another phone call last night saying that someone suggested I wasn't happy about all this, so we did mega-fast damage limitation. As it happens, Tarquin hadn't got round to a best man, so I'm now him."

Kristin stared at her husband-to-be. "I thought you asked Moss ages ago?"

Tarquin fiddled with his teaspoon. "I forgot I hadn't. I meant to, then that deal with Weales was about to go pear-shaped and I got involved there and well..." He smiled, deprecating. "I was—"

"Oblivious to anything else," Kristin said. "Just as well I love you and Moss is okay with it."

"I've told him he owes me some of that single malt he's bought *en primur*."

"Eh?" Audie said. "What's that?"

That was what Arietta wondered. Her French wasn't bad, but she thought whisky had to be aged a minimum of three years in the barrel to be Scotch. So how could he have bought some while it was newly produced?

"Whisky still in the barrel, not bottled, and as long as it's in the barrel, no duty paid on it yet. Duty is what you have to pay on a lot of goods," Moss explained to his daughter. "Complicated stuff, but if you think one barrel or one year's whisky might be exceptionally good, you can buy it early on."

"Sort of sneaky but legal?" Audie said with interest. "Sounds fun. A bit like betting on the Grand National when you all let me pick a horse."

"Oh it is," Tarquin assured her. "And if you back the wrong horse—or barrel—you can lose your money. Simplified but basically right."

"As in, don't spend money you can't afford," Moss said. "And before you ask, the whisky would still be very good whisky, it just might not be to your taste. Like different types of baked beans."

I bet that's the first time a single malt's been compared to a tin of baked beans.

"Like you made me give you a pound for the horse?"

"Just like that."

"Bummer."

"I'll hasten to add it's our own sweepstake," Moss said. "And it's a pound a person—family and friends only."

"Count me in next time," Arietta said. "I can manage a pound."

* * * *

"I still do not know how you persuaded me to do this." Arietta stared at Moss as he navigated the Ferrari over a narrow bridge. She sighed. "Or why you're prepared to risk this car on the roads we're going to have to drive over. It'll end up all bashed and battered."

They'd waved goodbye to Audie, Kristin and Tarquin after a late lunch, all relieved that what could have been a sensation had ended up as a bit of a 'well, it's over and done with and there's nothing to tell, really'. Newspapers hadn't been bothered about the way they all got on. As Moss had said with a grin, they wanted *'antagonism and confrontation'*.

Arietta was concerned they had set off in what she thought of as the wrong direction. Not that she knew which was the *right* direction, but they were heading south, and she had been certain Moss had said his house was north.

"I'm not driving all the way. This is only as far as the airport. We'll take my helicopter from there, land in the grounds of a nearby hotel and a car will take us to…" He hesitated. "My house."

That was high living with a capital H. She went over his words in her mind. "Yeah, you never did say much about where your house is." She'd teased about it being a caravan in the woods and he'd replied, "*two joined together*" and refused to add anything else except "*you'll see*".

"It's a surprise," he said for the umpteenth time.

"I don't like surprises," Arietta grumbled, and jumped when he tapped her knee.

"You'll like this one. I hope." He grinned. "After all, two caravans are better than one."

"Really?"

"So they say. You can tell me what you think when we get there."

Did he sound worried? All of a sudden Arietta realised she was behaving badly. After all, she'd agreed that to stop with him at his home was a good idea. "Sorry, what a cow. I'm excited to see it and wondering if I've got everything I need." *And scared that I'll hate it and he obviously loves it.*

"You've got your toothbrush, laptop, iPad, phone and clean knickers. What else?"

She sighed. "Lots, no doubt. I'm still thinking about the wedding. Kristin looks fed up and Tarquin worried. What are her parents like? Do they listen to anything Kristin says?"

"Not much. She said after they'd handed their address book over to her parents with stern instructions only to invite the people whose names they had starred, her mum pretended that she'd never heard

276

them say that. Kristin reckons a lot of people were surprised at the invitation, like you were. She sounded ready to slap her mum, and I can so see why. She's a snob to boot. Mrs B-T, not Kristin. She lost that bit of her ages ago, thank God."

"I can't help but feel a bit like a poor relative." Arietta laughed. "Woe is me, etcetera, etcetera?"

"You're no slouch, love, and you're with me. Which, after all the stuff in the newspapers some people would think it was weird that I'm there. We'll go united."

"Bit hard when you're down the front and I'm at the back but...hey, it's okay, I'm just doing the scaredy-cat routine." And she didn't like it one bit.

"We'll slay them that look down their noses at us. Imagine them in their nappies, works every time."

"You reckon?" Arietta asked grumpily. "Why can't they just elope and we'll go to the seaside or something?"

Moss slanted a glance at her.

What do I sound like?

"Sorry, I'm being a bovine again."

"Moo. Why are you scared? What on earth for?"

"Posh place. Posh people."

"Not if they've gone all-out address book. Tarquin confided in me that three of the addresses are his bookie, Kristin's chiropodist and their local chippy. As he said, *'all nice people, but not exactly friends'*."

"Poor people if they turn up. Maybe we can form a 'we are ordinary, not posh' club and we'll do the look down our noses thing. Or would that be up? Argh, sorry, why am I such a bloody wimp? I mean, they're only people, aren't they?"

Moss slowed the car and pulled into the side of the road. "Exactly. They pee and poo like everyone else."

Arietta sniggered. "I know. Really it's because I bet they're so blooming condescending at my"—she mimed quote marks—"good luck. You know, fancy a nobody being with *him*."

"Do many people know what you do?"

Arietta shrugged. "No idea. Probably not. I don't hide it but nor do I flaunt it and it wasn't mentioned in the paper. I use Etta C Thomas as my pen name. Thomas because Thomas nagged me to write the first one. And the invite was to Harriet anyway."

"I'd forgotten that. Brilliant. We'll be fine."

"We will?" Arietta asked doubtfully. He seemed so incredibly confident. She still wasn't sure she was doing the right thing.

Moss gave her a swift hug and a kiss on the cheek. "Oh yeah, you wait and see. Right, let's get on so we can get settled before dinner. Which reminds me, I've booked a table but we don't have to use it if you'd prefer to eat in our own place. Food can be sent to us."

"Room service?"

"Sort of and…no, wait and see." He winked. "It'll be a surprise."

Arietta shut her mouth again. He seemed to be saying a lot of that wait and see stuff, and she was not a patient person.

Her inner worrywart carried on niggling until they reached the airfield and Moss slowed the car near one of the hangers. A tall, grey-haired man strolled over as Moss opened Arietta's door.

"All ready, boss." He shook hands with Moss and turned to Arietta. "Ms Clare. I'm George Hobson."

Arietta smiled. "How do you do, Mr Hobson?" *What do you do, Mr Hobson?*

"Thanks, George." Moss put his hand on Arietta's arm. "Shall we go?"

They walked around the hanger and he pointed to his left. Arietta stopped walking and rocked on her heels. "A helicopter? You meant it?"

Moss nodded. "I did."

"How far is it?"

"About thirty miles from your house. Bit further from here. Isn't she a beauty?"

Arietta closed her eyes and wondered if she'd fallen down the rabbit hole. She opened them again and stared at Moss' amused expression. "You're crackers. We've driven fifteen miles in the wrong direction to do this? Screwy, Moss. Well screwy. If I put that sort of stuff in a book, it'd be marked down as fantasy, unreal and the sort of thing a bloke in an over-the-top romantic novel would do to impress the heroine."

Moss roared with laughter. "As you write historical novels, they'd definitely say you had a screw loose if you put one in one of your books."

Arietta rolled her eyes. "You know what I mean."

He sobered. "Yeah, but this way we control how we get there, make it look as if wherever we came from, this was the easiest way to travel, and finally, piss off dear Mr B-T, who can't afford one."

Arietta chuckled. "Poor man, blighted his life?" The more she heard of Kristin's parents, the less she thought she would like them. She looked at the helicopter again and gulped. It didn't look big enough for both of them, let alone a pilot. "Er, who's going to drive that thing?"

Moss dragged her towards it and opened the passenger side door. "I am." He lifted her in before she had time to utter one word, let alone protest she'd rather not.

Once he'd got in next to her, he handed her a pair of headphones. "Shove these on and let me do all the necessaries, then we'll get going."

Arietta twisted them in her hands. "This might be the time to tell you I get motion sick, even going up in a lift a few floors."

"There's a sick bag in the door pocket. By the time you realise we're up, we'll be down," Moss said in a cheerful voice, which grated on her tight-as-a-wire nerves. "Now hush while I get us on our way."

Arietta glared at him, but he appeared oblivious. As the helicopter rose, so did her bile. She swallowed hard, determined not to give in to what she considered was a stupid reaction. Stupid or not, it still got the better of her. She grabbed the bag, used it, found a bottle of water in her backpack and sipped cautiously. Her churning tummy did a few more lurches then decided to play ball. Either that or she had nothing else to part with.

"Okay?" Moss said in what she considered was far too damn cheerful a voice. "Won't be long. Look at that view. Great, isn't it?"

She firmed her lips, scared to open her mouth and either throw up again or shout like a shrew and tell him how she really was. She daren't nod or shake her head. She gave a very half-hearted thumbs-up, which she guessed he didn't notice.

"You can talk, you know. That's what the headphones are for."

"Nope, sick." That was as much as she could manage. Sod the view. She'd look at it when her head and the world had stopped spinning.

Luckily, that wasn't much later. Though whether she'd be able to get out of the helicopter under her own steam was doubtful. As the rotors slowed and stopped, Moss flicked switches and looked at her.

"Sheesh, you weren't joking, were you? At the risk of you thumping me later, you look like death warmed up."

Arietta thrust her sick bag at him. He took it, wrinkled his nose and dropped it into a larger rubbish bag.

"Poor love. Let's get you off here."

She liked the sound of that, though how it could be achieved without reactivating her upchuck reflex she had no idea.

It seemed Moss decided fast and furious was the way to go. Her world spun and steadied as she was lifted out of the machine and noticed through barely open eyes that she was deposited carefully onto the seat of a golf buggy. The forward-facing seat. She didn't bother to look properly, just leant back as best as she could, thankful to be on terra firma once more.

As the buggy rolled smoothly forward, she tried to gather her scattered wits. *What a way to arrive.* Sickly, headachy and no doubt peely-wally. White and wan.

Chapter Sixteen

A few minutes later she felt it was safe to speak. She wouldn't say the golf buggy would ever be a preferred way to travel — she felt every bump they went over — but at least she was in fresh air. "How far to your house?"

"Four, five minutes. It's on the other side of the hotel."

"The…what hotel?" What on earth was he talking about?

"Pannerburn Castle. Look." The golf buggy swung round a corner and at the end of a short avenue of trees the old, elegant mansion could be seen in all its aged — but updated — glory.

"Your house is in the grounds of the hotel where the wedding is being held and you never told me?" Her voice rose and her words ended on an astonished squeak.

"I wanted it to be a surprise."

"It's that all right." Arietta held on to the handle of the buggy as he drove across the avenue and down a side road marked Private. "Why, though?"

"You were so twitchy about it all, at first I kept quiet so as not to remind you about it, then I thought it might be nice to let you see we have our own space."

"I get that, and I'm looking forward to seeing it." Not one hundred percent accurate, but it would do. "Are there many houses here?"

He shook his head. "Apart from staff quarters behind the hotel and half a dozen guest cottages in the other direction, none. The owners decided against timeshare and so on. If you play the golf course you get preferential rates, but apart from that, it's an upmarket twenty-bedroomed hotel. And my home at the far side, well away from anyone else."

"Just yours? How come?" An idea came to her. "Do you own this place?"

"Um, I did, and I part do. It was left to me. Not in this state, I hasten to add, it was almost a ruin. Two inhabitable bedrooms as long as you remembered to put the buckets out for when it rained, one bathroom for the whole place and a cavernous room downstairs for everything else. It was spooky, falling around your ears and, as my mum put it, a liability. Which became *my* liability."

Arietta thought back to their very early conversations, when they were comparing notes about their nearest and dearest.

"The tatty, rundown falling-to-bits house your godmother left you? This is *it*?"

"The very one."

The way he'd described it, Arietta had thought it was more of a two-up two-down sort of place. Not a thirty-odd-roomed mansion.

"Wow." Somewhat of an inadequate reply. "Can I be nosy and ask how it went from that to this?"

"Course you can. Money and not mine. Mainly because I didn't have any. I was the original struggling actor. I sold it on very good legal advice to a syndicate with some caveats that they grudgingly agreed to. One was that the bit of land where my house is, is not part of the hotel but I get to enjoy all the benefits of the place. Which includes free golf and use of the spa and gym and so on. Right of way across the land from the heliport, and I don't pay to use that, ad infinitum, and reduced rates if I want to, how was it put? "Avail myself of any other activities the hotel chooses to allow."

"Like the wedding?"

"Like the wedding," Moss confirmed. "Though if I couldn't have done that Kristin's dad could have got some discounts. He was the guy who put the deal together for the syndicate. That was how I met Kristin. Arthur says now he wishes he'd been a bit more savvy, but admits he didn't think it would take off as well as it has. I'm just glad the advice given to me was sound. Anyway, almost there." He turned round another corner and pressed a switch on the front of the golf buggy to open the double gates they approached.

Arietta gasped again. The cottage might only be one-and-a-bit storeys, but in her mind that was where 'cottagey' ended. Built on a slight arc, it was in many ways a traditional style, but also very modern. Which was a contradiction in terms but the only way she could think to describe it.

"Wow."

As the gates closed behind them, Moss drew up outside the oak front door. "Like it so far?"

"It's gorgeous," Arietta said honestly. "Not at all like I imagined." Not that she'd had many preconceived ideas, just not this.

"Better?" Moss swung out of the buggy and held his hand out to her. "Welcome to Thuinich. That's Gaelic for settled. It seemed to fit."

"Much better." She joined him on the immaculate gravelled drive and, hand in hand, they headed to the door. "It does fit."

"Glad you think so as well." Moss opened the door with a flourish. "Come and explore your new, for as long as you want, abode," he said with a bow. "Shall I carry you over the threshold?"

"Not this time. You don't want to put your back out before your best man duty day."

He laughed. "I don't think that's likely, love, but I might trip, so I'll err on the side of caution. This next week will be hell on wheels, also known as action filming. I might have a stand-in for some of it, but not for everything. Get ready for one knackered me every night. At least it's daytime only, which is a bonus."

"I'll run your bath."

"And join me in it?"

"Just bath salts."

"Bummer, I'd prefer you."

"Won't that make your aches and pains worse?" she asked, deliberately trying to be wide-eyed and seemingly innocent.

"Nah, it'll just add pleasurable ones."

Arietta thought once more how she liked his style.

"Good thinking."

"I aim to oblige. Come on, let's get inside."

He drew her forward and into a round hall, which in turn led into a curved corridor with several doors opening off it. It seemed all the rooms were on the same side of the corridor, and they'd entered halfway down the longer side. Arietta itched to look around. Would it be rude to ask to be nosy?

Moss pre-empted her. "Want to have a look around while I get the cases in? Our room is the one at the end of the corridor to your right. The re-plastered bits are at the kitchen end."

How on earth she managed not to high five or shout "hell yeah," Arietta wasn't certain. "That would be great, thanks."

He nodded, seeming not at all fooled by her decorous reply. Arietta laughed. "I'm dying to."

See you in the kitchen when you're done. That's the last room in the other direction. Don't worry, I've a mini kitchen next to the bedroom. Well, a fridge, kettle and sink anyway. They came in handy when the place got flooded. Means we can have coffee or fizz in bed. Sorted."

Arietta grinned at him and it was his turn to laugh.

"I decided against a toaster. Crumbs in bed are so uncomfortable." Moss turned to go back to the golf buggy. "Fruit, now, is a different matter. Right. See you when you're ready."

The inside of the cottage — she'd call it that, seeing as Moss did — was also not at all as she had expected. Arietta wandered along the corridor, admired the view from the many windows, which faced the front of the house, and wondered about the logistics of who might be able to see in and how to stop them. Then she realised it was one-way glass. A good solution. She resisted glancing in the other rooms as she passed by. She wanted to see their room first.

Ours. Sounds good.

The last door at the end of the corridor was ajar. Arietta pushed it open wider, took three steps inside, rocked on her heels and whistled silently.

O...kay. It might not be enormous, and be dominated by the super-king-plus bed, covered in a soft green and blue spread which matched the curtains, but she reckoned she'd still fit two of her three bedrooms into it with space to spare.

In spite of its size, it was comfortable, welcoming and, she realised, personified what she loved about Moss. His restfulness, his sense of knowing—mostly— what was needed and when, and although nothing to do with the ambience of the room, the way he admitted when he was wrong.

There were two doors on the far side of the room. One led into a bathroom with a very large bath—no wonder he'd mentioned sharing—an oversized shower and two basins and the other to the tiny kitchen Moss had mentioned. She had a giggle at the tin of biscuits on the shelf. Toast crumbs weren't acceptable but digestive crumbs obviously were!

I could live here. That was a pleasant but sobering thought. What about her beloved cottage? Her garden?

Problems that might, maybe, need to be faced at a later date. For now she'd enjoy learning this little bit more about Moss, his life and how she might fit into it—if she needed to.

She'd have to ask Moss where he wanted her to put her clothes and so on. In fact, she'd have to find out what clothes she had with her and whether she'd need to take a wee trip home or to town to make sure she had everything she needed.

It was only for two weeks. With luck she could make do.

Arietta left the room, peered into the other two smaller but no less comfortable bedrooms, one very obviously Audie's, and headed past the open front door through where she could see Moss talking to a tall tweed-clad man over the gates. Moss said something, the other man nodded and with a wave of the hand Moss turned and headed back towards the house. Not wanting to be seen watching, Arietta turned into the lounge and had yet another wow moment. The views from the bedrooms were good, but this was stunning. Even though all the rooms looked in a similar direction, the curve of the corridor meant this was the only room so far that looked straight down the garden and onto a reed-fringed loch.

"Lochan Mairi," Moss said from behind her. "Named after my godmother when I sold the house. Before that, it appeared to be nameless. Just a wee bit of water. No fish, lots of tadpoles, nowhere deeper than three-foot-six, only large enough to swim for a dozen or so strokes either way. A garden pond almost. The far side of which is my boundary."

She was impressed, and remembered him mentioning tadpoles. Not all a fabrication, then. "You swim in it?"

"On occasion. It's not exactly bathwater temperature. Shall we start a tradition? Once a week, come rain or shine?"

"Maybe not." Even the thought of it brought her out in goosebumps. "The view is stunning, though. So is the house so far."

Moss smiled. "Phew. Think you'll be okay when I'm at work? Won't be lonely, or bored? You can use the hotel facilities, there's a map of all the walks around in the dresser and my study is free to be your study for now. We'll think about a proper one just for you when you're ready." The words 'if you are ever ready' hovered between them unspoken.

"Sounds great," Arietta said, and meant it. "Where's the kitchen?"

"Two doors along. Here. Dining room, kitchen. Would you like coffee now?"

"Please. I'm over my upchuck reflexes." If the kitchen was at the end of the corridor and there was only the dining room between them, where was his study?

Moss noticed her puzzled expression. "Okay, you want to know where the study is?"

She nodded. "Might be handy."

"Then follow me." He led the way back to the hall and pointed to a door she hadn't noticed. "The one on the other side is a loo, this leads to my eyrie, also known as my study." He opened the door and stood back. "After you, and take care, it's steep."

She soon saw what he meant. The door opened on to a gently spiralling staircase, which appeared to head over the downstairs rooms. It ended at a room set in the roof, with a window and a balcony overlooking the garden and loch. On the desk in front of the window was her laptop and a bulky bag where several books showed.

"It's over the lounge," she said with delight. "How fabulous, you'd never know it was here from the front. And that gorgeous vista again. I love it."

"I remember you saying you like a view when you work," Moss said diffidently. "So I asked Roddy, he's the guy who keeps an eye on the place for me, to get a desk here and arrange for those cupboards and shelves. We can change what you don't like or don't want." He waved towards a cupboard. "There is a wee fridge, kettle and cafetiere for you of course. Oh, and a loo through that door. Which was the cause of the flooding — some numpty didn't tighten joints properly or something. It's all fixed and useable now."

Thank goodness.

"That's great, but I thought you said it was *your* study?" If it hadn't been dust free, and but for the telescope in one corner, she would have deduced it was unused. "What's with the telescope? Are you a secret star gazer?"

He shrugged. "In theory it's my study, or so it was described on the plans of the house. In practice I hardly ever use it apart from bird watching — the feathered kind, dirty mind, hence the telescope given to me by my dad for my thirteenth birthday. I do like the thought of villains coming to a sticky end as you look out and see if you can see any herons, though."

If she hadn't already loved him, she would have fallen in love with him then.

* * * *

Over the next week or so, while Moss was at work, Arietta spent most of her days in the study. Writing, plotting or gazing at the view. She'd seen a heron, without recourse to the telescope, written the plot for a new book, not in her usual genre, and tentatively suggested it to her agent who loved the idea.

The first flurries of snow arrived, but luckily didn't settle, and even though it was cold, Arietta managed a walk every day. Sometimes just to the lochan and back and sometimes around the grounds of the hotel, which, as she explored, she fell in love with.

She braved the gym while it was empty – once – and decided she preferred to walk in the fresh air – and enjoyed a brisk half hour's swim most days. Then she'd go back to what she privately thought of as her eyrie and write, energised and enthused.

When Moss arrived home, cold, tired and hungry, Arietta was ready for conversation if he was up to it, or just sitting together if not.

She could definitely get used to it.

"I had the strangest message from Kristin today," she remarked ten days or so after they'd relocated to Thuinich. "It says don't bother with a hat, I promise no Alice bands, see you tomorrow at eight a.m. P.S. don't eat breakfast. If she's talking about Saturday" – the day of the wedding – "my poor hat will feel unloved, unwanted and neglected."

Moss laughed. "We'll go to the races and you can wear it then. I got one from Tarquin saying 'be at yours at eight a.m. tomorrow, have whisky handy'."

"At eight a.m.? Sounds strange. What do you think is going on?"

Moss speared a piece of lamb off his plate and ate it before he answered. "Dunno, but what is weird is that when I spoke to Audie on my way home, she never mentioned it. She was still going on about bleeping Alice bands, her word not mine. I didn't ask in case it's something she shouldn't know, but..." He shrugged and studied the tureen of vegetables. "Could I manage more? Yes, but I'll be good and I won't."

Arietta laughed as she stood up to clear the table. "That's because you've seen the apple sponge."

He held his hands in the air. "I cannot tell a lie, it's true. A man can resist extra veggies, he can't resist an Arietta Clare Apple Sponge. Bring it on."

"Custard?"

He gave her an incredulous look. "Are you kidding me? What else?"

"Cream, ice cream, as it is…?"

"All of the above except the as it is?"

Arietta shook her head. "In your dreams, Kirby, in your dreams."

"No room. All my dreams are full of you."

Aww.

"Is that why you mutter and say, 'not a chance, no way, get lost' in your sleep then?"

"*What?*" Moss almost shouted the word and looked flabbergasted. "I don't, I haven't." He stroked her cheek. "Oh, God, no."

Arietta patted his hand, immediately contrite. Why on earth had she replied in such an awful way?

It was that or cry and go all soppy.

"Not lately, no. There was one night you muttered something along those lines, ages ago, but you added 'Percy, you're an ass'. Well, I think that's what you said. I'm sorry, but I had a moment."

"A moment?" Moss sounded puzzled. "How do you mean?"

Arietta wound her arms around his neck. So not like her, but so she thought the very right thing to do. "It was that or burst into happy tears and make you all soggy. It was such a special thing to hear." She sniffed. "Oh shoot."

It was a good thing he understood, *and* he didn't have an early call the next morning.

* * * *

Arietta woke up as her alarm trilled. She'd hummed and hawed over whether to set her alarm and in the end thought maybe she should. Just in case.

The just in case had happened.

She shook Moss. "Wake up, we have an hour."

He smiled and reached for her. "Plenty of time. We can have several quickies in an hour."

"Moss," she said, exasperated. How was it possible to be aroused and worried at the same time? "Kristin and Tarquin will be here in under an hour. We need to get up and shower."

"Okay, you run it," he said obligingly. "I'll join you in a sec."

"Separately. We do not have time for…for… anything else," she finished in a lame way.

"Later?"

"Yes, later, now get moving. Use another shower. I am not greeting visitors in my birthday suit."

He sat up, wide awake, and mock leered. "You can greet me in it any time."

"Good, thank you, get up and…oh hell." She glanced at her phone. "Forty minutes and counting."

"They won't mind if we're less than wide awake," Moss grumbled as he threw back the duvet and shivered. "Brr, has the heating not come on?"

"It's on, but not got warm enough because we forgot to bring the time it comes on forward. It's cold outside by the look of it and it's started to snow again." Arietta had peered through the blinds. "It's settling. Thermals at the ready." She headed into the bathroom and took the second shortest shower on record, which included washing her hair.

Twenty minutes later her hair was almost dry and she'd managed a swift eyeliner and lippy application — if they were having visitors she wanted to look as if she hadn't scrambled into her clothes five minutes before, even if she had. Arietta dressed in warm cords and a long slouchy cashmere jumper, put her feet into her old and trusty fleece-lined Uggs and wondered if she could get away with gloves until she warmed up. Fingerless of course. Otherwise it would be hard to make the coffee.

However, gloveless, by the time Moss entered the kitchen, she'd warmed up and the view through the window showed the garden was white and the snowflakes bigger.

"Will they get here?" Arietta asked. "I'd hate for them to get stuck halfway up the M80 or over the moors."

Moss moved the coffee pot off the stove, where it had been bubbling away furiously. "I bet you they stopped at the hotel or in one of the cottages last night. I can't see them arriving here at eight if they didn't. Why I still don't know, but as I saw a certain car heading up the drive out of the study window when I went to see how it all looked out there, I can guess."

"You can? Who? What? Tell me?"

He shook his head. "Nope. Guess."

"Grrr. Moss, I'll tickle it out of you." Arietta advanced on him, her fingers outstretched.

Moss laughed and nipped behind the table. She pushed the table towards him at an angle, went the other way and effectively blocked him in.

Moss looked at the table, obviously considering…

"Don't you dare," Arietta warned. "It's got the coffee cups… Moss, you rotter."

He did a victory shimmer. He'd vaulted over and now poured coffee into the cups as if he didn't have a care in the world.

"Please give me a clue," Arietta begged. "Just one teensy tiny idea."

He hummed a few lines of a well-known and very recognisable song.

"What?" she said, astounded. "You think that?"

"Well, it would put a spoke in the B-Ts' snobbish wheels, wouldn't it?"

Chapter Seventeen

"I've never played mother of the bride, chief bridesmaid and half of the congregation before," Arietta whispered to Moss an hour later. "And never thought I'd do it in a fake fur coat and leather Uggs."

"Nor me in a padded parka and walking boots, but I love it, don't you? Shall we do it as well?"

"I'd prefer a secluded beach and warm sunshine," Arietta said as her heart missed a beat. Was that a proposal or a rhetorical question? "Or anywhere warm and non-midgiefied."

"I'll remember. Think of which beach." Moss grinned as she went hot and cold.

Really…ohhh…enough. He might not mean it.

"For now I'll concentrate on us not going A over T." Moss held her hand as they crunched through the snow — which had luckily stopped falling and allowed a weak and watery sun to show — towards a small, very small snow-covered marquee, in the middle of what in the summer was a flourishing rose garden.

It's more like a tent, but each to their own.

"Why on earth are they having it outside?"

"Romantic," Moss said as he held back the door flap to let them enter and once they were through dropped it down again. "Allegedly. Whew, thank goodness." He gestured towards a large patio heater that was doing its best to warm them and their surroundings.

For all it was a small space, it was cheerful and it *was* romantic, with soft flowing drapes and waterfalls of winter flowers that included lucky white heather and cyclamen. Music played softly in the background, which added to the ambience. However, it still wasn't warm enough to shed their coats.

"It's outside inside really," Moss said and dodged her playful swipe to his bum. "We're not eating out here, promise. What's the time?"

Arietta glanced at her watch. It wasn't easy, as she had the sleeves of the coat pulled well down over her wrists and the cuffs of her gloves well pulled up. "Three minutes to."

There was the sound of several people walking towards the marquee.

"And here they are," Moss said cheerfully. "I hope. Can't have a wedding without them."

"It's us and I don't have an Alice band on." Audie burst through the doorway and danced up to them. "Look, isn't it fab?" She pointed to her fake fur hat and jacket. She handed a bouquet of heather and greenery to Arietta. "We get these, aren't they fab as well?"

"Definitely. Lovely and perfect," Arietta replied. "Spot on."

"I get to wear jeans too," Audie said. "Warm."

"Oh yes," Arietta said. "I've got cords. And" — she lowered her voice — "thermals."

"I'm glad your clothes didn't stop at the jacket and hat," Moss said as Audie giggled. "Be a bit chilly."

"Daad, honestly." Audie shook her head and looked at Arietta. "How *do* you put up with him?"

"She loves me," Moss said complacently. "Ignores my wee ways."

"Well so do I love you, and put up with your wee ways," Audie said. "But you still make me groan."

"He makes me groan as well," Arietta assured her. "But as he makes good coffee, I forgive him."

"Oh well…" Audie said, and did a wiggly jiggle. "Ohh, here's Mum and Tarquin. Isn't it jell?"

"Oh yes," Arietta turned to Moss. "Jell?" she whispered. "Jealous?"

He did a tiny shake of the head. "Jelly bean, the best scene, only known to Audie and her mates, I reckon. Or well, jell as in well jealous, but in this case more likely the former."

"Fair enough." Arietta turned to the door—aka the flap—and smiled as a beaming Kristin, dressed very similarly to Arietta and Audie, entered arm and arm with Tarquin.

"Go on," she said to her groom. "Get up there with Moss. Then I'll natter to Arietta and Audie and be fashionably late."

"Too cold to be late, hon," Moss said. "Buck the trend."

"Please," Tarquin said fervently. "Before I forget my words."

"You won't." Moss dragged him forward at the same time as the celebrant entered and, with a word of welcome to them all, moved to the long, cloth-covered table at the far end of the tent.

"Oh God, thank you," Kristin said. "We couldn't face the bun fight and were overjoyed to be able to do this. Mum and Dad won't speak to me for years but I don't care. We can have the reception in our glad rags but this...this is more meaningful. It's for us, not them."

"I get that and I agree. Your day."

"Come on, Mum, let's do it." Audie kissed her mum and turned to Arietta. "We follow, don't we? Then they can say I do and we can go indoors and have some soup while they take pictures in the snow."

"You'll be in them," Kristin said. "Tough luck, I did warn you." She winked at Arietta. "Arietta will be okay."

Arietta bit back her grin. She hadn't known what was going on but reasoned she could take layers off but not add them if she didn't have them with her.

"What?" Audie blinked and turned to Arietta. "How? It's freezing. How will we cope?"

"Thermal knickers," Arietta said. "Will work wonders.

"Ah, that's why Mum wanted me to wear them. Bummer."

"Let's go, folks," Kristin said. "Before we freeze our" — she glanced at Audie — "bits off."

"Can I go back in for my knickers then?"

Thank goodness no one else is around to hear that.

"No time, as the celebrant's waiting," Kristin said. "Stand near the heater and think of the soup."

The short and simple ceremony was lovely. Kristin and Tarquin said their vows in clear voices, and when pronounced man and wife kissed each other, followed by a kiss to Audie and hugs for Arietta and Moss.

Arietta surreptitiously wiped her eyes as they signed the register after the bride and groom.

"Okay?" Moss held her close to him.

"Weddings get me here." She pressed her hand over her heart. "Especially ones that seem so right."

"It was spot on, wasn't it?"

"Oh yes. Short, simple and oh-so sweet."

Moss kissed her cheek. "I'll remember that. Adding in warm—"

Audie came up to hold both their hands and he didn't say any more.

Arietta wondered if she was happy or disappointed about that. A bit of both probably. It wasn't the time or the place to be put on the spot, even if it turned out to be a hypothetical question.

"Photos now," Audie said. "Mum says I won't have time to get cold. Come on, they're going outside."

"Yes, Miss Bossy."

Audie giggled. "Someone's got to be, and Arietta's being polite."

Moss groaned. "Someone's got to be," he parroted. "Let's go or they'll forget we're here."

The photographs in the snow were mercifully short and sweet, and the snowball fight as the photographer snapped them was amusing and fun, even if they did all end up with snow down their backs.

Audie had a demon aim.

"Got to be a cricketer," Moss commented as he shook his head and snow fell all over his shoulders. "Great shot, your mum now needs to wipe her face."

"So does your dad." Arietta rubbed a handful of snow over it then turned and ran towards the house.

His last snowball hit her on the back of her knees. She turned round and did a victory jiggle. "Hahahaha…urgh." Tarquin—who had the worst aim of them all—had actually hit someone.

"Ooops," he said. "That was meant for Moss. Ah, there's a man waving. I think our wedding feast awaits."

* * * *

A few hours later, stuffed to the gills, as Moss put it, and awash with champagne, Arietta and Moss walked back home arm and arm through the rapidly melting snow just as dusk was falling.

"That was lovely," Arietta said. "Magical in its own way, though I don't envy them telling the B-Ts."

"They'll have the celebration, though, and be seen to be seen. That's what matters to the B-Ts."

"Not my idea of heaven, but hey ho, each to their own."

"Will you go and get Audie as soon as she's said hello to her grandparents?" Arietta asked as they approached the cottage. "Or is she stopping up there overnight?"

"Here," Moss said as he unlocked the gate and relocked it behind them. "As we offered. She gets on well with her grandparents but in a place like the hotel they'd be hard-pressed to entertain her. She doesn't want to be in the cottage with her mum and Tarquin, and rightly so. Kristin will text when she's ready to come down, and I or we can pop up to get her in the buggy if I judge enough time has passed since the fizz. If not, I'll get one of the hotel's buggy to take us both ways."

"You didn't drink much," Arietta pointed out. "A glass and a half maybe? But I like the way you think."

Moss waited until they were inside, coats and boots off and sitting side by side with a cup of coffee, before he spoke again.

"Do you?" he asked. "Really?"

"Do I what?" Arietta replied, confused. What was he talking about?

"Like the way I think."

"Oh, right." He'd gone back to her comments outside. "Of course I do, I wouldn't be here otherwise."

"And you like Audie?"

What's not to like? She's lovely. "I love Audie," Arietta said truthfully. Her heart beat just that little bit faster. "She's a gem." What was he going to say?

"And you can cope with Kristin and Tarquin around and about?"

"In small doses. If I'm honest, they do get a bit wearing at times," Arietta said. "But they don't mean to. Well-meaning I reckon, but... Yeah, sorry."

Moss laughed. "I agree there. So, with all those provisos, do you think we could have our own magic day some time?"

"As long as it doesn't involve snow. What exactly do you mean?" She wanted it spelt out, preferably in words of one syllable.

"You know, my love. You do know."

She smiled and kissed him. "Of course I do — maybe. But I'd like it to be warm. I do not want to wear thermals."

He laughed. "Fair enfough. So if I do warm, intimate, just a few people and no, no thermals, my gorgeous Arietta, will you marry me? Be my wife, my love, forever?"

"I thought you'd never ask," Arietta said. "Of course I will."

"But not here?"

"Nope, not unless it's sun and no midges."

"Barbados," Moss said. "Definitely Barbados. Thom can be best man. Bridesmaids?"

"I better go for Audie and Kristin. Maggie can be my matron of honour and Tarquin whipper-in to keep us all in line. We'll have everyone from your family and mine and Thomas can be MC as well as best man and ogle the guests. Well," she temporised, "I'm betting on one guest creating havoc and upsetting the best man."

Moss raised his eyebrows. "And who is that?"

She grinned. "My mate Jan—and I can't wait for the fur to fly."

"Neither can I—as long as we are wed before."

Arietta laughed. "Oh, I promise that…or else."

"Good enough for me, my love. It's a plan."

Want to see more from this author? Here's a taster for you to enjoy!

Happy Ever After at Romansa Castle: The Catch Up
Raven McAllan

Coming 2023

Excerpt

Jan Fraser glanced idly out of the twentieth-floor window of her office and watched as several Star Ferries moved across the busy Hong Kong harbour from the Central Piers to TST in Kowloon like ants scurrying about their business. Not far from the shore, a rubbish sampan snagged some weeds and a bag of goodness knows what from Hong Kong harbour and a police boat went by on its way to some business or another.

She adored it. Every last bustling, noisy inch of downtown as well as the tranquil hills and trails of the islands and New Territories.

All of which made her all the more determined to discover — why her? Why did life decide now was the time to throw some curse balls in her direction?

It was no secret she loved her life as it was. Work, a great social circle, perfect — albeit tiny — house in Sai King, a lovely fishing village in the new territories, and the thought of a holiday due to her She relished the thought and the joy of getting out her suitcase and holiday clothes.

Now two things had put a spoke in her wheels.

The first, admittedly was only an annoying gnat of a spoke. An ex who out of the blue was about to descend on her – or so he thought. Which would have been a not so pleasant surprise if his sister hadn't warned her. Not a long text. Just, 'Thomas in HK soon 4 filming. Arr Thurs. Sez will call u. Has yr wrk addy, not from me!' The last three words were highlighted *and* written out in full. As Ari was a supporter of 'text speak', it showed how she wanted to emphasis the fact.

His forthcoming presence was irritating, but not the end of the world. Surely she was far enough over him – as in the other side of the world over him – to be civilised if he did turn up?

Say 'hello, no thanks, I don't want a meal, or a drink, to go up the peak on the tram or take a trip to Disneyworld'. Don't add I'd rather swim with sharks, or eat worms than spend my free time with you. Be polite and distant and hope I don't see him around the place. Be courteous and show him he means nothing to me any more. Even if the events that had led up to them splitting still gave her the shakes.

Sod him. Why couldn't he accept I had the chance of a lifetime as well as him? That we could survive for six months apart, and if we couldn't it was as well to find out sooner rather than later?

As it had happened they hadn't found out. Thomas had used the old chestnut "*if you loved me you'd come with me*". Jan had retorted, "*if you loved me you'd accept how important my chance is as well*", and instead said thanks but no thanks. In her mind his attitude was selfishness in the extreme. Two in a relationship meant give and take, not one give and one take. Or at least not the same one doing all the taking and the other having to do the giving.

Now it seemed he was about to appear in her life again.

Sod it. This time she'd be the selfish one, and if — *if* — they did meet up it would be on her terms. She grimaced then smiled reluctantly. She was reading an awful lot into the fact an old...old what...acquaintance was probably going to drop by to say hi. It could be no more than that.

It could be though. Argh. Enough. Jan gave herself a mental shake. Why worry about what might never happen?

Plus, if that wasn't enough to keep her awake at nights, her boss had just dropped another bombshell on her! On a Friday afternoon no less. Just before they'd all departed the building for the weekend.

A bombshell she couldn't really get out of. Mind you, if she were honest would she really want to if it didn't mean the postponement of her holiday? Jan thought about that for a second or two and admitted to herself — reluctantly — probably not.

The door behind her opened and she turned to smile at May, her friend and boss, who waved a white hanky in the air.

"Is it safe to come in?"

Jan shook her head in amusement. "Yes, and you might well wave that. Rotter."

"That's rotter, boss." May grinned. "Sorry, but who better to send? I accept it means putting your holiday off for a few weeks, but a, we'll pay for all the extra expense, and b, you were heading over there anyway. And c, you know darned well you're the one person who will break balls if need be."

"Sounds gruesome. And, *and*, note, I'm not due to be heading there until I've had a month in Portugal," Jan pointed out. "You're asking me to go to Scotland, the *west* of Scotland, in the main midge months. I've sold my midge net hat and run out of repellent. I'll be eaten alive."

May shook her head and laughed. "Buy a hat and repellent and put the cost on expenses. If we left it until after midge months, you'd have the hot humid summer here to contend with first."

"I'd be in Portugal. Hot and not humid." *Not like here.*

"Mosquitos."

"Vinho Verde."

"Sand flies, burnt nose, sweat rash."

"Nit-picker."

"I thought you said nose picker." May snorted. "I got over that ages ago. Well, three at least."

"Wow." Jan opened her eyes wide. "That long ago?"

"Still bite my nails though."

"Who doesn't?" Jan looked at her own red as in fire engine-coloured nails. She didn't—often—and had discovered if she got her nails done she was less likely to put a finger in her mouth and nibble. "Seriously though, it's not the time I'd prefer to spend around forest and water, posh hotel or not. After all, I doubt I'd be allowed to wear a midge net and smell of eau de citronella all the time." That, Jan admitted, was her preferred mode of dress during the high of the midge season. "With my trousers tucked into my socks and my hands up the sleeves of my jumper. I swear, the little blighters take one look at me, rub their wings or whatever together and think ooohhh, dinner. And breakfast, lunch and all snacks in between." She scratched her arms. "Makes me itch just thinking about it."

May dipped her head. "Okay, point taken. You and midges do not go well together. But, Jan, we really do need you at the hotel." She was all seriousness now. "The new owner is adamant he wants our help to pitch it to the right people. He doesn't want to close it to the public — well, not all the public — but there's a big, as in massive, superstar movie about to be filmed around there, and he needs advice on the best way to handle the situation. Not to antagonise anyone in any way."

"Close it for renovation," Jan said promptly. "There, sorted. Portugal here I come."

May laughed and shook her head. "Good try. He says not. There are a lot of people who own houses in the grounds. He can't stop those people turning up. They'll presume they are free to use the facilities as normal. You can't be expected to accept there's no golf or gym or whatever when it's in the deeds of your house you have unlimited, unrestricted use. And it is. In the deeds. He's checked and so have our law people. Not a cat in you-know-where's chance of wriggling out of it. If anything is broken or whatever the hotel is liable, and it costs them money, not the house owners."

"I can see that could be a problem." Jan stared out of the window and nodded as she thought furiously. A cruise ship was in the process of docking on the other side of the harbour and tugs and little boats were moving fussily around it. She never lost her sense of marvel at how busy the harbour was and how all the different types of craft managed to go about their business. A sampan dodged a tourist junk and someone shook a fist in the bigger boat's direction. Jan smiled. How she wished she could hear the conversation going on there. Swearing was recognisable in any language.

May coughed. "Earth to Jan."

"Where exactly are we talking about?" Jan asked and dragged her mind back to the subject in question. "It might help to know that. After all, it could be on the east coast and nigh on midgeless." She didn't think so for one minute, not the way May had been talking. "So?"

"That, sadly, is on a need-to-know basis," May replied in a regretful, 'sorry but it's not my doing' sort of way. "If you agree to head over and spend a month or two checking things out, giving advice and so on, I can, after you've signed a confidentiality clause, tell you where you'll be going. Not before, and unless—" She broke off and held her hands up in the air. "I know, I know, it should be you know what you're letting yourself into before you agree, but this isn't my decision. I can tell you it's all above board and the directors are adamant they want you. As a colleague I say that, as a mate I agree I'd be as fed up as you over it all and inclined to tell me and them—to f off. If a bit more politely."

Jan stared at May as she tried to remember something Arietta, her friend and warner of Thomas' imminent arrival in the city, had mentioned. Something about her—Arietta's—husband Moss possibly filming close to where they had a house in the west of Scotland and a lot of kerfuffle over it. Something to do with the film company not wanting there to be any chance of rubberneckers and the new owner of the nearby hotel adamant it couldn't shut its doors while the film-makers faffed about in the extensive grounds. No contracts had been signed, including Moss', and everyone was getting, in Arietta's words, "*a wee bit antsy*". Could it be that?

"Oh," Jan said much more nonchalantly than she felt. "Romansa Castle. Gaelic for romance. Moss Kirby's next movie. I heard there was a wee bit of a hoo-ha if it was to be filmed there."

May jumped and stared at Jan for several seconds. "What are you? A super sleuth? Where did you get that info? That is supposed to be top secret. Both the hoo- ha and the place."

Shoot, I hope I haven't got Arietta in trouble. She didn't say it was for my ears only. Blast, damn and fig rolls. "Really? Since when?"

"Since when what?"

"Since when is it top secret? That wasn't mentioned. Just that the hotel felt it couldn't shut. The film company had discussed it with the previous owners, I believe. If I've got it right, they were offered a deal that the majority felt they couldn't turn down and then as the film company hadn't got anything signed, he…she…they said there was nothing to honour. Or something," she finished lamely. Moss had been a part owner and had been so disgusted by the mentality of some of his co-owners he'd sold his share willingly. He said he was relieved to let the whole sorry mess and stupid arguments be sorted out by someone with more time. It might be a house associated with his family, but any thoughts of hanging on to his bit of it were long gone. He'd still got his new home and a fair bit of land where he and Jan lived whenever possible and was happy with it. Weirdly, Arietta had informed Jan, the land Moss still owned was not the land the film company wanted to use. If it had been life would perhaps have been simpler all round.

"So how are you in the know?" May persisted.

"I know someone who knows someone from around there."

"A lot of knows there when there shouldn't be, eh? Damn and blast." May sat down on Arietta's desk chair with a thump. The chair rocked and slid several feet backwards and spun around a to face the wall. One of May's coveted Jimmy Choos flew off her foot and headed towards the ceiling.

With a leap that would do justice to any rugby player, Jan caught it in mid-air and presented it to her friend with a grin. "Cinderella, your shoe."

May nodded regally. "Cinderella's would have stayed on," she pointed out as she slid her foot back into it and grinned. "Gah, I always forget your chair does that. Mine sticks."

"I make sure I do a full spin," Arietta said. "Might as well enjoy a wee burl around."

"Burl?"

"Spin. I forget you're not up to speed with your Scottish slang."

"I'm learning. Fair enough, but not now. Any more nuggets to share?"

Jan shook her head. "Don't think so."

"Then how about it? It's not compulsory, but—" May hesitated and worried her bottom lip with her teeth. A sure sign she was worried. "I honestly can't think of anyone better to go and advise them. Him. Or whoever. Plus, I've got a promise you can go first class both ways and to Portugal or wherever after the work part is done. If we do a good job, it could lead to a lot more prestigious contracts. Let's face it, we know we're good and doing well, but we can always try to do better." She winked. "Bigger bonuses."

Jan couldn't decide if she'd made her mind up or it had been made up for her. Either way, it appeared her immediate future was settled. "If, just *if*, I head there and try and see what can be done, then I go on holiday straight after?" She could go to Europe on the same plane she'd booked—she'd decided to fly via the Netherlands—and head to Scotland instead of the Algarve. Work could sort out the logistics—and any extra flights and accommodation. Portugal in September instead of July and August would probably be a better temperature anyway. "Then back to my job here?"

"Of course," May said promptly. "Why, yes."

Too promptly? Hmm.

"Why do you not sound so sure?" Jan asked on impulse, and with growing suspicion noticed a look of guilt flash over May's face. "What aren't you telling me?"

"Nothing." May didn't sound very convincing.

"If you don't fess up, the next time you walk out of one of your Jimmy Choos I'll accidentally heave it out of the window, or down the loo."

"Cruel." May sighed and wriggled her feet deeper into her footwear. "Okay, they did sort of wonder if you'd sort of want to do an extended stint with them, still work for us, but go on loan to them."

"What?" Jan's voice rose in a screech. "Stop over there and... Definitely no, no and no again. My home is here. I do not want to go back to Scotland to work for however long. What a crackpot idea, I might be crap at what they want anyway. Next."

"All right, keep your hair on. I'll pass that on in politer terms. If you get everything sorted faster, then you can add the rest of the time onto your holiday. Don't be surprised if someone tries to persuade you though. And before you ask, no, I don't know why you etcetera. I mean, do they know your nasty habits?"

Jan laughed, now the tense moment was over. "Rash statement, boss of mine. I might rush things so as to get more tanning time—or invent some really nauseous idiosyncrasies."

"Not you," May said shrewdly. "You're too conscientious."

"Ain't that true." Jan gave into the inevitable with, if not good grace, a resigned acceptance. "Okay, I give in…sort of. I'll do the month. When do I leave?"

"End of next month and be prepared for two months."

"Nope, one or no can go." Why was she being so ornery? Jan had no idea except for one of those something-weird-is-up itches she sometimes got. Usually when whatever she had to do and didn't want to went pear-shaped. Or she cocked up.

"Hard woman, I'll pass that on. What if they say you have to give them the option of another month?"

Jan high fived herself. "Then I stay here and go on holiday."

"Hmm. Right." May sounded almost resigned. "How we've got it so far gives you almost seven weeks to sort stuff out here and hand over anything that can't wait. Head off early and have a great weekend."

A great weekend with a lot to think about. However, Jan smiled at May. It wasn't the other woman's fault that Jan had to use one of her granny's favourite expressions, 'got her knickers in a twist'. "Yeah, you too."

One thing, it was a relief to know that she'd got that length of time at home before she headed overseas. Still grumpy at the way May had convinced her she'd have to do the job, and wondering what she'd got herself involved in—and with who—Jan logged off and closed her computer, tidied her desk and got her bag before she waited for the lift to deposit her on the ground floor of the office block where she worked, headed for the main door and paused.

Taxi, bus or boat? She had a choice of transport to take to get home. Whichever mode she chose it would take her a good hour to get to Sai Kung, the fishing village where she lived, but she reckoned it was worth it. Especially at weekends, when she could wander down to the water's edge and choose what fish she fancied for lunch. Watch the seller pick it out of its tank and hand it up to her, wrapped in paper and a plastic bag, via a long-handled hook. Co-workers and friends said they envied her, but never appeared to lose the opportunity to try to get her to move closer to the city centre or one of the other densely populated areas, where they said she would have lots of things to do. She didn't bother to point out she had enough of that where she lived. Just resisted their attempts. She enjoyed the contrast and didn't want hustle and bustle all the time. Plus, the journey to and from the central business district and her home was perfect for reading.

Just before she reached the door of her office, Martin, a colleague, hailed her. "Drink at the pier? Half a dozen of us going."

"Why not." It was Friday, she had nothing planned, and the convenient little red minibuses ran from Central to the end of her street until almost midnight.

The tiny bar by the piers where the ferries to a couple of the islands that dotted the sea around Hong Kong left from was laid-back, friendly and busy. Jan thrust her arm through the crook of Martin's arm as they fought their way through the usual crowds in the CBD area of Central and made their way to the harbourside with their co-workers. Maty had declined with a 'got me my man and a hot date in front of the TV'. Her husband was something high up in a bank and frequently overseas.

As ever, the throng sounded like a flock of cheerful parrots. It seemed as if all languages were represented, and she found it amusing to see how many she could identify. With a wry grin, Jan realised she could understand quite a lot of cuss words as well as 'excuse me', 'please' and 'thank you' in most of them.

An itch down her spine made her turn and look behind her, but she couldn't see any reason for it.

She mentally shrugged and put it down to Arietta's text and an errant hair that had decided to come lose and tickle her.

Thomas Clare stared at the laughing, vibrant woman who strode out of the multistorey office block arm in arm with a tall suited-and-booted male and headed in the opposite direction to where he was standing.

Bugger. She's got a bloke. What am I doing here? Why didn't I at least make her aware of my presence? Say hi, do the fancy meeting you stuff? Not let on I'd deliberately tried to see her? Sod it all, why am so dithery? It's just Jan. Except there was no 'just' about it.

So many random thoughts whirred in his mind as Jan and the unknown man walked farther away. Why hadn't his sister warned him?

Probably thought it would do me good. Besides, if I do do the 'hi' bit, Jan would probably ignore me, spit in my eye or laugh at my audacity and sense of self-importance, that I'd think she'd want to speak to me.

Which, sadly, he totally understood. With the hindsight of several years growing up, he could understand what a self-centred arrogant idiot he'd been. As an only son, with a sister who would tell him he was an idiot when need be but sadly wasn't always around to do that, and elderly parents who were of a generation who accepted that what he thought best *was* best, his ideas were antiquated at times. The time he and Jan were together was subsequently one of those times.

Hopefully he was now wiser as well as older.

He stared at the departing couple thoughtfully. Should he follow them? Would that be considered stalking? If he did walk their way and bump into them, what then? Say a casual, 'hello, fancy meeting you here'? Pretend he hadn't seen them? Admit he'd been hoping to speak to Jan? Ask her advice? Explain he was in Hong Kong for work as well?

Bloody hell, why is it all so flipping hard? Thom considered the options then shrugged. Sod it, he'd go for a drink and decide whether he could be bothered to cook—if shoving a ready meal in the microwave his forward-thinking apart-hotel provided could be called cooking—or grab something from one of the stalls dotted about the city and eat on the hoof.

Or splash out and eat in one of the bars or restaurants where I can people-watch. An evening of relaxation wasn't going to be on the cards once he started work the following day. He was only in Hong Kong for a month, and most of the time was accounted for. His role in the film wasn't the main one but, as he was told on numerous occasions, pivotal to the plot. Pivotal or not, he considered it a fabulous role and was, in his own words, chuffed to bits to be offered it. The time in Hong Kong was the best added perk ever. He loved the place, every last inch of it. From the blokes trying to sell him a suit, a watch or a handbag—all creative copies—to the flower sellers, high-end shops, trams, busses and boats. Everything pleased him. Even the sudden rainstorms.

Like the one at that moment which made the covered walkway even more popular and the umbrella sellers ditto.

Thom sauntered along the busy walkway, dodged several people talking rapidly into their phones, oblivious to their surroundings, and headed for the quayside down one of the many routes that could be taken.

As ever, the route was busy. It not only accessed the central business district but several shopping malls and streets and eventually the central escalator—the moving walkway that came down the peak first thing in the morning and went upwards for the rest of the day—and Lang Kwai Fong, the area where a lot of bars were situated.

Thom chuckled to himself as he remembered many a happy night there on past visits. Why had he left it so long to return to Hong Kong? It was one of his favourite places to visit.

Because Jan is here.

When she'd first moved there he'd sulked. He'd been offered a job in Australia and had thought Jan would jump at the chance to accompany him. Instead, she had told him she had been offered a fantastic job in Hong Kong and wasn't going to turn it down to spend six months in Australia whilst he spent his days—and probably a fair few nights—filming and she twiddled her thumbs and waited for him to find time to spend with her.

He'd sulked. Overreacted and, as his sister had kindly told him, "*spit his dummy out*".

By the time he'd got over his snit, Jan was in Hong Kong and he was on the other side of the world. When he'd flown home he'd gone via Hong Kong, spent a couple of nights there and wondered if he would see

Jan. He hadn't, of course, and had been too proud to beg Arietta to give him her address. He'd discovered her work address through a friend who had come across her by chance whilst looking for someone savvy enough to help out with a problem regarding his new hotel.

Zac Moncrieff had whistled when he'd seen her resume. *"This chick could be the one to smooth things over and be the answer to my prayers. What d'you think?"*

Thom had peered over Zac's shoulder. *Janetta Fraser.* His — or more correctly not his — Jan. A sharp, familiar prick of regret had caught him. The one that he always experienced when he remembered what he could have had and had thrown away. He'd realised Zac was staring at him, expecting a reply.

"That she'd cut off your balls and fry them up for the dog's dinner if you called her 'this chick'. No woman wants to be thought of as 'this chick'. Honestly, Zac."

Zac had grinned. *"Only to you. Anyway, what do you reckon?"*

Thom had shrugged. *"You could try I guess. Why her though? There must be lots of people who fit the bill."*

"I won't give you chapter and verse, but I just reckon she'd take no prisoners and get the job done."

"You could be right. Where is she working now?"

Zac had told him and Thom had looked the business up. So here he was, wandering through Hong Kong in a rainstorm having seen her from afar.

It had been fate, he decided, that not a week after that conversation with Zac, he'd been offered his present job and here he was.

For at least a month.

Surely that would be time to see if he could meet Jan and discover if that spark of awareness, that flare of arousal, was still there.

For goodness' sake, man, you might be an actor, but you're not rehearsing for a role in a hot romance. Enough. Thom chastised himself and noticed with relief it had stopped raining and the paths and lawns outside were steaming gently in the late evening sunshine.

"Beer, and a bite to eat," he said out loud and earned a strange look from a passer-by. He smiled self-consciously and ran his hand though his hair. He really had to stop his habit of talking to himself out loud, especially in public. Or, if he felt it necessary, at least pretend he was talking on his phone. He took some earbuds out of his pocket and plugged one into his ear. Hopefully better than nothing.

Of course, he reasoned, what would be even better would be to get out of the habit altogether.

Today's words of wisdom. Thom veered to one side and headed down one of the covered walkways that led directly to the waterfront, turned left and went towards where he hoped a favourite bar still existed. Not one he would have dreamt of going to in the rain, but now? If the steps everyone used as a seating area were still wet, he'd stand. Or buy something and pay for a plastic bag to plonk his butt on.

The pavements were as near as dammit dry. Thom bought a beer from one stall, succumbed to a burger and chips from another and sat halfway up the concrete steps so he had one lower to put his feet on and one higher to lean against. He ate his burger in double-quick time — he'd not realised how hungry he was until he'd scented the onions, and his stomach had rumbled. Once he'd wiped his greasy hands on a napkin and put the rubbish in the appropriate receptacle, he took his tablet out of his bag, pulled up his script and began to read in between mouthfuls of beer.

People walked in all directions, some sat nearby with their own drinks, others stood in groups chatting until their ferries arrived and they were taken across the harbour. Thom had half his mind on his surroundings and the rest on the script as he relished the clever writing. It would be a hit, he was damn sure of it, and boy was he happy he was part of it. He got to a part where his character had a big involvement and forgot everything except how he would play Sam Rolton, small-time crook and hopeless romantic who got tangled up with a private detective who thought he, Sam, was more of a scoundrel than he was. When they teamed up to solve a crime, things got interesting.

Thom had been hooked the first time he'd read the story and now was even more so. He scrolled back to the beginning of the scene, tuning out the hooting of the ferries as they came and went, the noise of the crowds and the engines of the vehicles on the nearby road.

It was only when he picked up his glass to find it was empty that he realised how long he'd been sitting there.

Night had fallen, and the street—and quayside— lights were on. The crowds had thinned out and the people that were around appeared less stressed and more chilled.

The Friday night feeling? Probably. Thom started at his glass thoughtfully. One more?

Why not. He didn't have anyone or anything to head home to. Or in his case, to head hotel to. The burger had taken the edge off his hunger, and if he was peckish later on, there were plenty of snack bars in the hotel's vicinity.

He'd have another pint.

He bought it and headed back to the steps only to see the place he'd been sitting was now occupied.

By someone he knew.

"Jan?"

Jan Fraser glanced up and froze. Her expression was wooden as she gave him the slightest of nods.

"Thomas? Fancy meeting you here." She didn't sound particularly enamoured at that.

"Fancy," he said and gestured to the step next to her. "May I?"

She shrugged. "I can't stop you, but please leave enough space for my companion. He's just gone to get our drinks."

As a mood depressor, she couldn't have done better. Thom inclined his head. "I wouldn't dream of usurping him."

Jan smiled. It didn't reach her eyes. "You couldn't."

It was enough for him to move to the other end of the steps and make sure he sat with his back to her.

About the Author

After 30 plus years in Scotland, Raven now lives near the east Yorkshire coast, with her long-suffering husband, who is used to rescuing the dinner, when she gets immersed in her writing, keeping her coffee pot warm and making sure the wine is chilled.

With a new home to decorate and a garden to plan, she's never short of things to do, but writing is always at the top of her list.

Her other hobbies include walking along the coast and spotting the wildlife, reading, researching, cros stitch and trying not to drop stitches as she endeavours to knit.

Being left-handed, and knitting right-handed, that's not always easy.

Raven loves to hear from readers. You can find her contact information, website details and author profile page at https://www.totallybound.com

Home of Erotic Romance

Sign up for our newsletter and find out about all our romance book releases, eBook sales and promotions, sneak peeks and FREE romance books!